When I Was Seven

Mary Ellen Bramwell

BLACK ROSE
writing™

The final approval for this literary material is granted by the author.

First printing

This is a work of fiction. Names, characters, businesses, places, events and incidents are either the products of the author's imagination or used in a fictitious manner. Any resemblance to actual persons, living or dead, or actual events is purely coincidental.

ISBN: 978-1-61296-759-2
PUBLISHED BY BLACK ROSE WRITING
www.blackrosewriting.com

Printed in the United States of America
Suggested retail price $16.95

When I Was Seven is printed in Calibri

This book, and my writing itself, would not exist without the loving support of my husband Allen, my children, especially Amy who is my most valuable and toughest critic, and my parents. Thanks also go to Paula, Black Rose Writing, my fellow authors, and my readers. You all enrich and impact my life in one way or another.

To my Jesse, who was seven when this story began.

*"When I was a child, I spake as a child,
I understood as a child, I thought as a child."*
– 1 Corinthians 13:11

When I Was Seven

The beach seemed abandoned, but we didn't care as we stripped off socks and shoes so we could wiggle our toes in the sand. Mom kept us back from the water – too cold, she said. But the sand had taken in the sun's rays, and the top layer was still warm.

The others started to walk down the beach while I sat down, content to run my fingers through the sand beside me. The more I dug, the colder it got, but I didn't care. I lifted handful after handful up into the air, letting it sift itself back through my fingers to the waiting ground below. The farther I dug and the colder it got, the wetter it got too. I turned over to kneel like a turtle on the beach, all the while digging and mounding the dirt, forming the foundation of the life-size castle I envisioned.

I dug for what must have been only minutes but felt like hours as I imagined myself the kind ruler of my castle. From a high turret, I would wave and then bow to the sand subjects of my kingdom, who adored me.

Just as I reached out to my loyal subjects, a sound startled me and I looked around, the magic of the moment evaporating in the air. What had I heard? It must have been a bird, but when I glanced at the sky above, it was bare. Dropping my gaze, I searched the shore. I could see for miles, but there was nothing and no one in sight, and I realized for the first time I was alone, completely alone.

The beach and I were one – abandoned.

Chapter 1

When I was seven, Grandma came to our house to live. It felt like something familiar, yet something that's hard to put into words. It's as if when she came she left the front door open. Only you're not sorry it's open 'cause you sense that spring has finally come. You rush to the door to discover that the world looks exactly the same as when you last looked, only it smells better and it makes you smile. And when you tell Mom, she looks up with tired eyes and doesn't see the difference. But I did.

━━━━━━━━━

I first met Grandma, well, probably the day I was born, only I don't remember it so much. I bet she would have held me in her arms 'cause I was so cute. And from what I've seen when grandmas get around new babies, I'll bet she made funny faces at me and googly noises to make me smile. I probably cried instead.

See when Lily was born, she cried a lot. I complained to Mom. But then she told me that babies can't talk yet, so if they want something, the only thing they can do is cry. It's their way of saying, "Hey, I'm hungry," or "Would you please get me that pacifier I just spit out of my mouth?" So, I'm guessing I cried, but I think it would have meant, "Hi."

My earliest memory of Grandma is way back when I was three or two. It's actually the furthest thing I can remember at all, 'cause for as long as I can remember, Grandma's been there. She's like an extra mom, but one who doesn't have to remind me to do my homework.

Grandmas don't have to worry about any of that anymore. They can just play games with their grandkids, and when they get tired of that, they can curl up to read stories and even take naps with us. It's pretty sweet.

So I was really happy when I heard Grandma was coming to stay. My friend Justin's grandma lives a long ways away and sometimes she flies in on an airplane to visit. When she does that, she stays for a few days, maybe even a couple of weeks. But that's not the kind of staying my Grandma was doing. Her apartment is actually really close by. That's where she moved after Grandpa died. She said her house was just too big without Grandpa there. I always thought a house stayed the same size, so I didn't understand how it got bigger just because someone left, but I guess it did. Grown-ups say a lot of things I don't understand, but I'm starting to understand more now that I'm seven.

The real reason Grandma came to stay was that she'd been sick. The good part, though, was that she was finally getting better. I know, because they were letting her out of the hospital. But Mom told me Grandma was pretty tired out from being sick, so we needed to let her rest. She said, "I know you like to play with Grandma, Lucas, but she's not going to be up to that right now. Okay, pumpkin?"

Mom calls me pumpkin sometimes because I have reddish hair and I was born in October. I like it 'cause I love pumpkin pie, so I think it really means she loves me. She usually touches the top of my head or squeezes my shoulder when she says it too. Her hands are always warm. It's like she's hugging me with her hands. I usually reach my arms up and she grabs me in a real hug. I love my mom, and that's part of why I love Grandma – she's a lot like Mom, only she calls me sweetie instead of pumpkin.

The day Grandma moved in was crazy. Dad and some of his friends went over to Grandma's apartment to get some of her things. They got clothes and books, but her bed came from somewhere else. Someone told me it was called a hospital bed. It was really big.

Mom and Dad decided that the best place to put it was in the dining room. At first, I thought that was so Grandma could just stay in bed to eat, but then I couldn't understand where we were supposed to sit since they took the dining room table apart and put it in the basement.

I tried to ask Dad about it, but he kept saying, "Ask me later, sport. I'm kind of busy right now." Then he winked at me and suggested I go find Lily or Justin. I went to find Mom instead.

She was in the laundry room folding clothes. "Where are we going to eat dinner?" I said.

She jumped a little. "Lucas, I didn't see you there. What did you say?"

"I was just wondering where we're going to eat dinner."

She gave me a puzzled look. "In the kitchen, like always."

"But when Grandma comes to have dinner with us, we eat in the dining room. Where are we going to eat since there's no table anymore?"

She stopped and stared at me and then gently took my arm and led me into the kitchen. She sat down on a kitchen chair and pulled me close so her eyes were level with mine. Her voice was quiet when she spoke. "This is different, Lucas. It's not like a big Sunday dinner or your birthday party. Grandma's … well, it's just different." She started to play with her hair. She has this long hair. When she works outside, she puts it in a ponytail, but other than that, it's always hanging down her back and over her shoulders. I'm not sure why she puts it up when she's outside 'cause it's about the same color as the dirt – kind of brownish. So, it wouldn't matter if it got dirt in it.

Moms can be confusing sometimes – like now. My mom plays with her hair when she's nervous, but I don't know why Grandma makes her nervous. When Mom was little, Grandma used to be her mom. And Grandma is really nice. She never makes *me* nervous.

When Mom didn't say any more, I said, "Can I go play outside?"

She must have forgotten I was there 'cause she kind of shook her head like she was waking up. "Sure," she finally said as she got up and disappeared back into the laundry room.

I shrugged my shoulders and started to head out, but the noise from the dining room sounded interesting, so I went there instead. By now, the bed was mostly put together. It was pretty tall off the ground, and Dad and his friends were moving different parts of the bed up and down with a button. I don't know if they were working on it or playing with it, but it looked like a cool bed. Grandma would be able to sit up and lie down and do whatever she wanted in it. Then

I noticed that the bed had railings on the sides, almost like a crib. They were putting the rails up and down, so I guess Grandma could choose where they went, but I'm not sure why she might want them up. When Lily was a baby, we were worried she would fall out of her crib, but Grandma wasn't a baby. I guess there was just a whole lot of stuff I still didn't understand about Grandma coming to live with us.

Once Grandma's bed was put together, I could hardly wait for her to come. It turned out I didn't have to wait long. She came in an ambulance from the hospital. It backed right up into our driveway. I thought that was cool, and I raced to the front door to get a better look, but Mom stopped me before I made it outside. "I'm sorry, pumpkin, but you're going to have to stay in here, out of the way." I was disappointed, but Mom looked pretty serious, so I ducked behind the front curtains. From there I could see everything going on outside.

It seemed weird that Grandma would come in an ambulance. I always thought ambulances took people from their houses to the hospital, never the other way around. I kept watching, but nothing much was happening. All the people had disappeared into the back of the ambulance, and I hadn't seen any of them come back out yet, so I went looking for Dad.

I found him in the dining room putting away his tools. My dad's tall; even bent over his tools he seemed big to me. He has a lot of bushy brown hair on top of his head. When he picks up Lily she loves to run her fingers through it. I don't think Dad likes it too much, though, 'cause sometimes she ends up pulling his hair, but he still lets her do it anyway. He just laughs and says, "Leave me some hair, will ya."

People say I have his hair, even though mine's reddish and his is brown. I think it's 'cause I have a lot of it, even after we cut it. It sticks up a lot too. Mom tries to keep it down, but it doesn't want to stay.

Grandma says I have my dad's nose, which is fine with me, since it's just right, not too long and pointy, but not too fat either. Mom's nose turns up a little and so does Lily's so I guess that's a girl kind of nose. I'm glad mine looks like my dad's.

I sat down on the floor so I could look up at Dad while he gathered his things. "How come Grandma came in an ambulance? We're not a hospital. We're not doctors," I said, starting to get

12

worried.

He stopped what he was doing and sat down on the floor next to me. "Sport, it's okay. Your grandma just doesn't have a lot of energy right now. So, it was easier to take her whole bed from the hospital, put it in an ambulance, and bring her here. Did you see the lights flashing?"

"No."

"Or hear a siren?"

"No, I didn't." I hadn't thought about those things.

"That's because it wasn't an emergency. They're just bringing her here to live."

"Oh." That part made sense. "But we're still not doctors, Dad! I'm learning more and more stuff at school, but I don't know enough yet. What do we do?" My alarm was growing.

He chuckled lightly. "Lucas, don't worry. She doesn't need much in the way of doctors right now, and when she does need a checkup, doctors and nurses will come visit Grandma at the house. We're just here to keep her company. You'll notice soon enough that she does a lot of sleeping these days. So mostly we'll just check on her and bring her some food and something to drink when she wants it. Can you handle that much?"

"Yeah, I can do that." I breathed a big sigh of relief. I didn't want Grandma to get sick all over again 'cause I didn't know how to take care of her. I had to get out of the way about then 'cause some medical people came in with Grandma in another hospital bed. I wasn't sure what we were going to do with two beds.

It turns out Grandma could move around okay and the guys that brought her were really strong, too. In just a jiffy they had her in her new bed and they were taking away the extra one. A nurse who had come with Grandma was checking her out to make sure she was okay. The nurse was holding Grandma's wrist and looking at her watch.

"What are you doing?"

The nurse looked up at me and smiled. "I'm checking her pulse. Your heart pumps blood throughout your body. That's how it keeps you alive. I'm just checking to see how fast her heart's pumping."

"Oh." I'd always wondered about that at my doctor checkups.

The nurse took Grandma's temperature and blood pressure too, explaining everything to me as she did it. When she finished, Grandma said, "Thank you so much. And will you make sure to tell the others how much I appreciate their help and kindness." That's my grandma. She's always super nice. She tells everybody thank you. She thanks me when I show her my schoolwork or when I draw her a picture, even when it's not my best one. She thanked me for playing a song for her on my recorder once, even though I got nervous and made a couple mistakes. It makes me feel good when she says thank you.

It's 'cause of Grandma that I started telling my teacher and my parents thank you all the time. My parents like it when I talk that way. They keep smiling when I say it 'cause they don't have to remind me to do it. But I'll tell you, it shocked the heck out of my teacher and my principal. I'll bet they would have given me a gold star on my forehead if they had one. I told Grandma about it. She said, "Good! Now just keep up the good work. And Lucas, thank you for telling me." I told you she always says thank you.

Dad was right about Grandma being tired. She fell asleep as soon as the ambulance left. A couple of chairs from the dining room table had been left in the room. I grabbed a book and took it into Grandma's new bedroom, but I didn't read much of it. Mostly I just sat in the chair and watched her sleep.

Grandma looked really pretty, even when she was sleeping. Her face looked like the pictures I've seen of angels 'cause it looked kind. I'm not sure how else to describe it. Even her hair lying on the pillow around her face seemed like a halo to me.

I don't think I'd ever looked at Grandma so closely before. I mean, I knew what she looked like, but we'd get so busy doing stuff that I didn't notice what made her look that way. I saw things that were familiar, but also things I hadn't before, like the lines on her face. She was starting to look like an apple that has been sitting around too long. It shrinks up and the skin gets all wrinkly, only hers wasn't too bad yet. I thought about touching her face to see what her skin felt like, but I was afraid that might wake her up. Mom was always telling me to be really quiet and careful when Lily was taking a nap so I wouldn't wake her. I figured I'd better do the same for Grandma.

One of my friends at school told me he didn't know his grandma.

It was either that she lived in another country and he'd never met her, or she died when he was a baby – I can't remember which. I couldn't imagine not having a grandma. You can tell grandmas anything, and they almost never get mad at you. They laugh at all your jokes, and they buy magazines and wrapping paper from you when you're trying to raise money for something. They just love you.

Mom came into the room, but instead of looking at Grandma, she was looking at me. "Pumpkin, are you okay?"

"Sure, Mom. Why?"

"Well, you've been sitting in here a long time. Don't you want to run around outside and play?"

"No. If it's okay, I'd just like to sit here with Grandma, you know, in case she wakes up and needs something or forgets that she's not at her house. I do that sometimes when I sleep at her apartment. I wake up and get a little scared until I remember where I am."

Mom didn't say much, just watched me as I watched Grandma. She was starting to make me nervous, but she finally left, saying, "I'll call you when dinner's ready."

Chapter 2

It was just Grandma and me, and my Mom and Dad of course, for a long time before Lily was born. That's probably why my grandma knows me so well. She even knows stuff about me that I don't even know. Like that first night she stayed at our house, she knew I wasn't going to like the Brussel sprouts Mom made for dinner, but I would like the ice cream bars, even though I'd never had either one before. She was right, too.

She also figured I would like to read before bed, so she asked me to read to her after dinner. Lily climbed up on Grandma's bed and I read stories to both of them until Mom sent us upstairs to bed.

The next day was Sunday, so I didn't have to get up early for school. When I finally woke up, I remembered Grandma was there. I raced downstairs to see her. She was sitting on the side of her bed combing her hair. Her hair is short and mostly straight, except it curves at the ends a bit. It looks messy, but I think it's supposed to look that way. It's brownish-red, but Mom says she gets the color out of a box, whatever that means.

"Good morning, Grandma."

"Hello, Lucas. I didn't see you there. Come here, and let me give you a hug."

I ran into her arms. "Did you sleep okay, Grandma?"

She smiled. "Yes, I did." I love it when she smiles. Her whole face, especially around her eyes, seems to crinkle up when she does. I told her once it reminded me of a crinkly potato chip and she laughed.

She brushed my hair off my forehead with her hands, and I reached up to touch her hair. "Grandma, how did you get this color out of a box?"

She laughed. "Well, you get crayons out a box, right?" I nodded 'cause that made sense. "I'm just coloring my hair instead of a picture."

"But, why? Didn't you like the other color?"

"No, I didn't." She laughed again. "My hair was turning gray, and I wanted it to stay the color it was when I was your age. What if I met one of my friends from when I was a kid? They wouldn't recognize me if I had gray hair, now would they?"

Grandma was always saying things like that that just made sense. I didn't have to think too hard about them. She reached out and hugged me as I started laughing with her.

When Grandma laughs, her eyes sparkle and they talk to me. They tell me how much she loves life and how much she loves me.

"What are you looking at, sweetie?"

"Your eyes. I think they're blue, but they might be indigo."

"Indigo? Where did you learn about indigo?"

"It's in my crayon box. It's my favorite color, even though I don't use my crayons much anymore. It just sounds cool, doesn't it? Like maybe it's from a different country or something."

"Oh, is that why I see you hide it in the toy drawer sometimes?"

I didn't know what to say. Grandma just looked at me over the top of her glasses. It's like she could see right through me and knew exactly what I was thinking. Grandma looks at me like that sometimes, and when she does, I know what *she's* thinking. She's not mad, just disappointed.

"I'm sorry, Grandma. It's just that I … I don't want Lily to break it. She breaks lots of crayons and I don't want to be mad at her, but I think I would be mad if she broke my indigo crayon."

Her face softened and she said, "I understand, she is only two and a half. Maybe when she's a little older, you can introduce her to indigo, and let her use it, exactly because it's special to you."

I nodded my head. That sounded like a good idea. She reached out and squeezed my hand.

Even though I like Grandma's eyes and her smile, the best part about her is her hands. She always has lotion in her purse, and if I ask her, she'll let me put some on. It smells good, not too much like flowers or something only a girl would like. It's some kind of fruit or

17

something, but mostly it smells like Grandma. The lotion makes her hands soft. I know 'cause she likes to rub my cheek with her hand. Sometimes she stops rubbing and just holds my face in her hands and smiles. I like that.

After we ate breakfast, Grandma took a nap. When she woke up she called me to her. Despite what Mom had said, Grandma said she was feeling pretty good and wanted to play with me.

I finally settled on my new army guys. We spread them out on her bed, some for her and some for me. She didn't even mind when I blew her guys up with my tank. She knocked them all over, then grabbed her chest and said, "Oh no, I'm shot, I'm shot! I'm dying … dying … dying." Then she fell over on the bed, and I started giggling.

Mom came into the room just about then, and she was not giggling. "I thought I told you that Grandma …" Then she stopped talking right in the middle of her sentence. She looked at Grandma who was starting to laugh, at me, at the army guys and back again. The edges of her mouth started to curl up. She was trying so hard not to laugh, but she finally couldn't help it and burst out laughing too. "Oh, never mind," she finally said, laughing her way back out of the room.

I looked at Grandma and smiled. I guess she's basically my best friend next to Justin. I love Mom and Dad too, but that's different. They have to tell me what to do and what not to do. It's their job. But grandmas can be your friend – if they want to. And my grandma, it seems, has always wanted to. That's probably why I love her.

We picked up the army guys, and then Grandma said, "If you want to go play with Justin, it's okay with me, sweetie."

"Don't you want to play anymore?"

"Well, I am still pretty weak, but it's more than that. It's okay for you to play with friends. You don't have to stay with me just because I've been sick. Will you do that for me?"

I smiled. "Sure, Grandma. I love you."

"I love you, too."

"Mom," I called, "can I go see if Justin can play?"

She poked her head in from the kitchen. "Sure, pumpkin, but grab some lunch first. I was just making some sandwiches. Would you like one?"

18

I loved sandwiches, so I ate two. Then I went to find Justin. He lives a few houses down the street and he's been my friend since I was five. His mom is super nice too. She's the one who answered the door.

"Hello, and who might you be?"

"I'm your neighbor from up the street." I smiled.

"Are you selling something? Because the only thing I'm interested in is someone who could make himself useful by eating some leftover cookies."

"I bet I could handle that."

She winked, reached out and hugged me, then called behind her, "Justin, Lucas is here to play."

After Justin and I ate chocolate chip cookies, we decided to play detective. It was one of our favorite things to do. Justin watches lots of cop movies on TV with his dad, so he always knows cool things to say when we catch a pretend bad guy, like, "Do ya' feel lucky, punk?" If his mom hears him, she rolls her eyes, but since she also laughs, we figure it's okay.

That day, we staked out the neighbor's cat. They call him Stripes, but we knew he was really the cat burglar, Shifty Shepard. It was easy to follow him when he walked along the top of the fence between the two yards, but when he jumped down, we had to try something new.

"I know! The knothole," Justin said.

We'd been using an old knothole in the fence for a long time. Justin's taller than me, so it used to be that only he could see through it. But now that I was getting so much older, I could see through it too, as long as I stood on tiptoes.

I got to the knothole first. "What do you see?" Justin said.

"Well, Shifty is on the prowl. He's moving toward the house. He's looking around to see if anyone's watching. Here, take a look."

"Ooh, you're right. We're about to catch him in the act. Oh, there he goes! Right into the doggy door. He's guilty all right."

"Now we just need to arrest him and question him," I said.

We both looked at each other. How were we going to arrest him when he was in the neighbor's house? And if we couldn't do that, what about the interrogation? After a minute, we both shrugged our shoulders.

We sat down on the ground to think of what to do next. All of a sudden Justin got a funny smile on his face and leaned in to whisper to me. "Do you want to help me build a doghouse?"

"Sure, but why are we whispering?"

"Because it's a secret."

"But why? You don't even have a dog." I almost forgot to whisper that time.

"Exactly." I must have looked confused because he said, "If I build a doghouse, Mom and Dad will have to get me a dog, but if they know I'm building a doghouse, they'll stop me before it's done. Then, for sure, I *won't* get a dog."

"Okay." I guess that made sense. "But I think we have to have a plan first. You know, decide what we want it to look like."

"Good thinking," Justin said and then raced inside to get paper and pencil. For the next twenty minutes or so we drew all kinds of doghouses. After we got tired of that, we went inside to play checkers.

When I went home later, Grandma was sitting up in bed reading a book. She looked up at me and smiled. Before I even told Mom I was home, I raced into Grandma's arms to give her a big hug.

"What have you been up to, sweetie?" Grandma said. From then until dinnertime, I talked and Grandma listened.

Chapter 3

I liked having Grandma at my house. Every day after school I would rush to her bed to see if she was awake. If she was, she'd make a space for me on her bed so she could listen to me talk about my day.

One day as I finished telling her about school, I said, "Aren't you glad you moved in here?"

"Sure, but what makes you say that?"

"'Cause now you get to see me more often!"

She laughed. "Absolutely, Lucas. But don't you miss the playroom at my apartment?"

I had to think about that. It had been an awesome place. "Not really, Grandma. Toys break, but Grandmas don't."

"Well, sometimes they do, darling. One day I'll go and join Grandpa in Heaven. Will you be okay when that happens?"

I cocked my head to the side. "I didn't know that, Grandma. I will miss you a lot."

"I know, but I won't really be gone, you just won't be able to see me, but I'll be able to see you. I'll watch out for you, too."

"Really? Are you sure you can't just stay?"

"I can stay for a little while, but not forever."

"Okay. You can go be with Grandpa, but not yet."

"All right. I just can't make any promises about how long I'll stay. That part's not up to me."

"Who is it up to?"

"That's up to God, Lucas. But He knows a lot more than we do, so He always makes good decisions, even if we don't always understand them."

I just nodded my head. "This is tricky stuff, Grandma. I don't think I understand it yet."

"That's okay, sweetie, not too many people do." She shook her head and got a far off look. "Not too many people do." She turned back to me, "Not even your mom, Lucas."

It turns out Grandma was right about that. I tried to talk to my mom about people dying and that maybe Grandma would die someday. She got upset and told me we should talk about something else.

Chapter 4

The next weekend after Grandma moved in, we went to her old apartment to finish moving her out. Justin's mom stayed at our house to sit with Grandma, and the rest of us went to the apartment, even Lily.

Her apartment looked different than normal. I think it's 'cause Grandma wasn't there and probably too 'cause of the boxes. Even the playroom overflowed with them; I couldn't see a single toy. When I had to go the bathroom, it felt like I was a mouse in a maze of cardboard looking for the cheese. I was just glad it was a short maze.

When I came out of the bathroom, I started looking at all the boxes. They were stacked almost to the ceiling, but the ones I could see had words written on them, like "For Iris," "Josie's clothes," or "Donate." Iris is my mom, and Josie is Grandma's name. Her name's really Josephine, but nobody ever calls her that, and I just call her Grandma.

I found a few boxes on the ground that hadn't been taped up yet, so I opened them to see what was inside. Most of them were boring, but then I found one full of books. It had cookbooks, books without any pictures, comic books and even some dinosaur books. No wonder Grandma was so interesting – she had interesting books even a boy like me would like. I didn't get to look at too many of them, though, 'cause people got mad when I started taking them out of the boxes to read.

"Lucas, we are trying to get everything sorted and *into* boxes. If you keep taking them out to read, we'll never get done. Why don't you go check on Lily?" Mom said. Boy, I knew we were packing up and all, but she usually liked it when I read books.

When I Was Seven

I remember one day when I was sick and stayed home from school, only I wasn't that sick. Mom brought a whole stack of books to my bed. She read every single one of them to me. Some of them made us laugh. Some of them got us scared, and Mom had to protect me until we got to the ending and found out everything was okay. Lily was still in Mom's tummy then, but she came out pretty soon after that. I started reading stories to Lily as soon I learned how to read by myself.

I could have read to Lily now – if the grown-ups had let me pick up a book. I found her in what used to look like Grandma's bedroom but now looked more like a cardboard heaven. Boxes were stacked against one wall and flat cardboard waiting to be folded into boxes was leaning against the other.

Lily was supposed to be asleep on the bed, but she was playing with Grandma's jewelry box instead. All I could see was the back of Lily's head where her blond curls were matted down, so maybe she had been asleep for a little while after all.

I don't know where she found the jewelry box, but it looked like it had been Grandma's for a long time. I could tell 'cause it had little white roses all around the sides and each one was full of dust. I couldn't see what the top looked like 'cause Lily had flipped it open and pulled most of the jewelry out onto the bed. A lot of necklaces were in a tangled mess, but Lily had one necklace hanging around her neck and bracelets and rings circled her wrists and fingers. Even more piles of stuff surrounded her. She looked up at me, smiled, and then returned to her treasure. "Pretty," was all she said, over and over again.

She was going to get in a lot of trouble, I could tell. But, since Lily's little, she gets away with a lot of stuff. So, I figured if I was standing there, I would probably be the one to get into trouble. I peeked out the door, but I couldn't see anyone. When I looked back at Lily, it didn't look like she had broken anything, so I climbed on the bed next to her. Maybe no one would mind after all, as long as we stayed out of the way.

Grandma, near as I could tell, only wore necklaces and earrings on special occasions. So it surprised me how much jewelry she had. Most of it was gold and silver, which made me think of pirate treasure.

Even though the jewelry box was fancy, I could picture it as a treasure chest, and the red lining inside was a great pirate color. All the jewelry was part of some vast wealth waiting to be plundered. Too bad Justin wasn't here to be my first mate, although I doubted Grandma would let us bury it in the backyard.

While Lily played with all the pirate gold, I noticed out of the corner of my eye a small loop of ribbon in the bottom of Grandma's jewelry box. The box was almost empty now, and the bottom was smooth red fabric. The ribbon was red too, and I probably wouldn't have seen it except an earring was tangled up in it. I got the earring undone and pulled it out, so the only thing left was that piece of red ribbon. It looked like it had gotten stuck underneath the red fabric and only a small part was poking out, right at the edge.

I grabbed hold of the ribbon and tried to pull it out, but it was stuck. I couldn't get it to budge. What would a pirate do? I spied one of Grandma's necklaces and got an idea. Soon I had the necklace threaded through the loop and then yanked on it, hard. All at once, the necklace broke in half and beads starting flying everywhere. Lily's eyes got wide. "Uh, oh," she whispered.

We both waited for someone to come and yell at us, but I guess they were too busy. I started to giggle just a little. Soon Lily did too, and we couldn't stop laughing at the beads all over the room. Even the necklace around Lily's neck started to jiggle with her laughter.

I started to pick up the scattered beads, but then I threw a few at Lily and she threw some back at me. That just made us giggle harder and louder. That's what did us in.

Mom was not happy.

When we had finished picking up every last bead, which I mostly did since Lily didn't help much, and when Mom had finished lecturing me but was still glaring, I gathered all the jewelry to put back in Grandma's case.

That's when I saw it. The bottom of Grandma's jewelry box had come up, revealing a small compartment. The little loop I pulled on was actually a handle. Even though I broke the necklace, the secret door had come open. Lying there in the very bottom of Grandma's jewelry case was a small ring with a light blue stone.

"Mom, look at this!"

She came closer. "Where did you find that?"

"It was hidden in a secret compartment at the bottom of Grandma's jewelry box."

She rolled her eyes at me. "Really, Lucas? That's just a cheap ring. I'm sure it wasn't hidden, just forgotten. If you throw it away, I'll bet Grandma won't even notice. Your imagination's running away with you."

"Okay, I'm sorry," I said, but I realized I didn't mean it. I guess it didn't really matter 'cause Mom just picked up Lily and left the room, leaving me to clean up the jewelry by myself.

I looked at the ring more closely. It was a dull looking gold, not shiny at all, and it was rather plain, a simple circle with the gem on top. Four prongs held the blue gem, but it was dirty. I licked my finger and washed it off with my spit. I had to admit it did look kind of cheap, so there didn't seem to be a reason to hide it. But that made me wonder all the more why it had been, 'cause in spite of what Mom said, that was a secret compartment, and the ring was definitely inside it. I put the ring in my pocket since I wasn't sure what else to do with it. Gently, I closed the secret door, then scooped up all of Grandma's jewelry and piled it back on top.

When I closed the lid, I found more dusty roses in a circle around a faded drawing of a little girl. She had rosy cheeks and a sly smile. It reminded me of Lily. Maybe Grandma got this jewelry box when she was a little girl like Lily. Only I couldn't imagine Lily with a jewelry box now – she'd just break it like she does everything else.

I set the box on the small bookshelf at the head of Grandma's bed. Someone would come along and pack it up later. I put my hand in my pocket and felt the ring. Maybe I could ask Grandma about it when we got back home. I'm sure she'd tell me all about it.

Chapter 5

It was late afternoon when we got home. Justin's mom was sitting by Grandma's bedside watching over her while she slept. I was surprised to find Justin there too. He was reading and apparently waiting for me to get back. When he saw me, he jerked his head to the left a couple of times, showing me we needed to go into the other room so we could talk.

Mom came in to check on Grandma, so we decided to go to the backyard for some privacy. We sat down on the grass with our backs against the house, and Justin pulled out a folded piece of paper. He smoothed it out on the ground so I could see what was on it. It was a drawing of a doghouse that looked just like the one Snoopy had. He smiled.

I opened my mouth to say something when I heard my mom's voice from inside. The dining room windows above us were open and the voices carried clearly on the breeze.

"Thanks for all your help, Allison."

"No problem. Your mom's a sweetheart. I enjoyed myself. She fell asleep just a short while ago for the first time all day. I think she wanted to keep me entertained, so I'm guessing she's pretty tired by now."

"I appreciate it. I don't always know how to talk to her myself. We've always been close, but I'm so afraid of what it will be like when she's gone that I … I don't know. I guess it's like I'm pretending none of this is real – that she's not staying at my house, that's she actually going to get better, that she's not …" The voices stopped, and all I heard was the faint sound of crying.

I wasn't sure what Mom was talking about. What would happen if

When I Was Seven

Grandma didn't get better? Then I heard the words that stopped my heart, "I don't want her to die, but there's nothing I can do about it."

Justin, I saw, was looking at his design and hadn't been listening to the conversation going on over our heads. He didn't look up at me, and I was glad. Until that moment I had thought Grandma had come to our house to live, but now I knew she had come to our house to die.

I find myself once again on the beach. I dig in the sand like before, but I only sift it through my fingers this time, distracted as I am. The remnants of my sand castle lie crushed and forgotten beside me. As my hands play mindlessly, I watch the horizon. It seems calm, but I know how storms can suddenly appear, so I am alert and tense.

I pull my knees up close to my chest and wrap my gritty hands around them, holding them close. Using my toes, I begin to burrow my bare feet into the cool sand. It seems like little protection from the pending storm, but I don't know what else to do or where I might go.

A cloud moves across the sun and I shiver in the sudden shadow. Where is everyone? They haven't forgotten me, have they? I imagine I should do something, but I have no idea what.

Just at that moment, I feel a hand on my shoulder, and I jump in surprise. As I turn, I see that it's my dad, come for me.

Chapter 6

Dad ordered pizza that night after all the busy work of moving Grandma's stuff. Justin stayed for dinner, and if Mom noticed he ate lots but I didn't even finish one slice, she didn't say anything.

I wanted to talk to Grandma or even Mom and Dad, but I wasn't sure how to start. Everyone seemed so tired, that I decided to wait for another day. Even Grandma fell asleep before Lily was off to bed. I sat in a chair beside her hospital bed just watching her sleep. I almost smiled when she started to snore with her head thrown back. I didn't realize Grandma snored, but I guess she did. I wondered what else I didn't know about her. Would I have enough time to find it all out before she was gone?

"Can I sleep on the couch in the living room tonight?" I said when it was my own bedtime.

"Why do you want to sleep there, Lucas?" Mom said.

"'Cause it's right next to Grandma's room. So, if she needs anything in the night or she gets scared, I'll be here to help her."

Mom's voice sounded kind of raspy when she responded. "That would be just fine, pumpkin." She encircled me in her arms and kissed the top of my head. "Why don't you go get ready for bed while Dad and I get things set up for you."

I hurried to put my pajamas on and brush my teeth. Knowing it would make Mom happy, I gathered up my dirty clothes and tossed them into the clothes hamper, not remembering the ring lying in the pocket of my jeans.

When I got back downstairs, I saw Mom and Dad had fixed me up a nice bed with pillows and blankets. Dad ruffled my hair, "Let us know if you need anything, and we'll come quick as a wink. Okay?"

I nodded as I snuggled into my bed with a smile on my face. It felt like camping, only more comfortable. I didn't fall asleep as quickly as Grandma did, but almost as fast.

Once, during the night, I thought I heard Grandma call out, but when I sat up and listened in her direction all I heard was the soft rumble of her snoring. I was still pretty sleepy, so I turned over and went back to sleep.

The next morning, I was actually hungry seeing as how I hadn't really eaten the night before. I could hear someone walking around upstairs, but since it was Sunday I figured whoever it was wouldn't be coming down anytime soon.

I found some leftover pizza in the fridge and helped myself to a slice and a glass of soda pop. Mom usually liked me to drink milk in the morning, but I figured if leftover pizza was an okay breakfast, leftover pop would be fine too.

When I was done eating, I went to check on Grandma. She had been sleeping when I woke up, but now she was sitting up, quietly reading.

"Good morning, sweetie. I see you slept close by last night. That was so thoughtful of you. Did you sleep okay?"

I nodded my head. "Grandma, are you dying?" I hadn't planned on asking her right away, but it was on my mind so much, it couldn't help just coming out of my mouth.

Her smile faded, but she didn't look sad. "Yes, Lucas. I am."

"Why didn't you tell me? Why didn't anyone tell me?"

"Well, I can only answer for myself, Lucas. Are you ready to listen to me? Really listen?"

"Of course I am." I wasn't sure why she even asked the question. I was standing right there, wasn't I, trying to talk to her?

"Because you weren't a few days ago."

"What are you talking about?"

"We talked the other day about how I might join Grandpa pretty soon, do you remember that?"

"Yes." I didn't like that she was turning out to be right.

"I've wanted to tell you, Lucas, but I could tell that day you weren't ready to listen. It would have been too much at once. So, I tried to get you thinking about the idea."

31

"Why? I don't understand why you couldn't have just told me then."

"Let me explain it this way. Do you remember when you learned to ride a bike?" I nodded. "Well, you started with training wheels. You had them to hold you up when you leaned too much one way or the other, but they allowed you to get used to pedaling your bike before having to learn to balance at the same time. You knew eventually those training wheels would come off, but since it was in the future, you didn't worry about it, did you?"

"I guess not."

"This is the same kind of thing. I hoped that if the idea I was going to die someday could sit in your head, it might find a way to get comfortable there. Then when you learned the whole truth, the idea of my death would already have a place to call home."

I wasn't sure why, but I understood what she was talking about. A few tears started to form at the sides of my eyes. I believed the night before that Grandma was dying, but now I knew for sure. "Why are you dying, Grandma?"

"It's time. Everyone has to die sometime of something. My time is now. I have cancer, Lucas. There are cancer bugs all over the inside of my body. They're eating away all the good stuff and only leaving more cancer bugs behind."

"Can't you get rid of the cancer bugs?"

"Sometimes doctors can. We tried for a long time, but in the end, we lost the war. I finally surrendered. Your mom wasn't too happy when I decided to quit treatments. She wasn't ready to accept that it wasn't working, but I knew, even before the doctor told me." She reached out to cradle my cheek with her hand. "Sometimes you just know."

"Why didn't Mom tell me?"

"She's just learning to accept it herself, Lucas. How could she explain it to you, when she can't even explain it to herself?"

"I guess that would be hard." It was all making sense now, but I didn't want it to. I reached over to hug Grandma. She held me in her arms for a long time, gently wiping the tears from my cheeks, but letting them fall for as long as I wanted.

The rest of the day was kind of a blur to me. I didn't want to think about Grandma dying, but I couldn't help it. Dad kept looking at me funny. I think he knew something was wrong, but he wasn't sure what.

In the afternoon when Lily took a nap, Mom decided to take a nap too. Even Grandma fell asleep. So Dad suggested we play a game. We pulled out some of our favorites and sat down on the floor to play. For a while, I forgot about real life.

As we put away the checkers after our third game, Dad bent his head down so he could look me in the eye. "What's up, Lucas?" He didn't usually call me Lucas, only when he was serious about something. I looked up, startled and wide-eyed. Dad laughed. "I'm sorry, sport. I'm not mad at you. You're not in trouble. It just seems like something's on your mind."

I breathed a sigh. "Yeah, I guess so. Grandma's dying. I asked her about it and she told me."

He nodded his head. "I wondered. It's hard to keep things from kids. What do you think about it?"

People didn't usually ask me what I thought, so his question made me feel a little grown up. "I don't like it, but I understand it."

His eyes opened wide. "I don't even understand it, Lucas. How can you?"

"I don't know. I just do. Grandpa left and Grandma has to go be with him sometime, doesn't she? It just makes sense."

He smiled and put his arm around me. "I guess it is that simple, isn't it?" After a minute, he whispered, almost like he was talking to himself, "I wish your mom could understand that."

Chapter 7

The next morning Mom woke me before Grandma was awake so I could get ready for school. I got dressed in my bedroom, but when I came downstairs to check on Grandma, she was still sleeping.

"Mom, maybe I should stay home to be with Grandma."

"Lucas, you need to go to school. She'll be here when you get home."

I guess that was true, but I wasn't sure it was true. Besides, I wanted to watch over her, and I wrinkled up my brow to try to tell Mom that.

She raised her eyebrows in response. "Really, Lucas, we'll take care of her while you're away." Then she nodded her head once – a sure sign the discussion was over.

I wasn't as sure about things as she was, but it appeared I didn't have a choice. Reluctantly I finished getting ready and walked the few blocks to school with Dad.

Just before entering school, I tried one last time. "Dad, I could do my schoolwork from home while Grandma's sleeping. I'm sure my teacher would understand."

He crouched down on the sidewalk in front of the school to get to my height. "Sport, your Grandma would want you to be at school. You can ask her yourself when you get home this afternoon, all right?"

I scrunched up my face at him. I wasn't sure I could trust Grandma's answer this afternoon once Mom and Dad had the chance to tell her what to say. This wasn't all right, but I wasn't sure how to convince anyone where I needed to be. "I'll ask her," I finally said, knowing it wasn't going to help.

School lasted forever that day. I kept watching the clock, wondering when I could go home. I tried to fall down in gym a few extra times, hoping for a big enough scrape that I would need to go home, but no luck there. I thought about telling the school nurse I felt like I was going to puke, which I kind of did, but there was a problem with that plan, too. I knew Mom wouldn't really believe me, but the bigger problem was Grandma made a big deal about telling the truth. I couldn't have that be the last thing Grandma remembered about me.

During recess, Justin found me sitting on the ground, drawing in the dirt with a stick. His hair was messy from playing, and it was hanging down in his eyes. He looked at me from underneath his hair. "What're you doing down there?" he said.

"Thinking."

"About what?"

"My grandma. She's dying, but they won't let me stay home to take care of her."

"Man, that's a bummer. Is she going to die today?"

"No, I don't think so."

Justin sat down beside me and didn't say anything else for a long time. Just before recess ended he swung his hair out of his eyes so he could look at me. "You know, I know a lot about dying, because of Stimpy."

I remembered Stimpy. He was Justin's gerbil who died last year. I nodded my head.

"I missed him at first, but it's not so bad now," Justin said. "My mom and dad are getting me a new gerbil as soon as school's out."

"What about the dog you want?"

He grinned, "They don't know about the dog yet. I figure I'll get the gerbil first and then tell them about the doghouse. A gerbil and a dog sound good, don't they? And you can play with them whenever you want."

"Thanks." The thought of playing with a new Stimpy sounded fun. But I knew it didn't work the same way with grandmas. It's not like you could replace her with a new one.

I remembered the day Stimpy died. They buried him in the backyard and then his whole family went bowling to take Justin's mind off Stimpy. I liked bowling, but not nearly as much as I liked

Grandma. No matter how much I thought about it, I couldn't figure out how anything would make up for Grandma being gone. Thinking about it just made me more anxious to get home to her. I got up and trudged back in from recess. Justin trudged right beside me.

Finally, school ended. It was a nice day, so Mom and Lily were outside waiting to walk me home. Lily liked to meet me as long as it wasn't raining or too cold. As we walked, too slowly if you ask me, something dawned on me. "Mom, who's sitting with Grandma?"

"No one is right now, Lucas. We'll only be gone a few minutes; she'll be just fine."

At that, I started running. Why wasn't anyone taking this seriously?!

When I got home, I was surprised to find Grandma sitting up in her bed, reading a book. She actually was fine.

"I was worried about you, Grandma. Were you okay today?"

"Yes, I was. Now, come sit down," she said, as she smiled and patted the bed beside her. When I was settled, she went on. "I can tell you're worried about me. I really appreciate that, but everyone needs a break sometime. I would love it if you spent the whole day with me, I really would." Ah, ha! She really did want me to stay home from school. But then she continued, "However, Lucas, I shouldn't be selfish. You have friends and teachers who need you, too. I'll just have to make do without you from time to time."

I looked at her, puzzled for a moment, but my face soon relaxed as I realized she was being honest with me. "I love you, Grandma," I said as I threw my arms around her.

"I love you, too, sweetie! Now, tell me about your day. What was the best part of school today?" She sounded just like my mom, only Mom hadn't been asking me that question lately. It seems she hadn't been asking me much at all, ever since Grandma had moved in.

I started to tell Grandma about school, but then I stopped. "To be honest, I had a hard time thinking about school today. I was thinking about you. Does it hurt? Cancer, does it hurt?"

She nodded before speaking. "Yes, cancer can hurt. But the doctors have given me some pain medications to help with it."

"Do they? Help, I mean?"

"Yes, they can. I don't like them, though."

36

Just then Mom poked her head in. She seemed a little distracted and only half smiled. "Lucas, don't forget to do your homework, okay, and make sure you don't wear Grandma out."

"Okay." When Mom left, I said, "She's sad about you dying, isn't she?"

"Of course she is."

"I'm sad, too, but I think she's worse."

"You can help her, you know."

"Me? How can *I* help? I'm only seven."

"You can listen."

"To what?"

"Just listen." I still was confused and she could tell. "You'll understand more as you do it, just listen." I wasn't sure what that meant, but I was willing to try it out.

I spent the rest of the afternoon near her bed doing my homework, even reading some of my book to Grandma. At one point I asked, "You're not getting too tired, are you?"

She reached out to touch my cheek. "Lucas, there will be days soon when I'll be too tired to even have a conversation with you, but for right now I can. So, I'm going to enjoy it. Is that okay with you?"

"Well, of course, Grandma. I just don't want to get in trouble with Mom for wearing you out."

Her eyes twinkled. "I wouldn't want her to be mad at me either," she said. Then she winked. "But for now, I think it's worth the risk."

When I went to bed that night on the couch, Dad touched the top of my head instead of messing up my hair like he usually did. Mom looked like she wanted to say something only she couldn't quite remember the words. I think it's 'cause her eyes got kind of watery. She gave me a big hug and whispered, "I love you, pumpkin, and I'm proud of you."

Dad doesn't say it as often as she does, but he did that night. "Love you, sport. You're a good man." He gave me a thumbs up and a nod as they both left the room.

I could hear them in the kitchen talking softly as I started to drift off to sleep. Mom said something and then Dad responded with, "Honey, she's been through a lot already. Maybe it's time to let her go. This is her decision." I sat up to listen. I didn't know if Grandma had meant eavesdropping was what I was supposed to do, but that's how I'd found out Grandma was dying in the first place, so I decided to take a chance.

"No, Pete! She's not done yet! The doctors can help her keep fighting it. I want my kids to grow up knowing their grandma. Lily's only two. How much will she remember? 'Grandma' will only be a title attached to the picture on the wall, nothing more."

"My mom's still around. Lily and Lucas will still have a grandma." I figured Mom gave him a dirty look 'cause he stopped talking for a minute. Then I heard Dad's voice again. "I know my mother isn't the warmest person in the world. I'm sorry about your mom. None of us are ready for her to die, but she's not dead yet. Let's enjoy the time she has left."

It was quiet for a few minutes, so I crept out of bed to peek into the kitchen. Dad was hugging Mom, and I think she was crying.

Chapter 8

The next day at the end of school, Mom wasn't waiting for me to walk home even though it was a nice day. So I walked home with Justin. We were used to doing that.

"Do you want to see my doghouse plans?" he said. "I've been making a list of all the supplies I'll need."

"Yeah, but can I see them later? My grandma needs me."

He just nodded his head. "Okay, I got your back."

"What does that mean?" I said. Justin says funny things like that all the time. They make me smile, even if I don't always understand them.

He shrugged his shoulders. "I'm not really sure, but my dad says it to his buddies. I think it means that watching over your Grandma is what you've got to do right now, and since that's what you've got to do, I'm okay with it."

I nodded. That made sense.

Justin nodded too. "You know, a man's got to do what a man's got to do."

It's nice to have a good friend like Justin. Part of me wanted to go play with him, but I was worried about Grandma.

When I came in the door, I could see Grandma was awake, but she looked groggy. "Are you okay, Grandma?"

"Right as rain, ..." She looked at me puzzled, then brightened and said, "Luke." She didn't ever call me Luke, and it almost seemed like she'd forgotten my name, but I knew that wasn't possible.

I didn't have any homework, so I asked her if she wanted to play a game. Grandma was always willing to play Crazy 8s or Old Maid with me.

She hesitated, then said, "Sure, I guess so."

I pulled out Crazy 8s. Grandma and I have played this game a lot, but something wasn't right this time. Grandma kept trying to play 6s as the wild cards, not the 8s like it's supposed to be. I had to tell her, "No, Grandma, the 6s aren't wild. You're going to have to draw a card."

She would say something like, "Oh, okay," and then she would draw a card, but pretty soon she was doing the same thing all over again. I decided it really didn't matter, so I let her play whatever card she wanted as the wild card. She won the game, but I didn't feel like either one of us was a winner. I gathered up the cards and then sat down on her bed facing her.

"Grandma, you're always saying to tell the truth, so I'm going to be honest with you. You're forgetting stuff more than normal. Is your head okay?"

She laughed. "Lucas, my head is definitely *not* okay." She stopped laughing and got a serious expression on her face. "Sometimes it feels like there's a big thunderstorm going on inside my brain. It's dark and cloudy and the claps of thunder keep drowning out the sound of my own thoughts." She shook her head. "I told you I didn't like taking my pain medications. Do you remember?"

I didn't, but I nodded anyway.

"I don't like them because they leave me confused. I understand that even the cancer, as it advances, might affect my thinking. It probably already has, but I know the medicine does." She looked right at me. "The doctor told me it's normal, but, Lucas, not being able to think clearly isn't normal. Does that sound normal to you?"

"No." I shook my head in case the word wasn't registering with her.

"I agree, it's not." She let out a big sigh, "But I guess I don't have much say in the matter. I am glad, though, that you were brave enough to say something to me about it. Everyone else is just too nice to say anything, but I know I'm getting mixed up more often." She let out a sigh, then said, "Will you do me a favor, Lucas?"

"Sure, Grandma." I'd do anything for her and I'm sure she knew it.

"Will you keep telling me when I say something strange? It helps me a bit to sort things out in my head. I don't know how much worse it's going to get before I die, but I hope not too much worse. So at least for now, will you do that for me?"

"Yes, Grandma," I said, although I wasn't sure it would really help. After all, she kept messing up in the game even after I tried to straighten her out. But if Grandma wanted it, then that's what I'd do.

I decided to let Grandma rest after that. I tucked blankets around her and kissed her cheek just like Mom does for me at night. Then I picked up the Crazy 8s deck and went to find Mom.

She was upstairs helping Lily pick up her room. "Mom, would you play Crazy 8s with me?"

"I thought you were playing with your grandma."

"Well, yeah, I was, but … Well, I guess she's kind of tired." I didn't want to talk about what happened. Talking about it made it real, and I guess I was hoping it wasn't. I must have been frowning 'cause Mom came over to me and lifted my face so I was looking up at her.

"Are you okay, pumpkin?"

I didn't want to look at her. I was afraid everything would spill right out of me – everything about Grandma and all the tears I was holding back. I looked at my feet and shuffled them a bit, but then I nodded my head.

She didn't say anything, just touched the top of my head and bent down to give me a big hug. "Sure. I'd love to play Crazy 8s with you."

Lily played with us even though we had to look at her cards and tell her what to play. Lily and I laughed and had so much fun that I didn't notice Mom wasn't laughing with us. I even forgot about Grandma for a while – at least until I looked at Mom. Her face looked old, older than Grandma's, older than it had been even the day before.

I reached up to touch her face with both my hands. "I know she's dying, Mom."

"What?"

"I know Grandma's dying, and it will be okay."

She didn't respond, just stared at the wall behind me for a long time. Finally, she whispered, "I'm not sure it will."

I don't know why, but I got a funny feeling she wasn't talking about Grandma anymore.

Chapter 9

Mom left to go make dinner, and I decided it would be a good idea to keep Lily busy and out of the way. It's funny how Grandma was the one dying, but Mom seemed to be the one needing the most help right now, only I wasn't sure why.

I sat down on the floor to play with Lily and her toys. Lily is an okay little sister. She likes to twirl her fingers in her curly hair, kind of like Mom does. Only with Lily, it gets funny 'cause sometimes her finger gets stuck in her curls and Mom has to untangle her hair to get the finger out. But I get in trouble if I laugh, so I don't anymore, at least not out loud.

She's usually pretty fun to play with, though, and I like being her big brother. "Hey, Lily, why don't we take some toys downstairs by Grandma. If she's awake, maybe she'll play with us." She nodded with a smile, so we gathered up some of her dolls then went to my room for my army guys and tanks.

When we got to the dining room it looked like Grandma's eyes were open, but she wasn't very awake. So we spread everything out in the living room to play. Lily didn't understand how to play with my army guys and tanks the right way, but she let me set up her dolls and then giggled and said, "Boom!" when I took them out with my tanks. She even had fun stomping over her fallen dolls with my conquering army guys.

When we got tired of that game, I said, "Let's read a story, okay?"

"Yes, yes!" She squealed while jumping up and down.

Lily always likes when I read her stories. She snuggles up next to me and gives me hugs. I guess I'd been spending so much time with Grandma lately that I'd been forgetting to read to Lily.

We grabbed some of our favorites and settled down on the couch.

That way Grandma could hear the stories, too. Lily loved every story. When I finished one, she would hand me the next one, saying, "More, more."

Before long, the entire stack of books was finished. "All done," Lily said.

Then we heard Grandma from her bed say, "Do you know what my favorite story was when I was little?"

"What was it?" I said, as we both ran to climb up beside her.

"Well, when I was a very little girl, kind of like Lily, my mother used to read me stories, too. I loved *Are You My Mother?* It's a story about a baby bird. The mother bird has lost her and keeps going from place to place, but no matter how much the mother looks she can't find her baby."

"Grandma, you got the story backward," I laughed. "It's the baby bird that looks for his mom, and in the end, he finds her."

"Oh," Grandma looked a little confused, but I guess she was just still tired.

That's when Mom called us in to dinner. She had made spaghetti, which is something everyone seems to like, only it was different this time. Mom made a plate up for Grandma so she could stay in bed to eat, but she never made a plate for herself. After helping us bless our food, she didn't say another word. It was strange too that Dad hadn't gotten home from work yet. That happened sometimes, but when it did, Mom always told us why – that he was working late or got caught in traffic or something.

I kept listening like Grandma told me to, but I was listening to silence. I guess that's important too.

"Where's Dad?" I finally said.

"He's late," Mom said without looking at me.

Dad came in the door as we were finishing up. He looked at Mom but didn't go to kiss her like he usually did. He just sat down and pulled food his way so he could pile it on his plate.

I was beginning to think you could listen with your eyes and not just your ears. When you did, it was amazing how much you could learn.

It was nice to escape when it was time to clear Grandma's dishes. Her eyes were bright and she smiled when she saw me. "Are you feeling okay? You seemed –"

"Fuzzy headed?" she said.

"Well, yeah."

"I was, but I think I'm a little better now."

"Good." I gave her a hug before taking her dishes back into the kitchen.

Dad was just finishing up. He ruffled my hair when he saw me and said, "How was your day, sport?"

I was glad he was talking again. I told him about the best parts of the day and then went to find Lily and Mom.

It was almost bedtime, and Mom was helping Lily into her pajamas. "I'll go get ready for bed, too," I said.

She smiled at me. "Thank you, Lucas." I was relieved to see her smile again. I hung on to that smile while I got my pajamas on, and for good measure, I decided to lay out my clothes for school the next day.

Jeans were my favorite, so I pulled out a clean pair from my drawer. When I laid them on the floor next to my t-shirt, I noticed a small lump in the pocket. Reaching inside, my fingers touched a ring, the one I had discovered in Grandma's jewelry box!

I raced downstairs to Grandma's side, glad to see she was still awake. "Grandma, I found something of yours." Using both hands, I held it up for her to see. She made a small sound like a gasp or a hiccup. Looking past the ring, what I saw startled me. Her expression looked strange. I couldn't tell if it was happy or sad. It sure wasn't excited, like I had expected. I quickly dropped the ring. "What is it, Grandma?"

"Where did you get that?" Her voice sounded scared.

"It was hidden in your jewelry box." She didn't respond, so I said, "I'll show you." I dropped the ring on her bed and ran to the basement to look for the boxes from Grandma's apartment. Fortunately, they were in front of our old boxes. I knew some of them were heavy, so I wasn't sure if I'd be able to find what I was looking for, but I finally spotted two boxes labeled "Bedroom." They were on the ground with one piled on top of the other.

Opening the top one, I almost laughed when I saw the jewelry box right on top. Scooping it up, I ran back upstairs but stopped suddenly at the top stair. Until that moment, I hadn't thought about Mom and Dad. I didn't know what they'd think about what I was doing, but if nothing else, they'd probably send me to bed before I had a chance to talk to Grandma anymore. I listened for a moment to make sure no one was close by, then tiptoed to Grandma's side.

She had picked up the ring and was moving it around in her fingers so she could look at it from all sides. When she heard me return, her head came up. She said nothing, but there was a strange, faraway look in her eye. I was starting to think I had done something bad.

"Here, let me show you." In a hurry, I opened the box and dumped all the necklaces and earrings on Grandma's bed. Then I turned the box so Grandma could see it. "There's a red ribbon in the bottom, and when you pull it, a secret door opens."

She handed me the ring and then reached into the box, fingering the ribbon, before pulling it up, exposing the now empty compartment. "Oh my, oh my," was all she said, but her face looked troubled.

"Did I do something wrong? Grandma, I'm sorry. I didn't mean to find it. I didn't know what was under the secret door. I didn't even know it was a secret door, honest. Should I throw it away?"

"No!" Then her face softened. "No, Lucas. It's okay. You didn't do anything wrong. May I see it, please?"

I handed her back the ring. She held it tightly and said nothing more. After a few minutes, I whispered, "What is it?"

"It's just a child's ring," she said, but so quietly I could barely hear it. Then she closed her hand around the ring and turned away from me. A few minutes later she appeared to be asleep, still clutching the ring. All I could do was gather her jewelry and put it all away, but it made me wonder why Grandma, of all people, hadn't been honest with me. It may be a child's ring, but it wasn't *just* a child's ring. Even I could tell that.

When I Was Seven

I shiver as I climb into the back seat of the car, and hugging myself, I rub my arms up and down in an attempt to get warm. My head jerks up at the sound of the car door shutting tight, enticing me to gaze back at the shore I have just left. It appears so calm, so static, but even as I watch, the waves roll forward, shutting off my view of where I crouched and sifted sand only moments before.

I reach over to roll the window down. The air is sharply pungent. I stick out my tongue thinking I might be able to taste the salt, and I almost can, it is so heavy on the breeze. The sound of crashing waves and gulls calling reaches my ears, and I turn to stare as the beach fades from view. I expect to return soon, but a worry starts to form that maybe I won't.

As I watch everything dwindle behind me, I strain to smell the last bits of sea air. It comes in waves, at once strong, then missing, before assaulting my senses again.

Thunder echoes in the distance, dancing toward us as we drive faster and faster into the newly falling rain that reaches for my arm through the open window. The scents and sounds from the beach disappear in the fierceness ahead.

Quicker than I could have imagined, everything behind me is gone – all of it.

Chapter 10

The next day and for a bunch of days after that, I tried to get Grandma to tell me more about the ring, but she wouldn't say anything. She'd just get a blank look on her face as if she wasn't home. But even though she wouldn't talk about it, I noticed the ring was never out of her sight.

Justin found me sitting on our front porch Friday afternoon. "Do you want to play today?"

"I guess so," I said. "Hey, Justin, have you ever known an old person?"

He had to think about it. "Well, there's my grandma and grandpa, and then my other grandma and grandpa, only I don't see the second ones so much. That's probably it, though."

"Well, do they tell you stuff?"

"Not really. Why?"

"My grandma used to tell me stuff, but now she won't, and I don't know why. See, I found this secret ring in a hidden compartment. I mean, *I* found it, so you'd think she'd tell *me* what it is." I slumped down, resting my head on my hands with my elbows on my knees. "But she won't."

"Wow. What's the ring like? Is it a diamond ring, like it's worth a whole lot of money? Maybe it's stolen."

"Nah. It's just a cheap-looking ring. I don't think anyone would steal it, but then why did she hide it in her jewelry box?"

"Hmm ... I don't know." He paused for a minute before brightening up. "Why don't we think about it while we work on my doghouse?"

I laughed. "Okay."

It started to rain on the way to Justin's, so we ducked inside his house, watching the water fall through his front window. "If it doesn't stop soon, we'll just work in the garage."

I nodded my head, but I wasn't really listening to him. His mom had just answered the phone by saying, "Hello, Iris. How's it going today?" All I could hear was her end of the conversation, so I wasn't sure what was being said, but I could tell Justin's mom was upset. She wasn't laughing and happy like she usually was. "So, what are you going to do? ... I'd put my foot down. He's partly responsible. ... Oh? I didn't know. I'm sorry. But that doesn't really change anything, does it? I mean, what's done is done ... Yeah, I guess so. Just hang in there, I'm sure it will all work out. ... Okay, so I *hope* it will all work out, even if I don't know how. ... Would you like me to come sit with your mom one of these days to give you a break? ... All right. Just let me know."

Justin was pulling on my arm. "Dude, didn't you hear me? It stopped raining!"

"Sorry, I guess not."

We headed out the back door and spent the next little while finding the perfect spot to start building a doghouse. Then we pulled some old boxes out of the garage that Justin sometimes used for forts. We placed them all around where we wanted to build so we could start working without detection. Our plan was working great until it started to rain again. We ran inside but left the cardboard where it was, not thinking about what happens when cardboard gets wet.

I went home a little later when it was clear the rain wasn't going to stop anytime soon. I stepped in the front door and was surprised Mom didn't hear me and holler to take my wet shoes off before walking on the carpet like she usually did. It's then that I heard voices.

I hurried to take off my shoes and then walked into the living room. Grandma and Mom were talking, but neither of them seemed to notice me.

"Please, just listen to me, Iris."

"Mom, you've got to stop worrying yourself about every little thing. Trust me."

"I do! Why do you think I asked for your help?"

"Mom, I hate to tell you this, but your mind is slipping. This ..." She was holding up the ring. "This is nothing. I honestly cannot deal with one more thing. It's nothing. Forget about it!" She threw the ring down and stormed out of the room, without ever realizing I was standing there.

It was a minute before Grandma looked up and saw me there. She beckoned me over to her and then wrapped me in her arms. After a minute, a teardrop landed on the top of my head.

"Grandma, what's wrong?"

"I don't know, Lucas. Maybe I am losing my mind." She picked up the ring and stared at it. "I thought this ring was something, but I guess it's just a plain old birthstone ring, after all."

"What's a birthstone ring?"

"Well, do you know what birthstones are?"

I shook my head.

"Each month of the year has a gem that represents the month. So, if you were born in February, like your mom, your birthstone is an amethyst. It's a purple stone. A birthstone ring is just what it sounds like – a ring with a birthstone on it."

"Oh." I hadn't expected the answer to make so much sense. "Then why are you so upset about the ring?"

"I'm not sure, Lucas." She stared at the ring in her hands and added, "I wish she'd just listen, then maybe I could find out for sure." She laid back on the bed while still clutching the ring.

"Do you want me to leave so you can take a nap, Grandma?"

"No, I'm just resting. I can still talk if you like."

"Okay. I was just over at Justin's helping him ..." I wasn't sure if I was supposed to talk about the doghouse yet, so I decided to change topics. "Grandma, can you tell me stories about when you were a little girl?"

Grandma turned her head. I thought it was so she could look at me, but she didn't. Her eyes seemed suddenly gray and cloudy, so I quickly added, "It's okay; you don't have to."

She acted startled when I spoke, finally looking at me like she'd forgotten I was there. After a minute she said, "No, it's okay. I was just trying to remember."

I sat on her bed waiting for her to begin, but she never did. She just stared, not at me, but at something I couldn't see. It's like she'd gone back in time but forgotten to take me with her.

After a while I tiptoed out, leaving Grandma lost somewhere in her memories, and went searching for Mom. She was in the laundry room, pulling clothes out of the dryer. I was still thinking about the ring, so I said, "When's Grandma's birthday?"

"Not 'til July. Why?"

"Just wondering." The birthstone ring must be Grandma's, but that didn't explain why it made her cry.

That night I had a hard time sleeping. Voices kept intruding on my dreams. "Why are you working late all the time now? It makes me think you're choosing it, just at a time when I need you even more."

"Well, I ..."

"You *are*? You're staying away on purpose?"

"Iris, I'm not good at this. I'm trying to sort things out, but I'm still here, aren't I?"

"Barely. Isn't it bad enough that my mother is dying? I can't do all the rest of this alone. Don't walk away. Please don't walk away!" Then I seemed to hear the sound of a door slamming.

I tossed and turned with my troubled dreams until I heard a different voice, this one closer. "Abby!" The noise scared me and I sat up and looked around. Then I heard it again.

"Abby, Abby Bear, where are you? Let's play kitten dragon again."

It was Grandma, but I didn't know what she was talking about. I crept into her room. Just a faint light was coming from a night light in the kitchen, but it was enough to see the outline of her bed.

"Grandma, it's me, Lucas. What's wrong? Who's Abby?"

I guess she didn't hear me 'cause she kept on talking. "You sit on the left because pumpkins can't dance. I'm going to hide now. Start when I count . . . 1, 10, 12, 23, dog, 5, blue."

"Grandma?" I was trying to shake her awake now, certain she was having a nightmare. "Grandma!"

I couldn't see her face in the dark, but I felt her move and she grew quiet.

"Grandma, are you okay?" I whispered.

"Yes, John, I'm okay," and then she seemed to go limp.

I stood by her bedside waiting for her to say something else, but after a few minutes, she began to snore softly. I stayed there for what felt like an hour to make sure she didn't have more bad dreams, and then I felt my way back through the shadows to my own bed on the couch.

I was pretty tired the next day. It's good it was the weekend and I didn't have to wake up early to go to school. When I did get up it was late and Grandma was sitting in her bed reading the newspaper.

Looking over at Grandma, she seemed to be fine now. I made my way over to her side. "Grandma, you must have had a bad dream last night 'cause you woke up and were talking all kinds of crazy stuff about pumpkins and kitten dragons."

"Oh. Did I? I don't remember, Lucas. I must have woken you up, dear. I'm so sorry."

"No, that's okay. But you called me John. Who's John?"

"I'm sorry, Lucas. I must have been thinking about your grandpa. His name was John. Did you know that?"

"No, I didn't. He was always just Grandpa to me."

"Did it scare you? When I started talking in my sleep?"

I thought about the night. It didn't scare me like spooky monsters, but it did scare me that maybe something was really wrong with Grandma. "I guess I was just worried that you were okay."

"Lucas, do you remember what I told you about my head being messed up these days, about the thunderstorm that clouds my brain?" I nodded. "Well, it does more than just confuse me. It makes it hard to see the right words sometimes. I was talking to your mom yesterday, and I think I was talking without really knowing what I was saying." She was shaking her head. "I don't like the way it feels. Sometimes I think that if I keep talking, I'll eventually find the right words. But I'm beginning to wonder if I should just stop talking altogether and wait for the storm to blow over." She smiled at me, a sad sort of smile. "I'm sorry, Lucas. I don't want you to worry about me. I'll be just fine."

"It's okay, Grandma. You always seem to get around to the right words in the end."

She smiled, a real smile this time. "You know, Lucas, I think you're able to sort me out when I can't sort myself out anymore." I looked puzzled, and then she laughed. "I'm sorry. I sometimes forget you're only seven. What's different about you is when you see or hear something that doesn't seem right, you ask about it."

"Yeah, I guess so."

"Your parents aren't nearly as observant as you are, so they're losing their ability to tell the difference. Maybe you can help them see what's real and what's not - when it's important."

"You think so?"

"I know so."

"But when is it important? How will I know?"

"Trust me, you'll know."

I wasn't so sure. I thought the ring was important, but no one else seemed to be acting like it was. Important didn't seem like a word I understood correctly. When I didn't say anything, Grandma said, "Will you at least try? For me?"

I wanted to ask her about the ring again and why it didn't qualify as important. I wanted to ask her why she needed me to help her when the adults couldn't. I wanted to ask her why she had to die now and leave me, but all I said was, "Yes, Grandma. I'll try."

"Good. Lucas, thank you for watching over me. You know, sometimes the knight can't slay the dragon, but that's okay because dragons have their place too." Then she rolled over and went to sleep.

I'm not sure I understood what she was saying. I think she was saying I was the knight, but I didn't know who or what the dragon was. I was watching over Grandma, but she wasn't the dragon I was supposed to slay. I guess I'd have to figure it out later. Maybe Justin would know.

Chapter 11

I made my way upstairs, still thinking about what Grandma had said. Entering my bedroom, I noticed something was off. It looked like someone had slept in my bed the night before, only I didn't know who or why. It was turning out to be a strange Saturday, as Saturdays go.

I threw some clothes on, hurried through breakfast, and went to go find Dad. He was outside cleaning up the yard. It was springtime and I could see daffodils and tulips coming up.

At first, he didn't notice me. He was sort of mumbling to himself. "Dad, are you okay?"

"Hi, sport. Do you want to help?" he said, without answering my question.

"Sure. Hey, Dad, do you know who slept in my bed last night?"

"Oh. I didn't think you'd notice."

"Well, yeah, the bed was made all funny, not as neat as the way Mom makes me do it."

"I, uh, I did. Was that okay?"

I tipped my head to the side and looked up at him. That didn't make any sense. "It's okay, but why?"

"Um … your mom was having a bad night and I didn't want to disturb her. Now, would you go grab that shovel for me?"

"Okay," I said as I shrugged my shoulders and did as he asked. After that, I helped Dad clean up and weed some of the flower beds and carry new plants around to places he wanted to put them. He didn't say another word. I finally broke the silence by asking, "Dad, did you know that Grandma sometimes talks crazy?"

He stopped what he was doing to look at me. "What are you

talking about?"

"She was talking crazy in her sleep last night. She called me John, and she mentioned strange stuff like pumpkins dancing. She was counting funny even though I know Grandma knows how to count for real, and –"

"Whoa, sport! That's a lot all at once. Slow down a minute. Yes, I know she gets confused, but what happened last night?"

I had to back up and tell him all about Grandma's nightmare and the things she said. He just nodded his head while he listened.

"You're right, sport. It doesn't make a lot of sense. I wouldn't worry about it, though. It's just part of what she's going through right now."

"But she told me if I wanted to help people I should listen. Do you think I should listen to this?"

"Listen? Well, I suppose it never hurts, but ..." He was scrunching up his forehead. Then his expression lightened and he laughed. "I mean, have you ever heard of someone playing kitten dragon?"

"No, I guess not. Thanks, Dad." As I walked away, I thought about that. Was kitten dragon the dragon I was supposed to slay and couldn't? Thinking about it made my brain hurt. I decided I'd go see if Justin could play.

Justin was kicking a soccer ball around in his front yard when I found him. "Do you know anything about dragons?" I said as soon as he saw me.

"What?"

"You know ... dragons, like knights slaying dragons."

"Yeah, I know what a dragon is, but I've never seen one. Why?"

"Oh, no reason. Forget about it."

"It's about your grandma, isn't it?"

"How'd you know?"

"'Cause all you talk about lately is your grandma."

I looked up to see if he was mad about that, but he was smiling. I shrugged my shoulders. "I guess you're right. She said something about how the knight can't always slay the dragon, but that it's okay.

I don't know what that means. She also said something about kitten dragon, but I don't know what that is either. Do you think it's the same dragon?"

He brushed his hair off his forehead and raised his eyebrows at me. "You think I know? I don't understand most of what my parents talk about. Do you need to understand it?"

"Hmm … I hadn't thought about that. I guess not, at least not right now."

"Okay. Then do you want to play soccer with me? It's kind of boring playing alone."

"Sure. I don't think Grandma will miss me too much right now."

We played until Mom called me home to eat. After lunch, I ran right back out to play. It felt good not being worried about Grandma for just a little while, even though thinking that way made me feel a little guilty.

Justin and I decided to work on his doghouse, but when we went out back we found the cardboard lying in soggy piles around where we wanted to build. Justin kicked the cardboard with his foot in frustration, but it didn't move. Instead, sprays of water bounced up. We looked at each other and started laughing. "Squirt guns!" we both said together.

Justin's mom met us at the door. She tried to frown at us, but we knew she couldn't keep a face like that for long. "Did I hear you say squirt guns?" We both nodded. "It may be late spring, but it's not that warm yet." The frown was wavering. We gave her sad looks and puppy dog eyes. "Oh, stop it you two," she laughed. "It really is too cold. Why don't you go play video games or something else that will turn your brains to mush."

We raced to Justin's basement to do just that. His mom called after us, "Lucas, would you like to stay for dinner? I'll order some pizza."

"You bet!"

"Okay, I'll call your mom and let her know you're staying."

I was tempted to stay and listen to what she might say to my mom, but the idea of unending video games sounded a lot more interesting.

It was almost dark when Justin walked me home. "I don't think she'll mind," he said when we reached my driveway.

"What?"

"Your grandma. I don't think she'll mind that you didn't stay with her all day today. She'll understand. My mom always says, 'Boys will be boys.' I think that means she knows that sometimes we just have to play. I'm sure your grandma understands that too."

I nodded my head, hoping he was right. "Hey, do you think I'm the knight?"

"Of course you're the knight." He rolled his eyes like it was a stupid question. "Who else would be your grandma's knight right now? You're watching out for her, aren't you?" I nodded. "And you're always trying to take care of her."

That's what I'd thought, but it was nice that he agreed. "Thanks, Justin. I'll see you later."

"Sure, dude, or should I say Sir Lucas?"

I was still laughing when I entered my house.

Chapter 12

"Abby! Abby Bear!" woke me again that night. I jumped up and raced to Grandma's side. Before I really thought about what I was doing, I was shaking Grandma awake.

"Grandma, Grandma! Who's Abby? Who's Abby Bear? What's going on?"

She rolled over and looked at me, only half awake. "Abby's my sister, John." Then she closed her eyes and was silent.

Well, I knew who John was, and now I guess I knew who Abby was, too. Since Grandma was already back asleep, I shrugged my shoulders, not too concerned anymore, and went back to my bed on the couch.

When I woke up Sunday morning, Grandma was still sleeping, so I went to find Mom. She was in the kitchen making pancakes, my favorite. "Mom, last night Grandma was talking in her sleep. She was talking about Abby."

"I'm sure she was just having a dream, Lucas."

"Yeah, I guess so, but do you know Abby?"

She stopped what she was doing and turned to face me. "Lucas, it was a dream. I don't know any Abby, but dreams are like that."

"But Grandma said Abby was her sister," I insisted.

"Lucas, calm down. Grandma doesn't have a sister – no sisters, no brothers – just her."

I wasn't sure who was talking crazy now. I wanted to argue with her, but she'd already turned back to making pancakes. I guess that was her way of saying our conversation was over. Sometimes I didn't like being a kid. It meant that people didn't think you knew what you were talking about, or you didn't hear things right, or you simply weren't smart enough to figure stuff out. It wasn't true. Well, maybe it was true sometimes, but not nearly as much as adults thought it was. My only choice seemed to be waiting for Grandma to wake up. I'd ask her to tell me about Abby.

I was glad I didn't have to wait long. She was up and ready for breakfast a few minutes later, so I took a plate of pancakes to her. As I set them down, I said, "Grandma, you mentioned your sister Abby last night, but Mom doesn't think you have a sister." I didn't get any farther.

"I was raised as an only child," Grandma said.

My mouth dropped open and my eyes grew wide. What was she saying? I looked at her, but her face was blank, no expression at all.

From behind me, I heard Mom say, "See, Lucas." Mom was leaning against the doorframe leading into the kitchen. I hadn't known she was there. When I looked up at her, she gave me a tired smile and turned back to the kitchen.

"Grandma?" I said turning to her, but she didn't acknowledge me, just stared at the breakfast in front of her, picking at it for a few minutes before abandoning it altogether.

I wasn't sure what to say, so I finally said, "Do you want anything else, Grandma?"

"Yes, could I have some wine, please."

"Grandma, you don't drink wine."

"I don't?" Her eyes were on me, but she wasn't seeing anything. "Could I have some . . . some . . . beer, then?"

I wasn't going to argue with Grandma anymore. Running into the kitchen, I grabbed Mom's sleeve. "Mom, Grandma asked for wine and then she asked for beer. She doesn't drink those things. What should I do?"

She looked alarmed and hurried with me back into Grandma's room, only to find her slumped over, asleep. After just a moment's hesitation, Mom said, "Let's take these dishes back into the kitchen."

As I helped gather things, I saw Mom brush up against Grandma's wrist and linger just a moment. I think she was checking to see if Grandma had a pulse, to make sure she was still alive. I could tell Mom didn't want me to see what she'd done, but I had. It scared me that Grandma might have died right then and there. I knew

Grandma was dying, but I wasn't ready for it to happen yet.

No wonder Mom looked stressed out all the time. She knew Grandma might not last one more day. I didn't know what to say to her. I set down the dishes and reached over to grab Mom in a big hug. I started to cry. I couldn't help myself. I thought my heart would break and I didn't know if I was crying for Grandma or for Mom or for myself.

Mom held me in her arms. I felt safe, and my tears soon stopped. I would save them for later. I didn't want to run out of tears before Grandma really died 'cause I knew I would need a lot of them then.

For once, I didn't want to talk. Mom waited there with me in Grandma's makeshift bedroom. We didn't say anything, didn't even clear away Grandma's dishes. We just moved to one of the nearby chairs to sit down. Mom pulled me onto her lap and let me decide if we would talk, and we didn't.

I don't know how long we were there. I think Dad looked in but quickly left. I guess he took care of Lily, but I don't know. I didn't really care.

After a long time, I whispered, "What's dying like?"

"I don't know, Lucas. I don't suppose any of us knows."

"I'll miss her."

"Yes. We'll all miss her," she said softly.

I knew Mom didn't like talking about it, but I was glad she did in that minute. I guess, too, Mom thought I was growing up a bit 'cause she didn't try to tell me everything would be all right like she usually does. She just held me there on her lap, wrapping her arms tightly around me, her body shaking slightly with her tears.

Chapter 13

The next few days weren't good ones for any of us. Grandma got really quiet. Sometimes I would hear her talking to herself, but I couldn't make sense of what she said. When I came in her room, she would catch the confused look in my eyes and stop talking altogether. I caught her rolling the small ring around in her fingers several times, looking at the light blue stone, but all she said was, "What did I do wrong?"

One afternoon I came home from school to find her holding the ring out in front of her, staring at it, and a small tear was rolling down the side of her face. I climbed up beside her and gave her a hug, but she pulled back, looking at me like she didn't know me anymore.

Not sure what to do, I reached out with my hand to gently touch her face like she often did to me. Her cheek was warm and damp. I gently patted her skin, then brushed her hair with my hand, softly so I wouldn't hurt her.

She stared into my face the whole time. Slowly I saw the light return to her eyes, and then her lips started to perk up in a hint of a smile. I reached over to hug her again, ever so softly. This time, she didn't back away, instead pulling me close and hugging me tightly, while still never saying a word.

The quieter Grandma got, the quieter Mom got too, only I didn't know if it was for the same reason. I walked around the house feeling lost – like somehow this wasn't my home anymore. I couldn't put my finger on what was wrong with everyone. If I'd known the ring would make Grandma so sad, I would have thrown it away when I first found it. But the ring wasn't the problem with Mom and Dad. I knew they were sad, but something else had changed, and it happened after they already knew about Grandma. I just wished someone would trust me enough to tell me what was going on.

That night I lay in bed wondering what to do. Mom and Dad had never taught me to pray, but Grandma showed me how. It definitely couldn't hurt. I got up, knelt down beside the couch, and started, "God, I'm just a little boy. I don't know how much I can do, but something's wrong and I can't fix it when I don't even know what it is. Please, help me fix something, and I hope that something is Grandma 'cause I don't have a lot of time left with her. In Jesus' name, Amen."

I felt peaceful for the first time in a long time, and I quickly and gently fell asleep. But I didn't sleep long. When I woke up, it was very dark outside, and I could hear the sound of Grandma's voice.

"Lucas, are you awake? I need you to come here."

I scurried out of bed, afraid something bad had happened, but glad at the same time Grandma was talking again. She was awake and clearly agitated. "What's wrong, Grandma?"

"Lucas, I don't know how much longer I'll live."

I knew she was going to die soon, and I'd been telling myself for a long time that it was okay. But the closer it actually got, the more I wasn't okay with it at all. I didn't know what to say in response.

She didn't say anything else at first, then she repeated herself, "I don't know how much longer I'll live." Pulling me to her, she put her hands on my cheeks and held my face close to hers. "Lucas, I want to see my sister again before I die."

"Your sister? Your sister, Abby?"

"Yes," her voice sounded desperate, like in the movies, but I wasn't sure why.

"But you said you didn't have a sister."

"I was raised as an only child, Lucas. Abby left me. I don't know what I did to make her leave or why she left, but she did. I never forgot her, though. The memory of her was buried in my mind, and I never stopped loving her. They couldn't take that away from me. Please, Lucas, help me. I want to see her before I die."

I knew Grandma had always treated me like a grown-up. And I liked it – until that very moment. How was I supposed to help her find her sister? I didn't want to disappoint her, but I didn't know what to do. "Do you want me to go get Mom? I'll bet she can help."

"I tried to talk to her already, Lucas. She wouldn't listen, just thought I was crazy. She almost had me convinced I *was*. But I'm not. Abby's out there, and I need to find her."

"Okay, Grandma. Do you know where she is? Maybe we can call her."

"No, Lucas, I don't." She looked lost, more like Lily might look than a grandma would. She grew silent again, silent and still. She looked like the squirrels I would see in the yard that froze when they knew they were being watched. Only instead of holding a nut, like the squirrels, Grandma was carefully holding the child's ring in her fingers. I waited for a few minutes, to see if she would say something else, but she didn't. I felt like I was all alone sitting there beside her.

I moved back to my bed on the couch, but I didn't sleep. When I finally heard noise above me, I raced upstairs. My parents' bedroom door was ajar. Peeking inside I could see Mom was still asleep, but I saw no sign of Dad. I looked in Lily's room. She was awake, playing with her dolls, rocking one softly in her arms. "Lily?"

"Shh. Baby sleeping."

"Oh, sorry," I whispered. "Do you know where Dad is?"

"Daddy over there," she said, pointing in the direction of my room.

Sure enough, I found Dad sitting on the edge of my bed, stretching. When he saw me, he said, "Hey, sport, why are you up so early?"

"Dad, Grandma woke me up in the night. She wants to see her sister before she dies. I don't know where she lives, but her name's Abby, and Grandma really, really wants to see her again. You've got to help me. She said she told Mom, but Mom wasn't listening. Please, Dad, what do I do?"

Dad didn't look the least bit concerned. "Sport, Grandma doesn't have a sister."

"That's what Mom said, but Grandma says she did, but Abby left them."

"Come here, Lucas." I sat down next to him and he put his arm around me. "Even you told me she's talking crazy, out of her head. Grandma had a baby girl once who died before she was even a day old. That was your mom's sister. That must be who Grandma's talking about. Her mind plays tricks on her these days. I'm sorry, sport." Dad ruffled my hair.

Was it really that simple, that Grandma was mixed up? I didn't think so, but how could I know for sure? I rubbed my eyes to clear the sleep out of them. I wasn't sure what to say or what to think. It felt like my head would explode with what Grandma had told me, only nobody seemed to care.

Even though I was tired, I was actually relieved when it was time to go to school. At least at school when I had a question I could figure out the answer, or if I got stuck, my teacher could help me since there always was a right answer and a wrong answer. It seemed that when you were an adult, the questions didn't always have just one answer, and sometimes they didn't have an answer at all. It made my head hurt to think about it.

Justin saw me when I entered the classroom. "What's up with you? You look terrible."

"I was awake almost all night because of my grandma."

He just nodded his head and slapped my back. I think that's something he sees his dad do with his buddies, but I understand it. It's like he said before that he's got my back. It made me feel good, and neither one of us needed to say anything else.

I sat down in my seat and starting thinking about summer vacation since school would be out soon. I was looking forward to it, but I was also a little worried. It was getting warmer outside, but inside my house was getting colder and more confusing. It left me with mixed up feelings about finishing the school year.

Just then my friend Rachel walked by. "It's my birthday today!"

"Really? Happy birthday."

"Well, not my actual birthday, but we're celebrating it today anyway." Since it was getting close to summer break, anyone who had a summer birthday could pick a day during school to celebrate it.

That afternoon we all made her a card, saying nice things about her. Rachel's mom brought in cupcakes she had made – chocolate with vanilla frosting and little colored chips on top.

Our teacher, Miss Sims, said, "Rachel, when is your real birthday?"

"July 21st."

I raised my hand. "My grandma's birthday is in July, too. She even has a birthstone ring for it."

"I do too!" Rachel said.

"Cool. My grandma's is blue."

Rachel scrunched up her face. "The birthstone for July is a ruby. It's red, not blue."

"My grandma wouldn't lie to me. It's blue."

"Lucas, she's right," Miss Sims said. "Ruby is the birthstone for July. Maybe your grandma just picked a color she liked."

I was mad and kind of embarrassed. The rest of the school day didn't go so well for me. I couldn't concentrate and I didn't even want to eat the cupcake Rachel's mom made. My life was just a mess.

It seems strange to be sitting in the sand again, even if it is a different beach with a different look and a different feel. The muscles in my hands, on memory alone, direct my fingers to dig and pile wet sand, but the resulting mound is shapeless. It was suggested I build a sand castle, but castles are for fairy tales and I've left fairy tales behind.

Instead, I sit and stare at the water, devoid of desire, empty of thought, waiting ... waiting for something I cannot describe or even understand. If there is a breeze, I do not feel it. Even the sun's rays are selfishly consumed by the clouds that crowd the horizon, but I do not care.

A sudden laugh makes me start, and my head snaps away from the water to search the beach-going crowd behind me, then drops in despair. It was nothing and no one. All I have are numberless grains of sand meeting a hungry ocean extending as far as the eye can see or the mind can imagine.

Chapter 14

When I got home from school, I checked on Grandma. She looked tired, but she wasn't asleep and her eyes looked clear. "Grandma, is this a good day? Can you talk to me?"

"Yes, Lucas. What's up, sweetheart?"

I saw the ring sitting on the small table, and I picked it up. "You told me this ring was a birthstone ring, but your birthday's in July and the birthstone for July is a red ruby. Why did you lie to me, Grandma?"

She looked even more worn out than she did a minute before. "I didn't lie to you. I may not tell you everything, and I know I get confused, but I don't lie." She looked a little bit mad, but then I was a little bit mad too.

"Then what is it?" I said, holding it in front of her.

"It was my sister's. She gave it to me to keep safe for her before … well, before she left." She took the ring from my hand and stared at it. "I've kept it hidden all these years, but she didn't want it back. She didn't want it anymore." Tears starting rolling down her face. "I kept hoping she would come back for it …," then so softly I almost didn't hear, "that she would come back for *me*."

I didn't understand what Grandma was saying. I wanted to ask her where her sister went and what happened when she left. The only thing I said was, "How did you know she didn't want the ring anymore if she was gone?"

"She never came back for it, did she?" I had to admit that made sense. "I need to see her before I die. I need to know what happened."

"I'll help you find her, Grandma. I promise I will."

"Lucas, that's a lot to ask of a seven-year-old."

"Well, who else is going to do it?"

She looked at me like she was looking through me – like she was checking out every thought that entered my head. "You've been listening to me when no one else would, haven't you? But this is not an easy task, Lucas."

"I know." I wasn't sure I did know, but it sounded like the right thing to say. "I won't give up until I find her."

At that, she smiled. She settled back on her pillow and said softly to no one in particular, "That's the key. You never give up, especially where love is involved." Tears once again formed at the corners of her eyes. She reached out to touch my cheek. "I love you, and I'm so proud of you." Mom once told me you could cry happy tears, and I guess that's what Grandma was doing now, only I didn't know how to tell for sure.

There were a lot more questions I wanted to ask, but just then Mom came into the room. She looked from Grandma to me. "Come with me, Lucas." I followed her into the kitchen. "What happened? Did you make Grandma cry?"

"Well, kind of. Grandma told me her ring was a birthstone ring, but she was born in July and the birthstone for July is red." She looked at me expectantly, clearly knowing that wasn't the whole story. I squirmed under her gaze, but continued, "I told Grandma she lied to me, but then she told me the ring was her sister's not hers, and then she started crying. She said her sister left her, but I don't know why she would leave or where she went. I'm sorry I made her cry, and I feel bad that I thought she was lying." I fell into my mom's arms and started to cry myself. I didn't know anymore what a little boy like me was supposed to do.

Mom just stroked the back of my head. When I settled down, I peeked up at Mom. She looked mad but calmly said, "Lucas, your grandma is going through enough already. She says things that don't make sense and then it bothers her later when she realizes how mixed up she got."

"Dad told me she had a baby that died. He thinks that's the person she's talking about, that she wants to see. But that doesn't make sense. A baby wouldn't have a ring."

Mom straightened up. It looked like I'd just made her angrier, but

I wasn't sure why. "Is that what Dad thinks, huh? Well, your grandma told me about the ring before. She was just confused; that's all there is to it. I told her it was nothing."

I couldn't look her in the eye, so I just nodded my head.

"Just sit with her and be her friend. She's in no shape to answer any questions. Please, Lucas, just leave it alone."

I nodded again, but she wasn't done. Mom lifted my head so her eyes could meet mine and her stare was hard as she added, "Do you understand me, Lucas? Don't bother your grandma about this. It's nothing."

I knew I was supposed to tell the truth, but I knew it wasn't "nothing." It was definitely something. Grandma was not *that* crazy in the head yet. Mom was still looking me in the eye, waiting for my answer. I didn't know what to do, so I nodded my head letting her know I had heard her and said, "I understand." I did understand what she was saying, but I didn't think she understood I had to help Grandma sort this out or maybe even sort it out for her. It was important, and I knew it.

Mom was satisfied, so she returned to what she was doing, leaving me standing there. I looked in on Grandma and saw she was sleeping quietly. I guess Mom figured she could trust me when Grandma was asleep. I hated to think she was wrong, but I needed to figure this out. I'd just have to find a way to help without bothering Grandma. That way I could at least keep part of my promise to Mom.

The hard part, though, was Mom didn't know I had another promise to keep. Grandma was always nice to me and helped me any way she could. Now it was my turn, and I had to try my very best. This was tougher than I thought it was going to be. If Mom and Dad weren't going to help, I would just have to find another way. But how was I going to do that? I needed a plan.

Chapter 15

Coming up with a plan was a whole different story from knowing you needed one. I nervously paced all over the house trying to think. When Mom raised her eyebrows at me as I passed through the kitchen for the fifth time, I moved to a chair next to Grandma's bed. But even then I had a hard time sitting still. My mind wasn't moving fast enough, so my legs started to move instead and then my fingers. I tried to sit on my hands to hold them still, knowing Mom would kick me out of there if she saw how restless I was. However, I couldn't seem to find a solution for my legs.

Lily walked by once and, looking at me, said, "Hafta go baffroom?" I didn't really need to, but I figured I might as well go anyway.

Mom has pictures all over our house. Some of them are of mountains and trees and nature stuff like that, but most of them are pictures of our family. I've never counted, but I know there has to be about a hundred of me and Lily and almost as many of Grandma – some with Grandpa before he died and a bunch after.

In the downstairs bathroom there was a small picture, the only one like it. I knew when I saw it what I could do, and I could do it without bothering Grandma.

"Mom," I said when I found her in the kitchen, "can I go visit Grandma Jenkins?"

She stared at me and I can't say she was smiling. "Uh . . ." came out of her, but that was it for a few minutes.

"I just saw her picture in the bathroom and thought ..." I wasn't sure what I was ready to tell her, so I just shrugged my shoulders. Then I put my hands in my pockets to keep from fidgeting.

She looked puzzled and little lines showed up between her eyebrows. I kept hoping she wouldn't ask me any questions 'cause I wasn't sure what else to say. "Uh, I guess so. When did you want to see her?"

"Um . . ." I really wanted to go talk to her right away, but I knew that would make Mom suspicious. I was making nervous balls of my hands in my pockets and I was sure any minute she'd notice. "Whenever," is what I finally said, shrugging my shoulders again, as if I didn't really care. Then I started to worry that maybe she wouldn't set it up at all, so I added, "Maybe I could visit her sometime this weekend, and just, you know, talk to her."

Mom finally looked like she understood something and nodded her head with a small smile, although I didn't know what it was she understood. I walked away, satisfied, to go find Lily. Behind me, I heard Mom call Dad at work, so I slowed down to see if I could catch what she was saying.

"Hey, Pete, it's me, don't hang up." Mom said. "It's about Lucas … Could you just set things aside for a few minutes and listen?" He must have agreed, because she went on, "He wants to visit your mom this weekend. Do you think you can call her?" I stopped around the corner so I could keep listening, even though I could only hear Mom's side of the conversation.

"I know," she said, "I just think he's getting worried about losing my mom and he wants to get to know his other grandma." She made a funny sound and then said, "You don't need to tell me, but I figure if I don't need to stay and visit with her, I'll be fine with the whole thing." Then the tone of her voice changed. "Pete, … do you think she'll make time for him?"

She was quiet for a minute and then said, "I *am* being nice. When has she ever made time for our kids? I wouldn't ask, but Lucas came to me and specifically asked to visit her and talk to her. What could I say?"

I thought she was done when she added, "Pete, I'm not going to keep him from her, but do you think it's a mistake? I don't want Lucas to be disappointed."

I thought about what I had overheard while I looked for Lily. I didn't know how visiting your grandma could be a mistake. I didn't really know Grandma Jenkins very well. We usually saw her at Christmas and sometimes on our birthdays, but that was pretty much it. If she came to our house, she never actually stayed too long. I guess I'd just have to see how things went. But I knew she didn't talk to my mom much, and I was counting on that. I figured Mom wouldn't tell her Grandma didn't have a sister, so maybe I could get the help we needed.

Dad didn't say anything to me about Grandma Jenkins that night, but I only saw him for a few minutes, he came home so late. The next morning, he got me up and out the door to school, but he didn't even drop a hint about any of it. I hoped he hadn't forgotten.

School passed quickly enough. At the end of the day, I went home with Justin. Mom had to take Grandma to a doctor's appointment or something like that. I liked going to Justin's right after school 'cause his mom always had a snack waiting. That day she had spicy cheese popcorn for us with juice boxes.

"Your mom makes the best snacks."

Justin shrugged his shoulders. "She only does it when a friend's coming over. If it's just me, I have to find some old dead fruit snacks in the cupboard."

"Oh, well, I guess this works out for both of us then."

He laughed. "Yeah, it's the only reason I invite you over."

We hurried to finish our snacks. It was a nice day and we wanted to take another crack at the doghouse. In the backyard, Justin showed me how he had dug four holes. We gathered some leftover wood from his garage along with some hammers and nails. Justin had built a few things with his dad, so he had permission to use what we were taking. The only problem, as we saw it, was that he wasn't allowed to use the saw. That meant whatever size our boards were was the size they were going to stay.

We spread out the drawing of the doghouse Justin had made, putting rocks on each corner to keep it from blowing away. Then we picked four of the biggest pieces of wood to be our posts by standing them up in the holes and then filling the dirt in around them. They were a little crooked but good enough, we figured. Then we started hammering two-by-fours onto those posts. We tried to line up one end of wood on one post and the other end on another post, but most of them were too long and they poked out beyond the post. "That's okay," Justin said. "It doesn't have to look good. The dog won't even notice."

Once we had three boards along the back, we nailed a couple onto each of the sides of the doghouse. We weren't sure how to make a door, so we just left the front side completely open. "There are a lot of gaps in the sides. Do you think we should put more wood on?" I said.

"Nah," Justin said. "That'll give him air conditioning. But we do need a roof. Help me go get the plywood we saw in the garage."

It wasn't a very big piece of plywood, which is good 'cause I don't know if we could have carried it if it was bigger. Together we lifted it up on top of the posts. It sat at a funny angle since the posts were different heights and angles, but we thought it looked great. We nailed it onto the two tallest posts. It must have taken us five or six nails in each one, but we were pretty happy when we were done. We hadn't even had to look at the drawing once to see what to do next.

It was nice to have a problem I knew I could solve. Now the only thing left to do was for Justin to ask for a dog.

That night Dad got home after the rest of us had finished dinner. He came and found me where I was playing with Lily. "Lucas, can you come here, please?"

I figured it was pretty serious since he was calling me Lucas. I cautiously made my way to where he stood in the doorway. "Yes, Dad?"

"I talked to your grandma, my mom, about you wanting to see her. She said that would be fine and offered to take you to lunch on Saturday. Would you like that?"

"Yes!" What a relief that I wasn't in trouble. And now maybe I could put my plan into action.

"Would you like me to come with you, sport?" Dad was acting relieved now too, but I wasn't sure why.

"No, I'll be fine." I quickly said. I hadn't thought about my mom or dad being there. That would ruin everything. Dad looked surprised by my response, and I wondered if he suspected something. "I mean, it should be okay, don't you think?"

"Yeah, I would think so."

That night when I climbed onto the couch to go to sleep, both

Mom and Dad came in to wish me a good night's sleep. It had just been one or the other of them lately, so I was glad to be able to give them both hugs. I smiled as I nestled into my bed even though both of their expressions looked a little worried.

Drifting off to sleep I could hear their voices coming from the kitchen. I couldn't make out all the words, but they sounded upset at something. Whatever it was, they were upset together 'cause I heard, "I agree," and "Yes, I know," a lot. Pretty soon their words floated away and sleep overtook me.

Chapter 16

When Saturday came, I could hardly wait for it to be lunchtime. I played a little with Justin in the morning. He thought my plan with Grandma Jenkins sounded like a great idea. "Way to be a real detective!" he said.

Mom showed up early to get me for some reason, but we got to play a little longer because she started talking to Justin's mom. "So, Lucas is going to spend time with your mother-in-law? How did that happen?"

"I'm not really sure. He just asked one day about her. When Pete called his mom, she was willing. I am a little worried how it's going to turn out, though."

"Yeah, I understand. You'll have to let me know what happens. But what about you and Pete? Has he come around yet?"

"No. He won't talk about it. It's like he thinks it'll go away if he ignores it."

"Like that'll work. What did the doctor say?"

"Nothing new, just come back in a month." Mom looked up and saw me listening to their conversation. She shifted uncomfortably, "Come on, Lucas. We need to get you ready to go."

Mom insisted I get dressed up for my lunch, and she kept telling me I needed to act like a gentleman. She even told me how I should talk, like remembering to say "please" and "thank you." She was really nervous, but I didn't understand why – it was just my grandma.

When Mom finally left me alone, I crept in to check on the

grandma who lived with us. I kind of thought of her as my real grandma and the other one as . . . well, I guess she would just be Grandma J for now. I'd figure out later what she really was to me.

I snuggled up to Grandma, right next to her on her bed. Her eyelids fluttered open and she looked at me. "Grandma," I whispered, "I'm going to get my other grandma's help to find your sister, Abby, okay?"

Grandma looked at me with a blank expression, then she slowly nodded her head. I threw my arms around her. "I love you, Grandma."

"I love you, too, sweetie," she whispered back.

Just then Dad came in with Grandma J right behind him. She was taller than my mom but not quite as tall as Dad, and she didn't have Grandma's smile. I tried to remember the last time I had seen her. It was probably at Christmas. I didn't think she was smiling then either. "Lucas, your Grandma Jenkins is here to take you to lunch. Are you ready?"

"Yes, Dad." I walked toward them both. I wasn't sure how to act towards Grandma J now that she was here. I finally decided to extend out my hand for a handshake. "How are you, Grandma?"

The sides of her mouth curled up ever so slightly. I wouldn't call it smiling, more like she was thinking about smiling. She took my hand and shook it. "I'm just fine, Lucas. Shall we go?"

"Yes, ma'am." I wasn't sure where the ma'am came from – I think I'd seen it in movies, but it seemed to fit better than "Grandma." Just then, I caught a glimpse of Mom a few steps behind Dad. She smiled at me and nodded. Clearly I had done something right. I figured more of the same would be a good idea, so I extended my arm to Grandma J for her to take. I know I had seen that in the movies.

Grandma J chuckled slightly then bent down to take my arm. I wasn't sure why it was funny, but at least she was happy.

In the car, I just kept thinking about how a gentleman would handle things. So, I said, "How are you this fine day?"

Her eyes danced just a little and she said, "I'm just fine, thank you. And you?"

"Fine, thank you. You look nice today."

She didn't respond, just nodded her head, but I could see that half-smile on her face again. I thought Mom would be proud of me, probably Justin too. I was handling this date just fine.

Lunch, it turns out, wasn't like any lunch I had ever had before. The restaurant was super fancy, and I was definitely the only kid anywhere in sight. The waiter brought us big menus and then told us what the special of the day was. I didn't even understand his words, but then again, I didn't understand too many of the words on the menu either. I thought I was a pretty good reader, but I couldn't make much sense of what I saw.

I looked up and noticed Grandma J wasn't looking at her menu; she was watching me. "Lucas, do you trust me?"

That was kind of a strange question, but I had no problem answering, "Sure, Grandma." Then I wondered if I should have said "ma'am" instead, but Grandma J didn't seem to notice. She just reached over and took the menu out of my hands.

"I'll take care of everything," was all she said. When the waiter returned, she ordered something for herself and then whispered something into his ear, while they both glanced at me. I guess I should have been nervous, but I wasn't. Even if I didn't know this grandma very well, I still trusted her. She was, after all, a grandma. That had to mean something.

I smiled wide when our food came. Grandma's plate looked fancy, but on mine was a hamburger and a pile of French fries. "This is awesome, Grandma!" Then the waiter placed a large chocolate shake next to my plate in a fancy glass. A bendy straw was poking out the top. "You're not like my other grandma, but I like you, too." I blurted out.

"No, I imagine I'm not much like her at all."

"Why is that?" I said, but then realized that might sound rude. I watched Grandma J's face to see if I had made a mistake. I guess not, because she laughed.

"Lucas, I like you. You say what you think, don't you?" I nodded my head. "I'll tell you why, since you asked. I'm not much of one for babies. Most people think they're very cute, and I suppose, in a way, they are. But I think they're messy and noisy and they can't carry on a good conversation. You, Master Lucas, can carry on a very nice conversation. I think I'm going to like getting to know you."

76

"Is that why you haven't spent much time with us, 'cause you don't like babies?"

She laughed again. "You are an honest child. The short answer is yes." She looked at me and I could tell she had more to say but was deciding whether to say it or not. "Lucas, I'll give you the same courtesy of being honest," she finally said. "Your mother and I didn't see eye to eye when we first met. She didn't have the best of manners, and I'm afraid I let that get in the way of getting to know her. Once I realized my mistake, it was too late. And then the babies started coming and that sealed the deal. You know, I've never told anyone that before."

"Really? How come?"

"I'm not sure. I guess there was no one to tell. Your grandpa and I were divorced a long time ago, and I never felt the need to confess to anyone else." She smiled at me, and I thought it was a really nice smile, so I smiled back. "Since we're being straight with each other, do you have any other questions for me?"

"Hmm, I guess I do, like how come your hair looks that way?"

She looked surprised, "What way?"

"Well, I like your hair, but it has a lot of gray in it, mixed in with the brown. My other grandma doesn't have any gray. She told me she chose a different color."

She didn't laugh, but she was smiling. "I'll bet a lot of people have wondered that, but they didn't have the courage to ask me." She cleared her throat. "I suppose I could color it like your other grandma does and most people for that matter, but Lucas, I like being me. I like looking this way, and I don't mind looking my age." The sparkle was back in her eyes. "Do you think I would look better without the gray hairs?"

"No, I don't think so. I was just wondering."

"Do you like your other grandma's hair better than mine?"

I didn't know how to answer that. I liked them both. "Well, I like how yours is curly like Lily's, but –"

She interrupted, "You don't need to say another word, Lucas. That was not a fair question to ask. Now, how would you like to come back to my house for the afternoon?"

I was glad she had changed the topic, and I liked the idea of spending more time with her. "Yes, that would be great."

"Good. I'll just call and let your father know, so he doesn't worry."

I don't think Dad believed Grandma J when she told him we were having "a delightful time," and it seemed like she was having a hard time convincing him. She finally said, "Would you like to speak with him yourself?" He must have said, "No," 'cause she didn't hand me the phone.

Right after that, we went to Grandma J's house. It looked a lot different than my other grandma's old house, and it wasn't much like our house either. There were a lot of fancy little statue-type things everywhere and big paintings on the walls. Nothing was out of place, and I didn't dare touch anything. My mouth hung open, and I just looked around like I was in a museum. "Grandma, are you rich?" I finally said.

I was getting used to her laughing whenever I asked a question. I just figured it meant she was happy. "Yes, I am. Does that make you like me better?"

I looked at her funny. Sometimes grown-ups said the strangest things. "No. Why would that make me like you better?"

"Well, some adults at least pretend to like you more when you have money."

"That's dumb. Money doesn't make you funny or nice or fun to play with. Do people just want you to buy them stuff?"

"Yes, Lucas, and I guess it's made me very wary about making friends. At one time I didn't want to share any of my money, but now I'm not so sure." She got quiet at the end of what she said, and I wasn't certain I'd heard her right.

"I'll bet you'd like to share, but only with people who are nice, not people who just want you to give them money." I thought about that a moment. "But I guess that would be hard 'cause that means you'd only want to give your money away to people who don't want it, and if they don't want it, then they might not take it if you give it to them. Is that right?"

"Lucas, I think you have hit the nail on the head." When I looked confused she added, "That means you've got it exactly right, young man." She smiled at me and then said, "Now, how would you like to play a game of checkers?"

I'd been having such a nice time I almost forgot why I'd wanted to see her in the first place. "Grandma, I do want to play checkers with you, but first I need your help. I don't want your money, but I have a big problem."

"Okay, Lucas. Why don't we have a seat, and then you can tell me all about it."

Her couch looked too expensive to sit on, but Grandma sat and then motioned for me to do the same, so I did. She looked at me, waiting for me to begin. I realized she actually was a lot like my other grandma. She was treating me more like a grown-up than most people, and she was taking me seriously.

"Okay, so here's the thing. My other grandma is pretty sick. She's dying actually." I wasn't sure how much she knew, so I figured it was best to lay everything out. She just nodded at what I'd said and let me go on. "Well, part of her being sick is that she talks crazy sometimes. She says stuff that my parents don't think means anything, but I think I figured out her crazy talk. When she talks crazy it doesn't usually make sense, but mostly she doesn't look at me like she knows who I am. So when she looks me in the eye, I believe everything she says." Grandma J tipped her head to the side and nodded like she believed me. "You trust me, don't you, Grandma?" The thought surprised and pleased me.

"Yes, Lucas. I believe you're telling me exactly what you see. I've learned over time things aren't always what they seem on the surface, but that's where we have to start. So, go ahead and tell me the rest of your story. Together we might just be able to figure out what it means."

I hadn't really thought about it that way before. I didn't know something could mean anything other than what it appeared to be. I wrinkled my forehead while I thought about that.

"Master Lucas," Grandma J interrupted, "don't worry. What's important is I believe you are telling the truth. Children aren't very confusing. I'd forgotten that. It's one of their redeeming features. Adults are another story, but you don't need to be concerned with that right now. Just tell me what you need my help with. I'll listen to whatever you have to say."

She trusted me, and I knew I could trust her, not just with lunch, but with everything. "Okay. So, here's what happened with my other grandma. She started talking about someone named Abby. Then she told me it was her sister. Only Mom says Grandma never had a sister and that I should stop bugging Grandma about it. But I think Abby's real."

"All right. Why do you think she's real? I'm not doubting your story, Lucas, but I get the sense you have reasons for believing there's a sister."

I was liking Grandma J more and more. "Yes, I do." I told her all about the birthstone ring hidden in Grandma's jewelry box and what Grandma had told me about it.

She nodded along with my story and then said. "Well, Lucas. What exactly do you need from me?"

"She told me she wants to see her sister before she dies. I mean, my other grandma wants to see Abby before she dies, but she doesn't know where Abby is. All she said was that Abby left her or something like that. I don't even know what that means. Please, Grandma, what do I do? How do I find her?"

Grandma J gently wiped the tears that had started to form at the corners of my eyes, then she patted my cheek. Her eyebrows had come together, and she was looking past me, thinking. "I'm not sure how to find her, but I'm pretty sure I can get someone to help us. You just let me take care of things." She smiled reassuringly at me, and I found myself smiling back. For the first time, I wasn't so worried about how to help my other grandma. "Would you like that checkers game now, Lucas?"

"Yes, I would, Grandma, or Grandma J." I stopped, perplexed. "What should I call you? Grandma to me is my other grandma 'cause I've been calling her that for a long time. I thought I'd call you Grandma J but that doesn't seem to fit either. Should I just keep calling you ma'am?"

She laughed just a little. "That is a bit of a dilemma, and you are right, just straight Grandma will never do. Hmm." She was quiet for a few minutes, then I saw her eyes brighten and she got a strange little grin on her face. "Lucas, why don't you call me Mamie. Think of it as being a friendlier way of calling me ma'am."

"Okay, Mamie." I liked the sound of it as it rolled off my tongue.

Chapter 17

When Mamie brought me home a couple hours later, both Mom and Dad met us at the door. They looked worried or surprised – I wasn't sure which. "Goodbye, Lucas. I'll be giving you a call soon," Mamie said over her shoulder as she walked back to her car.

Mom and Dad both looked at me with big eyes, but they didn't say anything, so I walked past them to go check on Grandma. "Lucas! Come back here," Mom called after me. I got the sense I was in trouble, but I wasn't sure why. I turned around and walked back to the two of them by the front door.

"Did I do something wrong?"

"Well, no," Mom said, her voice softer now. "We just wanted to know what you've been doing all this time."

"We played checkers, and she taught me how to play chess. It's kind of tricky, but I like it. Do you know how to play chess?"

"Yes," Mom hesitantly replied.

"And we had some snacks. She had this really good cheese that came in little circles and some fancy crackers. I'm not sure I liked the crackers, but the cheese was really good. And we also had chocolate covered blueberries! That was my favorite."

"That's what you were doing this whole time?" Dad said.

"Yeah, oh, and we talked a bunch, too – about all kinds of stuff." I'd had such a good time with Mamie, I almost forgot about the help I'd asked for, but I wasn't ready to tell Mom and Dad about that yet. "Could I go check on Grandma, now?"

I looked at Mom and then at Dad. I couldn't tell what their faces meant. They didn't actually say anything, but Mom nodded just a little in response. I figured that was good enough, so I hurried off to go see Grandma. As I walked away, I could hear them talking to each other behind me, but I couldn't tell what they said.

Grandma was sleeping quietly, except for an occasional snore that buzzed out through her lips. I wanted to tell her all about Mamie and how she was going to help us, but I didn't want to wake her. Before long, I had to leave her side 'cause Mom called me to help set the table for dinner.

It turns out I didn't have to wait long to speak to Grandma. When I took dinner to her, she was awake and moving around a bit. She smiled weakly at me, and said, "Hi, Lucas." It was so quiet I almost didn't hear it, but she was looking directly at me, so I could tell it was one of her good times.

"Grandma," I whispered, as I set her food down, "my other grandma, I call her Mamie now, is going to help us find Abby for you." Grandma smiled and nodded. "Grandma, I know you're very sick, but can you try to stay alive until we find Abby? We'll hurry, I promise."

"I will. Lucas, you are a sweetheart, thank you." She gave me a big hug that made me feel like everything was going to be all right.

I heard from Mamie just a few days later. When I came home from school on Monday, Mom casually said, "Your Grandma Jenkins called today. She wanted to talk to you."

"Really? Is she going to call me back, or should I call her?"

Mom didn't respond right away and I was just about to repeat my question when she said, "You can talk to your dad about it when he comes home from work." I tried to ask again, but she just walked away from me.

When Dad got home late that night, I rushed to him. "Grandma Jenkins called me today. Is it okay if I call her back?" I wasn't sure what the big deal was, but I did get the sense I needed to ask permission.

"Sure, sport," he said while ruffling my hair. "Would you like me to get her on the phone for you?"

"No, that's okay, Dad. She gave me her cell phone number and told me to call her anytime. I just wanted to make sure it was okay with you." I hurried off to call Mamie, but in the background I could hear Dad saying, "She gave you her cell number?"

Mamie answered after only one ring. "Hi, Lucas."

"How did you know it was me?"

"That's a good question. I'll tell you. I could see on the caller ID that the call was coming from your home, and Lucas, you're the only one in that family who has my cell phone number."

"Really? My dad doesn't even have it?"

"No, sir. Just you."

"Wow, that's cool." No wonder Dad was surprised.

"Now, about the other matter we spoke of, your Grandma's sister . . . I thought we would start by talking to a friend of mine. He handles my money for me, but he'll know who we should talk to. I called him today, and he can meet with the two of us tomorrow if you like."

"Tomorrow! That would be great! But I better ask my mom first."

"Yes, I suppose you're right. I'd like to pick you up right after you get home from school. Why don't you ask if that would be all right with her."

"Okay."

"And Lucas, you don't need to explain what we're doing. We'll tell her, but I don't think it's time yet."

"I know. I'll be right back." I set down the phone to go find Mom, but when I looked up Mom was right there and Dad was just behind her. I jumped a little and then laughed. "You scared me." They didn't laugh with me, so I shrugged my shoulders, and said, "Mom, is it okay if she picks me up after school tomorrow?"

She turned to look at Dad, then back at me. "Do you want to go?"

"Yes." I nodded my head in case she hadn't heard me.

She looked surprised, but simply said, "All right, then I guess it's okay."

Putting the phone back to my ear, I said, "Mamie, it's okay with Mom. I'll see you tomorrow!"

I hung up the phone and turned to face Mom. She looked so mad it scared me. "What did you just call her?" she said through gritted teeth.

"Mamie." I kept getting the idea that I was doing something wrong, but I couldn't figure out what it could possibly be.

"Why did you call her that?"

"Well, we didn't think Grandma really fit, since I already have Grandma, you know Grandma-in-the-other-room Grandma. So, we needed a different name. She decided Mamie would be a good idea." Mom didn't look any calmer, so I added, "Is it bad to call her that?"

She didn't answer me, just turned and walked away, but not without first giving Dad an angry look. Puzzled, I looked at him.

I didn't think he was going to say anything either at first. He just looked flustered, but he finally mumbled, "That's her name, Mamie Jenkins." Then he too turned and walked away.

I can't explain my fascination with the ocean – the beach, the endless sand, and the laughing waves. It's just there and always has been.

Today, the water intrigues me, makes me curious. I stand up and brush the sand from my clothes then move cautiously closer. There are others on the beach, but no one calls me back or warns me of danger. I take that as permission, so I step ever closer to the water, letting my bare feet settle gently in the sand with each step.

When the water first touches me, its coldness is startling, but I gradually get used to its feel. I watch as the waves tickle the shore, reaching in and then pulling back in jest to gauge the reaction. I stand immovable in the wet sand, letting the water wash over my feet and then retreat. With each passing wave, I notice myself settling further down into the sand until at first my toes and then my entire feet are completely swallowed by it. I look down and watch as I try to wiggle my toes, moving the sand from below until it cracks and a toe emerges.

It is free, but I am not.

Chapter 18

I could hardly get through school the next day I was so excited about Mamie picking me up. I told Justin all about it. He said he was jealous I got to go on an adventure. I have to admit sometimes it felt that way, but only when I wasn't worried that Grandma would die before I found her sister. It made me think that maybe being a detective was a lot harder than it looked on television.

Once I got home from school, I quickly kissed Grandma on the cheek then ran to watch for Mamie out the front window. When she pulled into the driveway, I hollered out to Mom, "She's here. I'll see you later." I still didn't know why calling her Mamie was bad, but I was trying not to say the name around my mom, and I figured it wouldn't hurt if I ran out to the car before Mamie could come to the door.

Mamie was surprised to see me running out to her, but a smile spread across her face as I got close. "Hi, Mamie," I said as I climbed into her car. Then I leaned over to hug her. It was probably the first time I had ever hugged her. She didn't hug me back at first, but then she put an arm around my back to pat it.

When I pulled back, she smiled and said, "Are you ready?"

"Yes, I am." As she pulled out of the driveway, I thought of a question I wanted to ask her. "Mamie, my mom was really upset yesterday when I called you Mamie. Why would she be mad about that?"

Mamie started laughing. "Oh, Lucas. I suppose I should explain. You see, young man, I'm not as nice a person as you think I am."

I didn't know if I should be worried or not. "What does that mean?"

Mamie chuckled slightly. "When your Mom and Dad got married, I wanted your mom to call me Mother. However, she thought I was not as good as her own mother and declined."

"She said that?"

"No, she didn't put it that way. She was actually quite nice in what she did say. I've forgotten the words she used, but I like to remember it the way I told you." She looked over at me with raised eyebrows and then winked. I think she wanted to see if I was still on her side. Not knowing what else to do, I just smiled back. "Well, that left your mother with a conundrum."

"What's a connud ..., comund ..."

"A conundrum?"

"Yeah, that."

"It means she had a rather confusing choice to make. What should she call me? She decided to try calling me by my name, Mamie."

"My dad told me that was your first name, but that's all he told me."

"Yes, I imagine it's not a pleasant memory. When your mother called me Mamie, I was furious. I told her in no uncertain terms that she was never to call me that again. I was not her equal, and she was exhibiting terrible manners by using my first name." Mamie let that sink in for a few quiet minutes.

"Then why did you tell me to call you that?" I finally said.

She looked down at me and then back at the road. "Because, Lucas, as I told you, I'm not as nice a person as you think I am."

The rest of the drive passed in silence. I wanted to tell Mamie she really was a good person, but she was right - what she'd done wasn't nice at all. I didn't know what to think or what I should say. I let out a big sigh of relief when we pulled up to the office of Mark Argent.

Mr. Argent met us by the front door and reached out to shake Mamie's hand. I noticed he was shorter than Mamie and he wore glasses on the end of his nose. I kept thinking they were going to fall off. He was very nice to Mamie, and he acted like he really liked her a lot – not in a boyfriend-girlfriend way, just a good friend way. But then I remembered what Mamie said about her money, and I wondered if he was just nice to her 'cause she had lots of money. I could see how it would be hard to tell the difference.

Soon he took us to the back, into his office. It was a dark office, but he walked to a window and opened the blinds, and it suddenly seemed a lot more cheerful. He pulled out a big, leather chair for Mamie and then a small, wooden chair for me before moving behind his desk to sit down. I noticed that even he didn't get to call her Mamie. He kept calling her "ma'am" or "Mrs. Jenkins."

When we were all sitting down, Mamie took charge. "Mark, this is my grandson I was telling you about. His name is Lucas. He has a matter of concern that is beyond my ability to handle. I know it's not your usual thing, but I assume you'll know who to contact to get the ball rolling." She then turned to me. "Lucas, would you like to tell Mr. Argent your story? You can tell him as much or as little as you like."

I was a little nervous telling a stranger all about Grandma and her sister, but I liked that Mamie trusted me to tell the story myself. It made me feel good. So I sat up straighter and turned to Mr. Argent. I was guessing he didn't need all the details of why I trusted what Grandma was telling me. If Mamie believed it from what I told her, I figured I could leave that part out.

"Well, Mr. Argent, my grandma – I mean my other grandma – is dying. She's living at my house long enough to die. I didn't know what I could do to help her, but then she told me she had a sister named Abby. I don't think she's seen her for a long time. My grandma told me she wants to see Abby before she dies, and she said she doesn't even know where she lives. That's what we," I looked at Mamie to make sure it really was "we" and she nodded her head. "Anyway, that's what we need help with. We need to find Abby."

Mr. Argent had his elbows on his desk with his hands clasped together under his chin, listening to me. When I stopped, he pulled his head back and put his fingertips together while he thought about it. "Lucas, do you know what your Grandma's last name was before she got married?"

"Isn't it the same one she has now?"

"No, Lucas. Often when women get married, especially in your grandma's era, they change their last names to match their husband's last name. The name they were born with is called their maiden name."

"You mean my mom's last name wasn't always Jenkins?"

"No, it wasn't, Lucas. Her name was Morgan, from her parents," Mamie said.

"Oh. I didn't know that. Well, no, I guess I don't know my grandma's maiden name."

"Okay. What about Abby? Has your Grandma ever mentioned a last name for her, from when she was little or even a married name?"

"No, sir."

"Okay, that makes it a lot more complicated. Do you think you could find out for us?"

"Probably not about any of Abby's last names, but I'm sure I could find out Grandma's other name."

"That's good. That would help a lot. Do you happen to know where your grandma grew up?"

I had to think about that one, but I couldn't remember any stories about where she came from. I had only known her in her big house and her apartment. "No, I don't, but I'm sure I can find that out, too."

"That would be great, Lucas. The more information we have, the easier it will be to track down her sister. I think our best bet would be to hire a private investigator." I knew all about private investigators from TV, but using one in real life was kind of exciting. Mr. Argent turned to Mamie, who nodded, which I guess was her way of saying, "Yes," meaning she would pay for it. I was suddenly very grateful. Mr. Argent continued by saying, "I'll do some checking to find some good references, but if we can narrow down the area she came from, it might make more sense to hire a P.I. from that area."

Mamie nodded her agreement. "Thank you, Mr. Argent. We'll be in touch with you when we have more information to share. Once we do, I'd like you to hire someone immediately. Time is of the essence."

I didn't quite understand what the last thing Mamie said meant, but it included the word "time" so I was guessing that she knew, like I did, that Grandma didn't have much of it left.

Chapter 19

When Mamie took me home after meeting with Mr. Argent, I quickly got out of the car and hurried inside, assuring Mamie that she didn't need to take me to the door. She didn't actually listen to me though 'cause next thing I knew she was inside the front door talking to my mom.

"Hello," my mom said. It came out sounding like ice, and I noticed she avoided calling Mamie by any name.

I wasn't worried Mamie was going to tell on me about what we were doing, but I listened, hoping she was being nice. That way it would be easier to get my parents to let me see her more often.

"Hello, Iris. How are you?"

"I'm fine."

"You look a little pale. Are you sure you're all right?"

"Yes, I'm … It's none of your business." It seemed like Mamie was playing nice, but Mom wasn't.

"Okay. How is Pete?"

"Feel free to ask him yourself," Mom said then moved to the front door, holding it open as a clear invitation for Mamie to leave. I was surprised by how rude she was being.

"I'll do that. Thanks for letting me have Lucas for a little while. He was delightful."

I smiled. I know she was helping me, but I would have liked her even if she wasn't. She was different from the other grown-ups I knew. I didn't know if that was good or bad, but I did know she made me happy.

As Mom shut the door soundly behind Mamie, I heard a noise from Grandma's room, and I hurried over to check on her. I was disappointed to find her sleeping. The noise must have been the sound of the sheets when she turned over. I sat down beside her bed to think about what to do. I wasn't sure if it was okay to ask my mom about Grandma growing up or not. I didn't want to let my secret out yet.

Grandma lay so still, and she wasn't snoring like usual. I watched as the blankets moved up and down, so I knew she was breathing, but I was still worried. I felt the same way I did the day I came home from school and couldn't find Mom. It was a day I had walked home with Justin. We said, "Goodbye," as I went in the front door, just like it was any other day, but it wasn't. The lights weren't on and it was deathly quiet. I called, "Mom. Mom! Mom?" everywhere I went – upstairs, in bedrooms, in bathrooms – but I couldn't find her anywhere. It seemed like forever before I finally went out to the backyard. Mom was pushing Lily on the swing, and they were laughing. I thought at first they were laughing at me and how scared I was, but then I realized they were just happy. I stood at the door for several minutes trying to fight back the tears that had nearly escaped. Mom didn't even see me at first. When she did, she smiled and waved me over to them.

She noticed I wasn't smiling. "What's wrong, Lucas? Did you have a bad day at school?"

"No. I came home and you weren't there. I couldn't find you anywhere." The tears were starting to slip out.

Mom stopped pushing the swing and wrapped me in a big hug. "I'm sorry, pumpkin. I didn't mean to scare you."

I hugged her to hold her there, to make sure she wasn't actually going anywhere, to convince myself she was real and hadn't left me all alone. I hugged her until my tears stopped flowing. I knew she had been there all along, but it started my mind thinking about what if she hadn't been. What if she did leave me or forgot about me? For the next month or so, I asked her to meet me at school at the end of the day. I told her I didn't want to walk home with Justin. I know she thought I was mad at him or something, but I didn't know how to explain it to her. I didn't even know how to explain it to myself.

That's what Grandma reminded me of, only I knew when she left, she wouldn't just be in the backyard. She'd be gone for good, and I wouldn't get her back. What I was seeing was the last of Grandma, fading away, growing dim.

The only light was my hope that I could find Abby for her. I kept waiting for her to wake up, so I could ask her my questions, but she just lay still, only occasionally turning over to sleep on a different side. I knew she'd wake up some time, but I was worried that every minute counted.

Finally, I went to find Mom. She was in the kitchen making dinner. She seemed upset. "Mom," I said, a little nervously, "are you mad at Mamie, I mean, Dad's mom?"

She stopped what she was doing and brushed the hair out of her face. "I don't know, Lucas. There's just a lot going on, and I'm not sure I know how I'm feeling about anything right now." She smiled weakly. "Did you want something, pumpkin?"

"Well, I was wondering if you could tell me stories about Grandma when she was my age?"

She hesitated, and I was worried she'd figure out why I was asking, but she just nodded and said, "I don't actually know that many stories about her."

"Oh," was all I could say. This wasn't turning out to be as easy as I thought it would. Mom had grown quiet, and so I sat patiently, wondering what she was thinking.

"Lucas, I guess I should know more stories about her childhood, but I can't actually think of any right now."

"Did she grow up around here somewhere?" I was hoping to learn something, anything.

"No, she grew up in Oregon, but she went to college out here in Virginia. That's where she met Dad, your grandpa."

"Oh, John."

She looked surprised, but simply said, "Yes, John."

"Do you know what Grandma's other name was? Her last name before she got married?"

By the look Mom gave me, I was worried I had just given everything away. "Why do you want to know?"

"I'm just curious. Your last name is Jenkins, but Grandma's last name is Morgan, so that means you used to be called Iris Morgan. I was wondering what Grandma used to be called."

That seemed to satisfy her, so she said, "Josephine Jones. In fact, I think when she was younger she used to be called JoJo."

"Really? That's cool. Thanks, Mom. Do you know any other stuff about Grandma?"

"Yes, I suppose so. What do you want to know?"

I wasn't sure what to ask, but I didn't want to waste my chance. "What were her mom and dad like?" I finally came up with.

She wrinkled up her forehead, thinking. "I don't know, Lucas. When I was growing up, I never met that set of grandparents. I knew my other grandparents, my dad's parents, but not my mom's. We never really talked about them much. I figured it was because they lived so far away or that maybe they were dead."

"Did Grandma ever go visit her mom and dad?" I couldn't imagine not seeing your parents much, even if you were married.

"No, I don't think she ever saw them after she got married, but I'm not sure. It can be pretty expensive to travel across the country, pumpkin, especially then. I don't think her parents were even able to come to her wedding. At least I don't remember seeing them in any of the wedding photos."

I was grateful to be getting some information, but it didn't seem like enough. The problem was I wasn't sure what else to ask, so I said, "Thanks, Mom. I didn't know that before." Then I decided to leave the room before she started asking *me* questions.

Since I knew Mom would be busy getting dinner ready for at least a few minutes, I found a phone upstairs and called Mamie on her cell phone.

She picked up quickly with, "Hello, Lucas."

"Hi, Mamie. I found out some of the stuff we need."

"Wow, that was fast. So, what did you learn?"

"Mom says Grandma's other name was Jones. She was Josephine Jones and she grew up in Oregon, but she didn't know any more than that. Do you think that will be enough?"

"Well, I certainly think that will be enough to get started. You've done great work, Lucas, just like a detective."

I smiled. "Thanks, Mamie. Oh, and she used to be called JoJo. I don't know if that will help, but that's what Mom said."

"At this point, Lucas, it can't hurt. I know the year your Grandma was born, so I'll add that to our information and give our friend, Mr.

Argent, a call right away and have him get started on it immediately. How does that sound?"

"That sounds great! Thanks!" Then I thought of something. "How do you know what year she was born?"

I heard her laugh before she said anything. "When your parents got married, I prided myself on the fact that I was a few years younger than she was. Somehow I thought it made me better than her."

"Why?"

"Lucas, you ask difficult questions. I suppose they're the questions I should have been asking all along. I'm not sure why it mattered. Women can be vain about their age, and I suppose I was."

"What does that mean?"

"Oh, it just means that I cared about my age way too much. Somehow I thought being old made me less attractive or less of something. You know, now that I explain it to you, it seems rather silly."

"So are you still vain?"

She made a funny sound. "Lucas, I don't know. I hope not. Lately, I've just decided some things don't matter as much as they used to."

"Is that why you have gray hair?"

She laughed. "Yes, it is. Have you ever thought about being a lawyer?"

"No. Why?"

"Because you ask questions no one has ever dared ask me before. You're getting at the truth of the matter, at truths I haven't even admitted to myself."

"Oh. Should I say, 'Sorry'?"

Her laugh was back. "No. If anyone should say that, it should be me."

I wasn't sure what to say next. I didn't think she was mad at me, but I wanted to change the subject all the same. "Well, thanks for helping me find Abby."

"You're welcome, young man. And Lucas, while we're waiting to hear back from Mr. Argent, would you like to come over to my house again?"

"I would love that! But you probably should work it out with my mom or even better my dad."

She laughed into the phone. "You're right, Lucas. That's a good idea. I'll call your dad later tonight, after he's happy from having a good supper."

"Oh. He doesn't usually come home in time for supper anymore."

"Really?" There was a different sound in her voice, and it wasn't happy anymore.

"No. He comes home pretty late, sometimes just as I'm going to bed."

"Hmm. How long has he been doing that?"

"Since a little after Grandma moved in. You know, not at first, but after she'd been here a few weeks. And I think he and Mom have been arguing a bunch too." Then I brightened up a bit, "But not about you. They're both mad about you together." It took only a second to realize what I'd said, "I mean, they're like together again. I- "

"It's okay, Lucas. I understand. Don't worry. And I'll get hold of your dad about you coming over again."

"Thanks." I was glad to hang up before I said anything else that was stupid.

Mamie did just what she said she would. Shortly before my bedtime, the phone rang. Mom answered, "Hello? Yes, he is."

Dad was in his office, but he came out when Mom called to him. Taking the phone he said, "Yes?" He looked a little surprised, but after a few words like "yes" and "okay," it all seemed to be set. I was excited until I saw his face darken. "What are you talking about? It's none of your business!" He paused for a bit and then said, more softly this time, "No, you can still see Lucas – for now, but stay out of the rest of it."

After Dad hung up, Mom looked at him to see what had happened, but he didn't even glance at her. Instead, he turned to me, "Sport, it seems your grandma is enjoying your company and would like to have you over to her place again this weekend." He had a curious expression on his face. "You've seen her a lot in the last few days." He waited, almost like he'd asked me a question, but I didn't know what I was supposed to say. When I said nothing, he shrugged his shoulders. "She seemed to think you wouldn't mind. I said she could pick you up on Saturday morning, but I can always call and cancel if you're not interested."

Adults can be so strange. I think he was asking me if I wanted to go, but he didn't actually ask the question. I was about to answer it anyway when I saw Mom's expression behind him. She sure looked like she wanted me to say no. Maybe it was so Dad would cancel on Mamie and maybe too 'cause she didn't want me to like Mamie, but I did. "Dad. I want to go." It almost felt like I was begging for something he had already said yes to. I saw Mom's face drop at my response.

Dad said, "Okay," and turned back to his office without another word to anyone. Mom just stared after him.

I decided not to hang around. Instead, I went to say goodnight to Grandma. She looked tired but brightened up when I came into her room. "Hi, Grandma," I said.

She smiled back, but the smile looked worn out like she'd used it one too many times. "Hi, Lucas," was her weary reply, but I noticed she was looking right at me, so I figured I could talk to her and tell it like it is, as Justin would say.

"Grandma, are you in there?"

She nodded.

I looked around to see if anyone was close by, then I whispered, "Grandma, Mamie and I were talking to a guy named Mr. Argent. He's going to help us find your sister."

She smiled and sank back into her pillow. "Yes. That's good." She still looked tired, but her eyes were happy. It *was* good.

"And you know what, Grandma? Mamie's pretty nice when you get to know her. She's not the same as you, but I like her too." I didn't want to hurt her feelings, so I added, "Is that okay if I like both of you?"

Grandma chuckled a little. "Lucas, that's wonderful. I'm glad you have two grandmas in your life." She coughed a little but waved me off when I tried to help. "I didn't see either of my grandmas much when I was growing up. A child should have someone who spoils him."

I climbed up onto her bed to give her a hug and snuggle next to her. She put her arm around me and held me tight. After a while, I whispered, "Grandma, I like Mamie, but she'll never be you. I wish you didn't have to die."

"Oh, Lucas, I know, sweetheart. I know."

I kept trying to save my tears, but they just started leaking out of my eyes again. "Grandma, where will you go when you die?"

Grandma reached up to my face and gently wiped away my tears. "I'll go to Heaven, and be with your Grandpa."

"But where's Heaven?"

"It's all around us or maybe above us. I'm not absolutely sure. But I do know it's close by."

"How do you know that?"

"Well, I know I'll be able to watch over you, and how could I do that if I wasn't close by?"

I had to admit that made a lot of sense. "Do you know what it's like to die?"

"Well, seeing as I've never done it before, it's going to be a new experience for me. But I like to think of it as going on a trip to see old family and friends. Only you don't have to worry about packing a bag or forgetting your toothbrush."

I started laughing. "You help things make sense to me, Grandma." I hugged her even tighter. She winced just a little, and I jumped back. "Did I hurt you?"

"Don't worry. I'm okay. It hurts a bit whether you hug me or not, so, if you don't mind, I'd rather have your hugs."

I reached out and hugged her again, being careful not to squeeze too hard. "Grandma, you always know just the right thing to say, but how come you stop talking sometimes?"

"Well, because I can't always figure out if I'm making sense, it just seems more peaceful to quietly listen or even try to sleep through it." That seemed to make sense, so I nodded my head. "I'm always hopeful that things will be clearer when I wake up," she added.

"Are they?"

"Sometimes, and that's enough to give me hope."

"Grandma, how come you always tell me stuff like this? You tell me everything."

"Is that okay with you?"

"Well, yeah it is. You make me feel like I'm smart 'cause you trust me with stuff. I mean, you're telling me all this and you told me about Abby. I don't feel seven when I'm with you."

"How old do you feel?"

"Oh, really old, like twenty or something."

She smiled. "I'm glad."

Then I thought of something else. "How come my mom didn't know about your sister before?"

Grandma got so quiet that I was worried she was going to stop talking again, but then she looked at me and I knew she was just searching for the right words. "It was all such a long time ago. I believe everyone wanted me to forget about her, and for a time I tried. On the surface, it seems I succeeded, but in reality, I just couldn't do it. So, instead, I kept her in my mind like an imaginary playmate, but I never spoke of her – to anyone."

"Wow, Grandma. Then why did you tell me?"

"Sweetheart, you trust what I say, and, to be honest, seeing her ring did something to me. It reminded me that those whispers in my dreams were real. I tried to tell your mom, but you have to admit, it doesn't make much sense. So when she didn't believe me, I started to doubt myself. However, the more I thought about it, the more I knew it was true." She touched my cheek and said, "I need to see her before I die. I miss her. I always have."

I could tell all this talking was wearing Grandma out. "I hope we find her then. I just hope we do." Grandma slowly nodded her head. "Goodnight, Grandma. I'll see you in the morning." She smiled and closed her eyes.

Chapter 20

When I woke up the next morning, I hurried to Grandma's bedside. Once I looked at Grandma's face, I knew. Her eyes were open but they weren't looking at anything in particular. They just stared or wandered around the room. She focused on me for just a moment and whispered, "Not today," and then the eyes were elsewhere again. My shoulders slumped. After last night, I was hoping today would be another good day, but I could tell it wasn't going to be.

I went off to school, but my heart was sad. I missed Grandma, and she wasn't even dead yet. Justin asked me what was wrong, and so did my teacher. I just shrugged my shoulders. I didn't want to talk about it. I was afraid I might start crying in front of them. Justin nodded his head and said, "Lucas, I've got this." Then he put his hand on the shoulder of our teacher and said, "Let me explain." I didn't hear what he said. He had steered our teacher in the other direction, away from me and was whispering and talking with his hands. I would have smiled if I thought I could.

After school, I hurried to Grandma's side to see how she was doing. "How was school?" I was just about to answer, but then she added, "John, did you put the cat out?" When she saw the expression on my face, she went silent, shaking her head like she was trying to get rid of the cobwebs inside, but it didn't work.

Mom came into the room a few minutes later, and Grandma perked up again. "Will you ask John to pick up a gallon of milk on his way home from work?"

I looked up at Mom, wondering what she'd say. She smiled at me with a tired smile and said, "Mom, we'll take care of everything, don't you worry." I was glad she said something 'cause I never knew what to say. She then placed her hand on my shoulder and gave it a little squeeze. I suppose it was better than any words she could have given me.

On Thursday, I came home from school to see Grandma sitting up in bed, brushing her hair. I thought she might be back until I drew closer. She had the same cloudy look to her eyes. Quietly, I said, "Hi, Grandma."

She looked up, startled at the sound of my voice. "Who are you?"

I would rather have had her call me John than to not even know me at all. I felt small and afraid. "Grandma, it's me, Lucas."

She stared at me for a long time, then a smile eased onto her face and her eyes began to clear. "Yes, I know you. How was your day at school?"

And just like that, she was back. I didn't know how long it would last, though, so I started talking fast, wanting to get in as much as possible. I told her about my homework and all my tests and everything I'd done at school.

Grandma smiled as I talked and would say a few words every once in a while, like, "That's nice," or "Good job." I was glad 'cause then I knew she still was there.

I talked so long that Grandma fell asleep and started snoring before I was done, but I decided to keep on talking. It felt good to be talking to her again. I was hoping she could hear me in her sleep.

After dinner, I helped Mom clear the table. I was still smiling from being able to talk to Grandma.

Mom wasn't in as good a mood as I was, though. Dad wasn't home yet, and she kept muttering under her breath. I remembered how Grandma had told me to listen, but I couldn't understand what Mom was saying. All I caught was my dad's name, Pete.

I interrupted her muttering by saying, "Why are you mad at Dad?"

Mom jerked her head up, but then her gaze moved from my face to something behind me. Dad was standing in the doorway. "Do you want to answer that question, Pete?"

Dad stood there with his mouth open. He finally said in a crisp voice, "I've been the one wronged here. I think I'm exhibiting a great deal of patience."

"You? You've been wronged? What are you talking about? Haven't you been listening to me?" She turned away in exasperation, back to the dishes in the sink.

Dad started to say something in response, but I was back in Grandma's room by the time he did. I climbed up beside my sleeping Grandma and covered my ears. I woke up the next morning, curled into a ball, in the same spot.

―――――――――――

Friday after school, Justin and I walked home together. I had gone to school as if nothing else were happening in the world, but it was hard to hide things from Justin.

"How's your Grandma?"

I smiled, thinking of her. "She was home yesterday."

He stopped mid-step. "Isn't she always home?"

"Well, she's always home at my house, but sometimes she's not really there. Do you know what I mean?"

"Not really. Is it like if you call someone and they don't answer the phone, so all you can do is leave a message?"

"Yeah, I guess so, only I don't get to leave a message. I just have to wait and call back, hoping she's home next time."

He nodded his head like he understood. "I thought maybe you started smiling 'cause there's only one more week of school left. Then you can stay home with your grandma."

I laughed. "Well, yeah, that does make me happy. I guess there are lots of things to be happy about. Oh, and I get to see Mamie again tomorrow."

"Awesome!" he said and gave me a high five.

"Hey, have you asked your parents about a dog yet?"

He kicked the ground with his feet, sending dirt into the air. "Nah. They haven't even mentioned the gerbil lately." Then he brightened up. "But I will. Don't worry. I'll ask."

The rest of the walk home we played Bugs: Dead and Alive. It's a game we made up. Justin and I count all the bugs we see, both dead and alive. The winner is the one who spots the most. But since we count dead and alive separately, sometimes we squash a bug on the sidewalk, just so we can count him twice. I won this time.

It turned out Grandma was in between good and bad when I came home. She was awake, and her eyes were clear, but she didn't have much to say. I tried to ask about her day, but she didn't say anything. I even asked if she knew who I was. She at least nodded her head to that, but then she turned away. I think she was telling me she was there but didn't trust herself enough to speak. So I left her alone.

I was so excited to spend Saturday with Mamie that I woke up early. No one else was even awake yet. I got myself a bowl of cereal, and I put my dishes in the sink when I was done. I guess I should remember to do that more often, but I did it so Mom would be in a good mood when Mamie came.

When I finished putting all my breakfast stuff away, I looked at the clock on the microwave. It said 7:32. I didn't think Mamie was coming until 10:00, so I had way too much time to wait.

I peeked in on Grandma to see if she was still asleep, and I was disappointed to see that she was. I sat cross-legged on one of the nearby chairs to watch her. She mumbled in her sleep sometimes, but nothing I could understand.

Her blanket had different kinds of flowers all over it. I watched them, imagining they were growing as they moved up and down with every breath Grandma took. I put my head in my hands and tried to match my breathing to hers, but mine was steadier than hers. Finally, I got up to check the clock on the microwave again. It was 7:47. It was going to be a very long morning.

Returning to my chair near Grandma, I started swinging my legs and looking around for something else to do. Grandma's jewelry box was sitting on the table beside her bed. I listened to the house, but it was still sleeping, so I carefully picked up the box and put it on my lap, being careful not to make a sound. Opening it up, the first thing I saw was the ring. It seemed so little up against all her other jewelry. No wonder Mom had thought it was nothing. I put it on my thumb so I wouldn't lose it and started to sort through the rest of Grandma's things.

I remembered most of them from when Lily and I had played with them at Grandma's old apartment. But this time, I wondered if each of them had a story to tell. Where did Grandma get them? Did someone give them to her? Some of them had round beads and others dangled. One small necklace, I guess it was probably a bracelet, had little things hanging from it. One was a crab; another was a tall tower-like thing. It also had a big boat, a totem pole, a Christmas tree, and a plain old fish. I was so busy looking at it that I jumped when Mom said, "You're up early." She looked pretty tired.

Not knowing if I was in trouble for messing in Grandma's jewelry box, I shoved the bracelet back in her box as I looked up at Mom. I guess it wasn't a problem 'cause she just said, "Did you find anything interesting?" and then moved on into the kitchen.

I took the ring off my thumb and placed it gently on top of Grandma's other jewelry, but I pulled out the bracelet and followed Mom into the kitchen. "Mom, look at this. Isn't it cool?"

She took it in her hands. "That is, Lucas. It's a charm bracelet. Each of these is called a charm. You can pick whatever ones you want to put on it. I had one myself when I was younger, but I have no idea where it is now." She handed it back to me. "Would you like some breakfast?"

"No thanks, Mom. I already had some."

"Oh?" she said, followed by another, "Oh," when she saw my dishes in the sink. She looked at me and I just smiled.

The rest of the morning I tried to keep busy while I waited for Mamie to show up. I tried reading a book, but I couldn't concentrate and kept reading the same page over and over again. I tried pulling my army guys out, but I didn't really care which side won. I stopped trying anything else after that and just walked back and forth around the house.

Mom said I looked like a caged animal with all my pacing. I knew it bothered her that I was going off with Mamie, but I didn't know what to do about that. "Mom," I finally said, "I think you'd like Mamie now. She said she messed up with you before and that she's not a very nice person."

"She said that?"

"Well, something like that, and that she should say 'Sorry.' I really like her, Mom. She's different, but I like how she's different, and she …" I caught myself. I almost told Mom how much she was helping me find Grandma's sister. "She … she makes me smile."

Mom gave me a look that seemed caught between puzzled and angry. "I'm glad you like her, but my relationship with her is complicated."

"She says she doesn't like babies, and that's part of the reason she hasn't been around much," I offered. I didn't want to make excuses for Mamie, but I was hoping Mom might give her a second chance. It didn't appear to be working, though, because she just looked upset.

"If you're trying to help her case, you're not. I told you it's complicated, Lucas. You wouldn't understand."

I didn't know if I would understand or not, and I wasn't so sure Mom was actually happy that I liked Mamie. "Why is it complicated?"

"Lucas," she let out a sigh, "it just is, okay. She's never once tried to like me or even get to know me. I really tried to be nice to her, but she could never be bothered with me. And now … I just don't know, Lucas, she's never taken time for you before. I just hope she really *is* being nice to you, that she's not just using you somehow."

"How could she use me? I don't know how to do much yet."

She sighed again. "Lucas, I told you it was complicated. I'm sorry I said anything. I hope you have a good time with her today, I really do," she said and then turned away. I guess she wasn't going to say anything else.

I still didn't understand what was so complicated or what was wrong with being used. When I thought about it, Justin and I used each other all the time. It just meant we were friends, like the time I used his back like a table one morning, so I could hurry and finish doing the homework sheet I'd forgotten about. Or the time he used my back and my shoulders to climb up so he could see over our back fence to watch for invading armies or to see if the grass was greener on the other side of our fence like his mom talked about. None of those were things I guessed Mamie would want, and I couldn't think of anything else she might use me for. I shrugged my shoulders and decided Mom was just mixed up.

I wandered back into Grandma's room. I smiled when I saw she was awake, but stopped when I looked at her eyes. They were glazed over. Mom brought her in some breakfast on a tray and set it to the side of her bed, but Grandma didn't look hungry.

"Grandma, do you want some breakfast?"

She looked at me but didn't say yes or no. When Lily was younger, I could get her to eat when Mom and Dad couldn't. I figured I'd try with Grandma. It had to be pretty much the same. I picked up a forkful of pancake and held it out for her. "Grandma, open up. I've got some pancake for you."

She stared at me, then the fork, and then opened her mouth. I fed her a bite of pancake and then another and another. I kept feeding her until she finally shook her head, but by then, there were only two bites of pancake left. I handed Grandma her glass of milk and she drank it down.

Smiling to myself, I gathered up her dishes to go put in the kitchen sink. As I turned, I almost ran into Mom. I don't know how long she'd been standing there leaning against the doorframe, watching. She smiled slightly at me and stood back to let me pass.

I went back to sit with Grandma until she drifted off to sleep. Then I tried really hard to not look like a caged animal to Mom. I was relieved when Mamie showed up 'cause Mom still hadn't said another word to me after our conversation about Mamie. I was beginning to think that finding Grandma's sister was going to be a whole lot easier than trying to understand Mom.

Mamie and I spent the rest of the day together. We started by going to a park Mamie knew about. It had all kinds of fun stuff to climb on and swing from. Mamie sat on a bench and put on a big, floppy hat and some sunglasses while she watched me.

After a couple of hours, she asked if I was hungry. I was, so she drove us to a fast-food place for lunch. I got chicken nuggets, fries, and a drink. Mamie got a burger and fries. "I didn't know you ate this kind of food, Mamie."

"Of course I do. My body may be old, but my mind isn't. I even like ice cream cones and popsicles."

"Really?"

"Well, maybe not as much as you do, but I still enjoy them on occasion."

Mamie was full of surprises. I liked her more and more every time I saw her. I wanted to tell her all about my week at school and how Grandma was doing, but I didn't get much out 'cause I was trying to remember not to talk with my mouth full. Once I forgot, and I saw Mamie's eyebrows go up. I quickly put my hand over my mouth, and then without thinking said, "I'm sorry," only I still had a mouthful of food. I immediately realized my mistake and my eyes flew open wide as I clamped both hands over my mouth.

Mamie tipped her head and gave me a searching look, then burst out laughing. "You know, dear boy, I do believe I have been a little too full of myself over the years. I do appreciate good manners, but even I make mistakes."

I smiled but said nothing – since I still had a mouthful of food.

After that, we went to Mamie's house. She took me on a tour of her house since I had only seen a little of it before. I forgot to count how many bedrooms and bathrooms it had, but it was a lot, especially for just one old lady. My favorite room was her library.

"Wow, Mamie, I didn't know people could have their own libraries." The shelves were so high I couldn't reach the top ones, and I didn't think Mamie could either. "How do you get those books down?" I said, pointing to books near the ceiling.

She chuckled and said, "With this." It was a ladder on wheels and it rode around the room.

"Wow," was all I could say. "Can I check out a book sometime?"

She laughed again. "No." I looked at her in surprise. Then she added, "But you may have any books you like."

"Wow, Justin would really like this. Can I bring him over to show him sometime?"

"Sure. Is Justin your friend from down the street?"

"Uh huh. I play with him all the time. Sometimes I go home from school with him, like when Mom has a doctor's appointment or something."

Mamie raised her eyebrows. "Has your mom been going to the doctor a lot lately?"

I had to think about that. "I'm not sure. I hear her talk about doctor's appointments, but I think she mostly goes while I'm at school. I thought they were all for Grandma."

"But don't your grandmother's doctors come visit her at your house?"

"Yeah, I guess so." I shrugged my shoulders.

"Justin's mom must be a good friend of your mother's. Is that right?"

"Yeah. I love it when Mom comes to get me from Justin's house instead of calling. They start talking and talking and we get to keep playing."

Mamie got a small smile on her face. "That must be nice. Well, we'll have to bring Justin over one of these days then, won't we?"

I nodded as I looked around the room some more. That's when I spotted a chess board built right into a table. We had played in a different room before and with a different board.

She saw my gaze and said, "Would you like to play?"

All I had to do was nod.

I was tired but happy by the time I returned home around dinnertime. Mamie walked me to the door, but she didn't stay. As she was stepping off the porch on her way to her car, she called back, "Lucas, I'll come pick you up after school on Tuesday again. I already cleared it with your father. It appears Mr. Argent might have some news for us."

I whirled around. "Really?"

She smiled. "Well, I don't know what he has to tell us, but he wanted to talk."

I jumped up and down. "Oh, good!"

Just then Dad stepped out to see what the noise was about. I wasn't sure what to say. "Lucas and I are working on a wonderful surprise," Mamie chimed in, "and I just informed him of our next step. So, I'm sure you'll let him keep it a secret until the time is right." Then before Dad could respond, Mamie winked at me and practically danced her way back to her car.

When I Was Seven

The ocean water never gets any warmer, I notice. When I am so cold that I begin to shake, I move out of its reach so the sun will dry my skin and take away the chill. But I can't seem to leave the water for long. It's intoxicating in its danger. I return to stand waist deep in it and turn to gaze at the shore I have left behind. After only a short time, my footsteps leading into the water have been erased, all trace of my path having dissolved before my very eyes.

Occasionally the adults, for there are no other children, beckon me to return, to leave the water, but they are not insistent. It is only a call for show, to please each other that they care. I may only be a child, but I can tell the difference.

So I stay in the water, even as I begin to shiver. Every so often a piece of seaweed drifts in or out with the waves and it tickles my legs. One long piece wraps itself around me and I reach into the ocean to release it. Coming back out of the water, I shake my arms and the long strands of my hair that are now damp, hoping to fend off any further chills.

Gazing around me, I see the gulls floating in large arcs, riding the currents of the air. I wish I could fly. But where would I go? The thought disturbs me, and I turn away. On the beach, I hear the people laughing and talking, content with their choices. I am not.

I turn to the sea. It stretches farther than I can imagine. Blue and bumpy, always in motion, yet it does not speak to me. It tells me nothing of what hides beneath its surface or who might take refuge there. Where, I wonder, does it all end?

If I were to walk out far enough, would anyone notice that I am gone? Will they look for me? Will they miss me when I am no more?

Chapter 21

I thought Tuesday would never arrive. It was almost like waiting for Christmas, only worse 'cause I didn't know if there were going to be any presents or a lump of coal instead.

Monday night I lay on the couch, tossing and turning. When I finally fell asleep, it was a fitful sleep. I dreamed that Dad came home from work really late. Mom must have been waiting for him 'cause I heard her say, "Welcome home, Pete. Can we talk?"

"Yeah, whatever."

"I think I finally figured it out. It's not about what you want or don't want. It's that you think I lied to you, that I betrayed you."

"Well, it's obvious, isn't it?"

"No, it's not! Why can't you trust me? I'm not lying to you, Pete."

It seemed strange for a dream, because that's all there was, and I didn't have pictures in my head to go with it, only the words.

When I got up in the morning, I didn't see Mom. Dad made me a lunch and then dropped me off at school on his way to work.

At the end of school on Tuesday, I ran the whole way home with Justin chasing behind me. Sure enough, Mamie was waiting for me in the driveway. I ran inside to dump off my backpack and give Mom a kiss before running right back out the door.

When I got in the car, she said, "Mr. Argent isn't available for another hour, but I thought we could spend the time together before our appointment. Is that okay with you?"

I was disappointed that I still had to wait, but the thought of spending time with Mamie was a good one. "Sure," I said and smiled for good measure.

Mamie was about to start the car but then stopped. "What's wrong, Lucas?"

I guess I wasn't fooling anyone. "I'm just so nervous. I don't want to disappoint Grandma. I'm her only chance, and I'm afraid I might mess up. I just have to find Abby for her."

Mamie reached over and put her hands on both sides of my face. "Master Lucas, you are not alone in this search. If there is something to be found, we're going to find it – together. If *we* don't find Abby, it will only be because it's not possible, not because you 'messed up.' Okay?" I didn't immediately respond, so she said, "Lucas, look at me. It's going to be okay. You're doing the very best you can, and that's all anyone can expect of you. Do you understand?"

I nodded my head, but my smile hadn't found its way back yet.

"Do you really believe your grandma would be disappointed in you, after all you're trying to do for her? I thought you knew she loved you with all her heart." She cocked her head, waiting for a reply.

Mamie had a point, but with a rush I said, "But maybe she'll stop loving me if I can't find Abby for her. It's the only thing she's ever asked me to do, I mean that's important."

Mamie gathered me in her arms. "Oh, sweetie, no one could ever stop loving you." I felt her hand smoothing my hair and her touch began to calm me down. "I'm sure your grandma would never have let you try to find Abby if she'd known it would cause you such worry. I believe she told you about Abby because you're the person she trusts the most with this special quest. You are her knight."

"I guess so." I looked up at her, and said, "You know, she told me something about a knight, but I didn't understand it. She said sometimes the knight can't slay the dragon, but that's okay 'cause the dragon has to live too. If I'm the knight, what's the dragon? Is the dragon about finding Abby?"

Mamie didn't speak but she pulled me closer and began to stroke my hair. I could feel the way her breath came and went, but still she said nothing. When she finally spoke, I could barely hear her words. "No. The dragon is death." She paused and I could feel her breathing even stronger. "Lucas, death is, unfortunately, a normal part of life, and no one can change that. There's nothing either one of us can do about it."

I looked up at her face and was surprised to see a tear running down her cheek. "Why are you crying, Mamie?"

"Because Lucas, your grandmother is … well, she's special to you. She's a good person … a better person than I am. If anyone deserves to see you grow up, she does. I haven't earned this like she has." She took a deep breath before continuing. "I'm so sorry that you will lose her. I have grown to love you so, and I wish you didn't have to go through the hurt of losing your grandmother. If I could take her place, I would."

It was my turn to throw my arms around Mamie. "I wish she didn't have to die either, but I wouldn't want to lose you. I love you, Mamie." At that, she really started to cry.

"I'm so sorry it took me such a long time to get to know you, Lucas. I'm glad you wanted my help, that you needed me." She dabbed at her tears with a tissue. "What I thought was just a little adventure has become the most important journey of my life. I didn't know anyone could teach this old dog new tricks, but apparently I hadn't counted on a seven-year-old like you." She smiled, all finished with crying. "What do you say we go get an ice cream cone then head over to see Mr. Argent?"

I grinned and nodded my head.

A short time later, while I was still licking the last of my sticky fingers, we were called back to Mr. Argent's office. Mamie could tell I was still nervous when we sat down, so she reached over and held my hand. Her hand completely covered mine and felt warm and comforting. She didn't even seem to mind that my hand was still a little sticky. I smiled at her.

"I heard back from the private eye I hired," Mr. Argent began. "He had troubles finding any evidence of an Abby Jones. He looked for birth records of Abby, Abbey with an 'e', Abigail Jones and came up empty. Jones is, of course, a common name and there were some

Abbys, but none of them were close to the right age."

My stomach started to sink. Even though I had been worried, I always assumed the grown-ups wouldn't have any trouble finding Abby. The TV detectives always get their man. I figured this would be the same. Mamie squeezed my hand, but I couldn't take my eyes off Mr. Argent.

He cleared his throat and began again. "The P.I. also checked for a Josephine Jones, but did not find any record of her birth either."

I didn't know what that meant. Grandma was certainly born sometime. I looked at Mamie for an explanation. She was staring at Mr. Argent. "So, what you're saying is that they weren't born in Oregon. That's all you've really learned so far, isn't it?"

He nodded. "Basically, that's what that piece of information tells us, but there is more. The P.I. did some newspaper searches and found reference to JoJo Jones during what would have been her senior year of high school. She received some local scholarship money for college. There was quite a write-up. That led him to her high school yearbook. She went to high school in a small town not too far from the capital city of Salem." He paused, but wouldn't look at either of us.

Mamie eyed him suspiciously. "What is it? What else did you learn?" she said.

"I'm sorry, but Josephine or JoJo was an only child. The seniors can make a tribute to their families and list their parents and siblings. JoJo Jones only lists her parents, and what the yearbook implies, the newspaper article confirms. It even explicitly states that she is the only child of Robert and Patsy Jones. I'm sorry," he said again while shaking his head.

I jumped up, ripping my hand out of Mamie's grasp. "What do you mean? Do you think my grandma's just making it all up?"

"Well, son, sometimes old people become delusional," he said, still not looking me in the eye. I didn't even know what his words meant, but I knew I didn't like them.

Then I heard a voice from behind me. It was Mamie, but it didn't sound like her. It was strong and I could feel it in my bones. "Mr. Argent, this is not a trivial matter. It is a dying woman's last wish, to be reunited with her sister. If you don't have enough courage to see

112

this through to find what is not obvious, I will find someone who does." I turned to look at her, unable to believe my ears, but she wasn't done yet. "Mr. Argent, this is the most important thing I have ever done for my grandson, and it is the most important thing he has ever done for his grandmother. Are you going to help us, or shall I walk out this door?"

Mr. Argent's expression changed. "Oh, of course I'll help. I just ... umm ... I just need to regroup a little."

"I don't believe that was your initial plan at all. You completely dismissed us." She fixed him with a hard stare. "I will give you a second chance, but only a second chance." Turning to me, she said, "Lucas, what else has your grandmother said? I believe Abby is real, just as much as you do. Is there anything else you can think of that might help?"

"Well," I was thinking as hard as I could, "Grandma has a birthstone ring of Abby's. It's light blue. But she also told me she was raised as an only child and . . ." I knew there had to be more. Then I remembered. "She said Abby left her. Everyone wanted her to forget all about Abby. But she never did." I looked at both of them. "Does that help?"

They both started to talk at once. "She could have run away."

"Or gone away to college."

"Or maybe, just maybe, she died young."

"Yes, for some families, the grief is too much and they just try to push it aside and forget about the child."

"Are there other possibilities?" Mamie said.

"I imagine 'leaving' could mean all kinds of things, but I'm not sure what," Mr. Argent said.

They were so busy talking about ideas that I think they forgot I was standing there. "I don't know what it means," I finally said, "but please don't give up. I love my grandma, and I don't want to tell her that I couldn't find Abby. I just can't do that."

They both turned to look at me, but to my surprise, Mr. Argent was the first to speak. "I'll call the private eye right now. He might even have more ideas than we do. I'll make sure he gets right on it." Mr. Argent looked like a different person from who he was a few minutes before. He seemed just as determined as Mamie. I didn't know if it came from Mamie's mood or if he was just trying to make Mamie happy 'cause of all her money. I suppose I didn't really care.

When we left Mr. Argent's office, I threw my arms around Mamie. "Thank you so much for helping me. I knew you would, but I didn't know that you *really* would. I mean, well, ... like what you just did. Thanks, Mamie."

She returned my hug. "I did it for you, Lucas. I did it for you." Then she pulled back so she could look directly at me. "I won't give up, either. We're in this together until the end, if that's all right with you."

I just smiled in reply. I must be the luckiest kid in the world to have two awesome grandmas.

"You know, Lucas, I have an idea."

"What?"

"When I take you home, why don't we stop at Justin's house? I can talk to his mom and see if it would be all right for Justin to come with you to my house sometime."

"Sure."

When we got to Justin's house, his mom answered the door. She looked surprised to see the two of us. Then I realized she'd probably never met Mamie before. "Hi, Mrs. Cook, this is my other grandma. Her name's Mamie. And Mamie, this is Justin's mom. Her name's Allison." I added with a whisper to Mamie, "but I don't ever call her that."

Mamie smiled. "I'll just take a minute because I've got to get Lucas back home. But I was wondering if sometime Justin could come with Lucas to my place. I'd love to have the two of them together."

"Well, I don't know. I guess so. I imagine I'll just need to check with my husband first."

"No problem. Take your time. You've no doubt heard stories about me."

"I ... well –"

Mamie put her hand up. "No need. They're all true, but I'm trying to turn over a new leaf."

Justin's mom laughed nervously. "Okay, fair enough. Your honesty is a bit disarming, but I can respect that. I'm sure Justin would love to join you sometime."

Mamie smiled. I turned to go back to her car, assuming we were done, but I was wrong. "One more thing, Allison. I know Iris isn't ready to make things public, but I'm wondering if you could help me. I'd like to get her a gift while she's ..." She glanced in my direction. "While she's got a bun in the oven. You know, something now just for her and then something later for ..."

"Oh. I didn't know that you knew. Umm, sure. I think that would be nice."

"Do you have any suggestions? Or her clothing size?"

"I'm not sure, but I can think about it and find out some sizes for you. You just caught me a little off-guard. Can I get your phone number?"

"Sure. And, if you don't mind, I'd like it to be a surprise."

"Of course."

They exchanged phone numbers, and then Mamie scurried me off to the car. It took us maybe two minutes to get to my house. Before I got out, I said, "What does turn over a new leaf mean?"

"It means trying something new, in my case, trying to be nicer."

"Is that true? Are you? I mean you're nice to me, but are you trying to be nicer to my mom?"

"Yes, I am. Although ..."

"What?"

"Let's just say old habits are hard to break."

I nodded my head and started to open the car door when I remembered something else. "What's a bun in the oven? I don't think my mom is baking anything today."

She laughed and got a mischievous look in her eye. "It's nothing you need to worry about right now. I just needed to verify a suspicion of mine."

I shrugged my shoulders and ran inside, waving goodbye to her from the front porch.

Chapter 22

I couldn't believe we were finally getting to the last few days of school before summer vacation. It's the worst time of year to sit in a classroom. The warm air makes it hard to concentrate on lessons, and even the teachers seem ready to bolt outside. Every day Justin tried to catch my eye from across the room, making faces to see if he could get me to laugh. He finally succeeded on the last day when I couldn't hold it in any longer. Our teacher just smiled and kept talking.

We always have a field day on the last day of school to celebrate. We run relay races and play carnival games, ending the day with water balloons. Justin and I teamed up to throw them at the teachers and the cutest girls. Then we faced off with each other.

"Do you feel lucky?" Justin said as he eyed me, holding the biggest water balloon I had seen all day.

"Yes!" I yelled as my balloon made a direct hit. I was laughing so hard, I never saw it coming. His balloon soaked every inch of me. Even my ears were dripping. That's what friends are for.

When the final bell rang, I was shocked to remember Grandma. I felt guilty for not thinking about her at all that day. Justin understood when I ran all the way home to see her. She stirred when I came near and reached out to me. I moved right beside her and she placed her hand on my cheek, gently cradling it while she looked at me and smiled. "How was work today?" she said. Before I had a chance to correct her, she saw the look in my eye and said, "Never mind." Then she went silent.

I stayed silent as well. We sat that way for a long time, the only movement being Grandma's thumb softly rubbing my cheek.

Finally, she dropped her arm to her side and closed her eyes. I carefully tiptoed away. When I had almost made my way out of the room, I heard her softly say, "I'm proud of you, Lucas," and then she slept.

Waking up Saturday morning, I rubbed my eyes, wondering what my first day of summer vacation might hold. Sitting up on the couch, I tried to listen like Grandma had told me to do. I could hear Dad banging around in the garage, probably pulling out the lawnmower. Lily was upstairs singing to her dolls. I didn't hear Mom at first, but eventually she came down the stairs and looked in on Grandma who was still sleeping.

When I followed her into the kitchen for breakfast, she looked up at me. She seemed tired and sad, but she gave me a big smile and said, "Good morning, Lucas." She didn't say anything else, so I started listening with my eyes.

I watched as Mom took breakfast to Grandma when she woke up and made sure she ate. Then Mom fixed Grandma's hair and even put a little makeup on her. They talked a little, but mostly Mom just sat at Grandma's side, holding her hand or carefully stroking her hair with the palm of her hand. Lily came and joined them too, lying down on Grandma's bed right beside her to snuggle. They were quiet, but no one seemed to mind.

When Lily scampered down to go play with her toys and Mom stood up to clear away the breakfast dishes, I moved to Grandma's side. She was resting. I don't know if she was actually asleep or not, but I didn't want to disturb her either way.

Grandma was starting to look different, I noticed. Her cheeks seemed smaller and her skin looser, like there was too much of one and not enough of the other. Even the color of her skin seemed to be changing. Where she used to be colorful Play-Doh, she was now the grayish clay from art class.

I watched her breathing and wondered if Mom and Lily ever did the same thing. Did they notice how her fingers sometimes twitched as she slept or that she was likely to snore? Did they sit here long enough to find out?

Just then, Mom poked her head in. "Lucas," she whispered, "Would you like a snack? Lily's having some yogurt and fruit." Reluctantly I left Grandma's side to join Lily and Mom in the kitchen, and somehow, in that moment, I felt closer to them.

I was just about to ask Mom if I could go play with Justin when there was a knock on the front door. It was Justin's dad, Mr. Cook. "Is your dad around?"

I nodded. "I think he's in the garage or somewhere outside."

Justin's dad walked over to the garage, and I followed. Dad was inside, messing around with the lawnmower. "Hey, Pete, do you have some time to lend me a hand? You've got to see what my kid did." He was chuckling.

"Sure. What is it?"

"Did you know he built a doghouse? He just asked for a dog and told me he already had a house ready for it. It's the funniest doghouse you've ever seen."

"That I'd like to see." Then Dad noticed me standing there. "Do you want to come along?" Of course I did. "Did you know anything about this?" I just grinned and shrugged my shoulders.

"So, Dan, what are you going to do about the dog?" Dad asked as we walked up the street.

"I'm going to buy him a dog, of course. If he was willing to work that hard just to get ready to ask, I think he can handle the real thing. What a funny kid."

Wow! I couldn't believe it. His plan worked. As we came within sight, Justin spotted me and came running. "Guess what?"

"You're getting a dog!"

"Yep." I'd never seen him smile quite so wide before.

By the end of the afternoon, and after an order of pizza for lunch, our two dads had built a new doghouse. Justin and I had to admit it looked a lot better than what we'd built.

On the way home, Dad was as cheerful as I'd seen him in a while. "You two are quite something. I sometimes forget how much even a child can accomplish when he wants to badly enough." He ruffled my hair and said, "I love you, sport."

The first thing I noticed once we got inside was that Grandma was awake. I think Lily and Mom were both napping upstairs because it was pretty quiet. Hurrying to Grandma's bedside, I could tell right away it would be a good afternoon. Her eyes were bright, and she was looking right at me.

"Hi, Lucas. Are you having a good day now that school's out?"

I was surprised she remembered it was summer vacation. "Yes, just wait 'til I tell you about Justin's doghouse." Then I thought of something. "Did you have a dog when you were a kid?"

"I don't think so, but Abby might have had a pet of some kind." She reached out in her familiar way to touch my cheek. "Lucas, I didn't get enough time with her growing up. Thank you for bringing her back to me."

"But I haven't. I haven't found her yet."

"I know, but a piece of her is back in my heart, a piece I wouldn't allow myself to have until you reminded me it was missing. You know, I'd forgotten so many things, but I'm getting glimpses back. Abby and I used to love to play on the swing set. Sometimes she would push me and then run right underneath me. It would make me soar so high I would pretend I was flying. I loved the feel of swinging free and letting myself rock gently back and forth until the swing would slow down almost to a stop. Then Abby would push me again, or I would give her a turn and push her as hard as I could."

While Grandma talked, I think she forgot I was there. She seemed to be back with Abby when they were little, lost in the memory of it.

"We used to play kitten dragon," she continued. "It was one of my favorite games. It was really just playing school, and Abby would be my teacher. We must have started playing it when I was very small because I remember that I couldn't figure out how to say kindergarten. It was such a big word. So, I called it kitten dragon." Abby's ring was sitting on the bedside table, and Grandma reached over and picked it up, twirling it in her fingers while she talked. "I thought school was going to be some wild adventure with a name like that. When Abby pulled out books and crayons, I thought she must be hiding something about what real school was like. She was already in

119

school, and I just figured it was all a big secret, like a secret club.

"When I finally was old enough to go to school myself, I was scared but excited, not knowing what to expect from kitten dragon. I have to say I was disappointed to learn it was just like what Abby had played with me. Then I realized I was kind of relieved too, to realize I didn't have to fight a dragon. I liked it after that."

"I liked kindergarten, too," I said. She jumped at the sound of my voice and stared at me as if she wondered where I'd come from. "I'm sorry, Grandma. I shouldn't have said anything."

"No, no. You're just fine. When the memories come, they can overtake me, and I forget what's going on right around me. Lucas, have you ever heard people say that right before you die your life flashes before your eyes? Well, mine seems to be meandering at its own pace. It must mean I still have a little time left."

"I hope so, Grandma. I'm not ready for you to die." I didn't say it, but I was also worried I might not find Abby in time.

"Lucas, no one thinks they're ready to let someone else go, but you are going to surprise yourself. You're going to be okay. It's your mom I'm worried about. When I die, it will catch her by surprise, even though it's not a secret."

"What do you mean?"

"Well, her idea is to deny the whole idea of my death, and then maybe it just won't happen. I can't get her to talk about it. If I bring it up, she refuses to listen and usually ends up leaving the room." She picked up my hand and squeezed it. "But, Lucas, you are stronger than you realize. Who knows, maybe you'll even end up being the one to help your mom."

I hadn't thought about that before. "Grandma, how old are you?"

"I'm 60. Why do you ask, sweetie?"

"Well, Dad says you're really young to die, but 60 sounds kind of old. Do you think you're too young to die?"

"That's a complicated question. I guess I never really thought I would die at 60. I figured I'd live to maybe 80. But living is about more than a number of years."

"What's it about, then?"

"It's about what you do with the time you have, not how much time there is. Life hasn't been easy. It took time for me to figure out how to make the best of it, but I finally decided I was going to be a happy person. I could make it my purpose in life always to find a way to be nice to others, even if they weren't nice to me. I have no regrets, Lucas. I can die in peace."

"But what about Abby?"

Her voice grew soft. "Except for Abby. Yes, I have no regrets, except for Abby."

Chapter 23

Abby. I dreamed about Abby Sunday night, even though I didn't know what she looked like. She was calling to me, saying, "Where's Josie? I want to see her. Where is she?" It's like we were in different parts of a big maze. We could see each other over the short walls, but we couldn't figure out how to reach each other.

I woke up breathing hard. When I looked toward Grandma's bed, a nurse was by her side and so was Mom. No one seemed worried, but I was.

Racing upstairs to the phone in Mom's bedroom, I called Mamie's number. When she answered, I burst out, "Have you heard anything yet? Do you know where Abby is?"

"No, I'm sorry, Lucas. I don't have any word yet. Mr. Argent tells me the P.I. is still checking on different angles. I'll let you know as soon as I know something."

I wanted to take a deep breath and accept what she was telling me, but time seemed to be running out. It felt like life was a big hourglass, and there just wasn't enough sand left in Grandma's glass to do what needed to be done. "We just have to find Abby quickly. I'm getting scared."

"I know, Lucas. We're doing what we can. Try not to worry. We'll find her."

"Okay. Thanks, Mamie. I'll talk to you later." I just stared at the carpet, not sure how to make Grandma's time slow down and the private investigator's speed up. If I'd been looking up, I would've been better prepared.

"Just what do you think you're doing?!"

I jerked my head up to find Mom's face only a few inches from mine. It was red and fiery. I didn't know how much she had heard, but clearly it was enough. From the way she looked, I'd never been in this much trouble before. When I didn't say anything, she said, "I believe I asked you a question, young man. Would you care to explain yourself?"

I didn't know how to explain, but being silent was clearly not a good choice. "I … I was looking for Abby … for Grandma. She wants to see her, and I promised to find her."

"I told you to leave that alone! There is no Abby. You're upsetting everyone by looking for someone who doesn't exist. I can't believe you would go to *her* to help you after promising me …" She stopped talking, just sputtering instead and shaking her head. All her words seemed lost, and she looked like a bomb that was ready to explode. She threw her arm to the side, pointing toward my bedroom. I didn't ask what that meant – I just ran as fast as possible to my room and climbed on my bed.

The bed was slightly messed up and smelled like Dad. I didn't come in here much these days, only to change clothes and grab some toys or books. I didn't know how long I was supposed to stay, but I was guessing I should get comfortable.

Mom brought me breakfast and later lunch without ever saying a single word. I found some books and Legos to keep myself entertained in the meantime.

In the afternoon, after she woke up from her nap, Lily crept in to play with me. I had to shush her while we played, but it was easy to forget about being quiet. Mom caught us after I'd shushed Lily three times. She shot me a look while she marched Lily out the door.

When you have time to examine a room from top to bottom, you also have time to plan. By the time Dad came home, mine was in place.

Mom and Dad called me downstairs after dinner. Before they could say anything, I asked, "How come you're home so early, Dad?"

He was mad, probably partly because of my question, but I didn't care. "Your mother called me."

After that, I didn't really listen to what they said. I figured they hadn't been listening to me, so why should I listen to them. When they were done, I told them I was tired, and I was going to sleep upstairs tonight. Then I marched up the steps.

I almost fell asleep a couple of times, and I pretended to be asleep when they each came to check on me. When the whole house was quiet, I got dressed and pulled the backpack I had hidden out of the closet. It had some clothes, my toothbrush and toothpaste, my two favorite army guys and a pack of gum.

It was easier to sneak downstairs than I thought it would be. Everyone was sound asleep. I even peeked into Mom and Dad's room to make sure Dad was sleeping in their bed. I drew a sigh of relief when I saw he was.

Taking the phone from the kitchen, I snuck into the basement just to be sure I didn't wake anyone and called Mamie. I'm pretty sure I woke her up, but I didn't think I had another option. She answered on the fourth ring.

"What's up, Lucas?" She sounded pretty groggy, but she didn't say anything about what time it was.

"Can you come pick me up? I'm running away."

"Oh really?" Her voice already sounded a lot more awake.

"Yes."

"Do you want to tell me why?"

"I'll tell you later. Can you come get me now?"

"Sure. I'll be over in a few minutes."

There was one more thing I had to ask, only I wasn't as confident about this one. "Would you let me live with you?" I squeaked out.

"Were you worried about that?"

I nodded my head, then realized she couldn't see it through the phone. "Yes."

I heard her familiar chuckle. "You don't need to worry about that, Lucas, not ever. You are always welcome in my home, my life, anything you like. I'll see you soon."

I tiptoed up out of the basement, returned the phone to the kitchen, and went to see Grandma. She was the only thing I didn't want to leave, and maybe Lily. I hadn't thought about missing them. I started to think about how much I was going to miss Mom and Dad too, but then I remembered why I was running away in the first place. I quickly kissed Grandma on the forehead, then as quietly as possible, slipped out the front door.

Mamie looked surprised to see me waiting on the curb for her. I thought she would just pull over so I could jump in for a quick getaway, but she turned into our driveway instead.

"Quick, Mamie, before anyone notices I'm gone," I said while reaching for the door handle.

"Wait just a minute, Master Lucas. Don't you want to say goodbye to your grandma?"

"I already did. Let's go." She was acting like we had all the time in the world to escape.

"Okay. Did you write a note for your parents, so they won't worry?"

"Well, no, but I don't care if they worry."

"Are you sure? If they're really worried, they might call the police."

She was making sense, and I wasn't happy about it. "Okay, I'll go write a note," I said, grudgingly.

I trudged back to the front door. Thankfully, I hadn't locked it behind me. I almost forgot to be quiet, but the first squeak of the door reminded me, and I slowed down so it wouldn't make another sound.

It took only a few minutes to find paper and pencil for a note. I wrote:

I'm running away from home
because you don't believe me.
Lucas

When I looked up from finishing my note, Mamie was standing over me, and I jumped. I didn't know she'd even come into the house. "You scared me, Mamie. Okay, I'm ready now."

"What didn't they believe, Lucas? About Abby?"

"Yes. Mom heard me talking to you on the phone today. I guess I said Abby's name. She was really mad, so mad she could hardly talk to me."

"Well, I can understand why you're upset then. Why don't we go sit on the couch and talk about it."

"But we've got to hurry before someone wakes up and catches us." I didn't seem to be getting through to her. She was acting like maybe she hadn't even heard me. She just kept walking into the living room and then sat down on the couch as if we were in no hurry at all.

I just stood there with my backpack on and my hands on my hips. Did people just not listen to seven-year-olds?

"Lucas, please, sit down." I didn't budge. "Lucas, I know you're anxious to get going, and I'm more than happy to have you at my house, but I think it would help to think this through a little bit. Please, sit down." She patted the cushion next to hers, and I reluctantly sat, but I folded my arms to let her know I wasn't happy about it.

"Okay, I understand you want to run away." I nodded my head. "And you want to find your grandma's sister for her." Again, I nodded. "Well, do you plan on coming back anytime?"

I hadn't thought about that. "I don't know."

"Let's consider your options. If you don't want to come back, then what are you going to do when you find Abby? Wouldn't you want to bring her back here, to see her sister?"

"I guess so."

"That would mean coming back, wouldn't it?"

"Yes." I wasn't sure I liked where she was going with this.

"If you're planning on coming back, don't you think it would be best to try to work things out with your parents now? I mean you'd end up having to work things out with them anyway. It'll be a lot easier to do it now rather than later … you know, after you've run away and all."

I didn't like that she was making sense. I had been so sure I wanted to run away. "Don't you want me?" I said very quietly.

She grabbed me in a huge hug. "Like I said before, Lucas, I would love to have you. I just don't think this is the way to do it. You'd get tired of me after a while, and you'd miss your bed and your toys, and even your family. I think you should stay."

It just made me sad, not in the same way I was sad about Grandma dying, but sad in like the way I'm sad when Christmas is over and I have to wait a whole 'nother year for the next one to come. I thought my plan was good, but Mamie was right.

"Maybe you could talk to your parents about spending the night at my house every so often. It would be just you and me."

I smiled, that did sound good. "I'd like staying at your house." Right then Mom and Dad walked in the room.

Mom had the note I'd left in the kitchen, and it was shaking in her hand. She looked just as angry as she did the day before, only this time, she was looking at Mamie and not me. "Get out!" She pointed toward the front door as if Mamie didn't know the way. I guess Mom liked pointing when she was mad.

"I was just talking with Lucas about staying –"

"I heard what you were talking to him about – staying at your house. Well, it's not going to happen. It's bad enough that he wanted to run away, but it's worse that you were helping him do it. Was this your idea?"

"No, Mom, that's not what happened, I –"

She turned on me. "I don't remember asking you to speak. Go up to your room right now."

"But –"

"You'd better go." It was Mamie talking.

"But she doesn't understand. You didn't –"

"It's okay, Lucas. I'm a big girl. I can take care of myself. This will all get sorted out eventually. Just scurry off to bed." Then she gave me a little smile and a wink. She was trying to save me from getting into worse trouble.

I did as she said, but I lingered on the stairs, trying to listen. I was expecting Mom to continue yelling at her, but I guess Mamie didn't give her the chance. "If you two weren't so busy being upset at each other maybe you would have noticed how much your son cares about his grandmother in the other room. And maybe, just maybe, you might have believed him – and believed her."

It was deathly quiet for a moment, then Mamie said, "I'll let myself out." I heard the front door open, and then Mamie's voice one last time. "Just remember, things aren't always what they seem." Then I heard the front door close behind her.

When I Was Seven

The wind has picked up, and it's playing with my hair, whipping it across my face and into my eyes, but I determine to keep searching. I've been looking for seashells, especially a conch shell so I can put it to my ear and hear the ocean when I'm back in my bedroom, but I'm not finding much. Bits of broken shells, however, litter the sand. I bend down, spotting a larger piece. It's a simple clamshell half, but it's mostly intact.

I hold it in my hands, running my fingers along the soft interior, then touching the bumpy ridges and roughness of the outside. I find it oddly familiar and comforting.

A voice distracts me, calling me to where a beach blanket has been spread. Lunch is waiting. I run back, tightly clutching the shell.

Later, after we shake the sand from the blanket and pack the cooler into the car, I climb into the back seat. Lying down, I fall asleep on the ride home.

In the dark, next to our empty picnic spot, the clamshell rests upon the sand, lost and completely forgotten.

Chapter 24

I slept in my bed for a few hours, but when the sky started to lighten up outside my window, I crept down the stairs. Partway down, I heard voices and paused. Mom and Dad were talking. I couldn't make out all the words, but I heard enough to understand something. They were mad about me trying to run away, and they thought it was all Mamie's idea. But the really important thing was they were so mad about that, they seemed to have forgotten to be mad about me looking for Abby. At least they didn't mention it. That part made me happy.

When I got downstairs, I checked on Grandma to see if she was all right. Then I climbed back onto the couch and went back to sleep with a smile on my face.

When I woke up, the last of the nurses and doctors were leaving. I must have been pretty tired. I guess that happens when you stay up most of the night. I wondered where Mom was, but I wasn't actually very eager to find out.

Grandma looked groggy, but she wasn't sleeping. She looked up at me when I got close. "Will you get me my pain medicine, John?"

I knew what that meant, so I hurried to the kitchen. Mom was there. I was a little afraid to talk to her, but in this case, it didn't matter. "Grandma needs her pain medicine," was all I needed to say.

I stayed by Mom's side while she gave Grandma her medicine. I knew Grandma had a lot of pain, but it seemed to be getting worse lately. She gripped my hand after taking her medicine and said, "Thank you." The pills always made things worse. I know they helped her pain, but they messed up her head. She'd say more crazy stuff or just not talk at all, sometimes simply because she was sleeping more. It made me sad, but I understood.

While Grandma was still holding my hand, I looked at Mom. "I just love Grandma, that's all. Mamie came over 'cause I called her. I asked if I could live with her, and she said I could, but then she talked me out of running away. It wasn't her fault."

She didn't respond, but she nodded her head before leaving the room.

I sat with Grandma for several hours that day and the next. By then, she had mostly disappeared. She would show up for a few minutes here and there, but there was nothing I could do to bring her up if she was gone. All I could do was wait and hope for the moments that came. It was a lonely wait.

I'm sure Mom noticed me sitting by Grandma's bedside hour after hour, but she left me alone. She didn't seem to be as mad anymore. We didn't talk about what had happened and I made sure not to bring up Abby. I hadn't given up on finding her, but I still had to wait to hear back from Mamie, once she heard from Mr. Argent. The only way to stay busy and not go crazy thinking about it seemed to be watching over Grandma.

One day as I sat by her side, I heard the doorbell. Justin was already peeking through the side window by the time I got to the door. When I opened it, he said, "Look! Do you want to meet Buster, my new dog?" Buster was so cute. We played with him the rest of the day, except when the puppy was so exhausted he fell asleep.

It was easy to play with Justin. He understood about Grandma, so I didn't have to explain why I got quiet sometimes. Mostly it was nice to be nothing more than a kid.

The next day, when I was reading a book to Lily, I heard a knock on the door. I figured it was Justin again. Before I could reach the door, Mom came from the kitchen and opened it.

I let out a gasp when I saw it was Mamie. I wondered what Mom would do.

"I know it's more polite to call first, but we seem to get disconnected every time I try," Mamie said.

"Hmm," is all Mom said.

"So, I was wondering if I might speak with Lucas." She saw me standing close by and threw me a reassuring smile. Mom didn't budge. She was holding the door open, and at the same time blocking Mamie from coming in with her outstretched arm.

"Lucas told me about that night. He said you called him and suggested he come live with you. Is that correct?" I started to object, but Mom gave me a look that immediately shut me up. "Well?"

"I don't like to contradict the young man. Heaven knows I don't want him to get into any further trouble, but I doubt that's what he really told you."

"Why do you say that?" I couldn't tell if she was mad at Mamie for what she said, or just surprised that she was right.

"Even if that were true, which it's not, it doesn't sound like him. He would be much more likely to take the blame himself to protect someone else."

"Really?" Mom said, more softly this time.

"He's a very sweet child. If you want the truth, he did want to run away that night, but please, don't be too hard on him. I just think that at seven, he didn't quite understand what his options were. He called me to come get him. I'll admit, I thought about just whisking him away with me."

Mom was smiling and nodding, like she'd just won.

"But," Mamie continued, "I knew that wouldn't be right. I couldn't do it. So, I tried to convince him to stay, to point out what he would miss by leaving."

"Oh," Mom said, all the fight out of her voice.

"However, if it makes you feel better about what you think of me, Iris, if I hadn't been able to convince him to stay, I would have taken him with me."

I wasn't sure why she said that. It wasn't going to help us. I didn't know if my parents would ever let me go to her house again after she said that.

Mom was quiet for a minute, then burst out in laughter. "You know, I can believe that. I think you're actually being honest with me, and your story matches his. I can't say that I completely trust you, but you're welcome to talk to Lucas. Just don't ask us to be friends."

"Fair enough," Mamie said.

My mouth was still hanging open by the time Mom had shut the door and Mamie was by my side. She winked at me. "I told you it would be all right." She winked again, "And of course, we just got very lucky." I had to laugh at that.

"So, Lucas, how are you doing? I've missed you," Mamie said.

"It's only been a few days."

"I know, but I still missed you."

I threw my arms around her, "I've missed you too."

"Well, this isn't just a social call." She saw my confused look and said, "I didn't just come by to say hi." She cleared her throat and got down to business. "I've been talking to Mr. Argent, and I wanted to tell you about the conversation I had with him."

I couldn't tell from her tone of voice if Mr. Argent had found Abby or not, and that made me kind of nervous. Cautiously, I said, "Is there good news?"

Just then Mom came back into the room. She had put Lily's shoes on her and grabbed her purse. "Lucas, grab your shoes, we need to go."

"Where are we going?"

"I have an appointment. Hurry up."

"Iris," Mamie was speaking very softly. "Would it be okay if he stayed here? I can watch him and keep an eye on your mother. I'll even keep Lily if you like."

Mom gave a little laugh. "No, I don't think so."

"Well, who's staying with your mother?"

"Allison, from up the street."

"Well, if you'd let me, I could stay, and Allison can check up on me from time to time to make sure I'm handling things okay. That would free her up as well. I really don't have anything on my schedule for the rest of the day."

I could tell Mom was thinking about it because she hesitated. I took advantage of the silence. "Could I stay, Mom? I know where everything is, so I can show … uh, this grandma … where to find stuff."

"Is she planning on bringing Justin with her?" Mamie said. That was her mistake, and I think she saw it as soon as the words left her mouth.

"How do you know that Allison is Justin's mom?"

Mamie just shrugged her shoulders and said, "Lucas." I guess that satisfied Mom 'cause her shoulders relaxed. "I'll tell you what. You can have the keys to my car, so you'll know I'm not taking off with Justin without your permission."

Mom sighed. "Okay, and you can keep your keys. I ... uh, I guess I should say thanks. Allison will be up in a few minutes. I'll text her what's going on." She pulled out pen and paper and jotted something down. "Here's my phone number if you need to reach me." Then she swept out the door, pulling Lily along behind her.

When the door closed behind them, Mamie gave me a reassuring smile. "Now then, let's get down to business. Mr. Argent." I braced for what she might say. She wasn't smiling anymore. "Lucas, I got off the phone with him and immediately tried to call you. However, your mother apparently wasn't taking my calls, so I came over to tell you in person. It's better this way, anyway.

"There's no good way to say this. The private investigator found nothing. He didn't find any evidence of Abby as a runaway or having disappeared. Apparently, he looked into childhood deaths over a large period of time and found no Abby Jones or any variation of that name. I'm sorry. It's not good news."

I thought I was ready for that, but I didn't even know what to say. It turns out I didn't have to know what to say 'cause Mamie had plenty to say for the both of us.

"Lucas, Mr. Argent went into great detail about all the different things the P. I. delved into. It seems whatever stone he picked up, he found nothing underneath, no evidence of our Abby. From his efforts earlier, he had found a number of Abby or Abigail Joneses, but none of them seemed to be the right age. So, this time around, he extended his research to include any of them within twenty years of age of your grandma. That's why it took so long to hear back from him."

Her tone grew soft. "Lucas, he tracked down every single one of them. None of them had a sister named Josephine. None of them share the same parents. None of them even lived in the same small town where he found evidence of your grandma, or even close to it for that matter. He combed through birth records and death records, even school yearbooks. The private investigator came up empty handed."

I couldn't believe what she was telling me. I felt a horrible feeling in the pit of my stomach, and I thought I might throw up. Mamie started to talk again, but I wasn't listening to her words – I couldn't listen, they hurt too much. What was I going to do? I trusted Grandma was telling me the truth, but I didn't understand any of this. Nothing made sense, and I wasn't sure how I was going to tell Grandma I had failed in her one request, her last wish. I didn't realize I was crying until I felt a teardrop splash on my arm. It startled me into realizing I was bawling like a little baby, only with no sound. I wiped the tears away with the backs of my hands and tried to stop the new ones that just kept coming. Through my silent sobs, Mamie's voice finally broke through.

"Lucas, did you hear what I said? Mr. Argent has declared the case closed. He's paid the private investigator and filed it away as a wild fantasy dreamed up by an eccentric old lady and a naïve little boy."

I did hear what she said that time. I didn't know what all the words meant by themselves, but I knew what they meant all together. Mr. Argent thought we were all crazy – me, Mamie and Grandma. He didn't believe a word I said. I wasn't sure why Mamie wanted to make sure I was listening to her tell me that. It just made me mad, and I frowned. When I looked up, though, I was surprised to see a hint of a smile on her face.

"Lucas, I fired his skinny, little … Let's just say Mr. Argent is no longer in my employ."

Chapter 25

I didn't know you could feel happy, sad, and mad all at the same time, but I was doing just that. Mamie hadn't given up, so I knew there was still hope. The emotions I had left over from the bad news, though, hadn't all gone away. "Mamie, what do we do now?"

Before she had a chance to answer, Justin's mom walked in the door. She looked at Mamie and said, "Oh! I didn't know you would be here. I didn't think Iris would ..."

"Trust me?" Mamie finished.

Justin's mom stared at Mamie for a minute, then slowly nodded her head. "Well, yes."

"I guess you didn't get her text yet."

"To be honest, I haven't looked."

"Well, when Iris was getting ready to leave, I was already here talking to Lucas. So she agreed to let us stay, on the condition that you check up on us. And no, to answer your question, she doesn't trust me."

Justin's mom was nodding her head and smiling. "I like you, even if you did weasel information out of me the other day." She chuckled to herself. "I suppose I would have done the same thing. Tell me, though, honestly this time, why did you want to know? I'm guessing it wasn't just curiosity."

"No. It appears my son is acting like a jack ...," Mamie looked at me, "a jerk. I'm hoping to find the chance to talk some sense into him."

"Good luck with that, but it's certainly worth a try. Well, I think you're all good here. You certainly don't need me." She winked at Mamie. "I'll tell Iris everything is peachy and that I've gone back home. Justin's at his cousin's house, so I think I'll go get some cleaning done ... or maybe I'll just read a book." She was smiling as she walked towards the door. As she was about to leave, she turned back to Mamie. "Do you think you could step outside with me for just a minute. I think there's something else you should know."

When Mamie came back in she had a puzzled look on her face, but she quickly pasted on a smile when she saw me. "All right then. Are you okay?"

"Yes, but what should we do about finding Abby?"

She gave me her biggest smile, and I knew she had a plan. Then she said, "I haven't the faintest idea," but she was still smiling.

I waited for her to say something else. I thought grown-ups always had a plan. After a few minutes of staring at her smile, I had to admit that maybe I was wrong about that. "Maybe we could talk to Grandma some more?" I said.

"That's a great idea. Let's do it."

I wasn't sure if it was a great idea or not, but it seemed to be the only one we had at the moment. I'm guessing I should have been scared that a seven-year-old was the only one who had any ideas at all, but I tried not to think about it. I was more worried that Grandma wouldn't have anything to say to us, either 'cause she didn't know anything else or simply 'cause she wasn't home. I didn't dare tell Mamie how I sometimes waited for hours to get five minutes with Grandma.

We approached Grandma's bed, one of us on each side, but Grandma was sleeping away. I looked at Mamie and shrugged my shoulders. I certainly wasn't going to wake her, but I didn't know what Mamie would do – we didn't have all day. That thought reminded me that Mom would be coming home sometime, although I didn't know when. This would never work if she were here.

Mamie pulled up a chair and it seemed she was willing to wait things out. So, I copied her and sat down in the nearest chair. I was usually patient watching Grandma sleep, but Mamie being there made me nervous. I didn't know what she was thinking or what we should do. I started to fidget, jiggling my feet and bouncing my legs. This was not going well.

Mamie's voice, even at a whisper, startled me. "Lucas, can you show me your grandmother's ring, the one that belonged to Abby?"

Glad to have something to do, I jumped up and moved to the bedside table that held the jewelry box. Opening it slowly, I could see Abby's ring right on top. I reached across the bed to hand the ring to Mamie. That movement was enough to rouse Grandma, and she started to stir, then blink open her eyes. When her gaze settled on me, she smiled weakly. I looked up at Mamie to see if she was watching, and Grandma turned to follow my gaze. Upon seeing Mamie, her eyes flew open wide. "Mamie," she said.

"Yes, Josie, it's me. Back to the scene of the crime."

I hadn't thought about the fact that my mom would have told Grandma all about her troubles with Mamie. I wondered if these two were friends or maybe enemies, but it turns out whatever they had been, they were going to get along just fine now.

"Mamie?" was all Grandma could get out.

"Your grandson here has been very concerned about helping you find your sister. I hope he told you I was trying to help." When Grandma nodded, she continued, "It seems we keep running into dead ends. Which means, I suppose, that we just have to back up until we find a different road to follow."

She held up Abby's ring so Grandma could see it. "This must be the ring that started it all, Josie." Again Grandma nodded. Mamie fixed her eyes on my grandma. "Is there anything else you can tell us?"

Grandma just returned her stare. I wasn't sure if she didn't remember anything else or if the words just weren't cooperating today. Mamie reached over and took Grandma's hand in hers. "I understand," she whispered so softly I almost didn't hear it. Mamie twirled the ring in her free hand much like I had seen Grandma do. "Who would have thought, a child's ring," she said to herself. She patted Grandma's hand and then handed her the ring, which Grandma took carefully into her own grasp.

"You know, Lucas, I've got an idea!" She was suddenly excited.

"What?"

"If the ring brought back memories of Abby, maybe there are more things of hers that will trigger memories. What do you think?"

"Well, I know there's a whole bunch of Grandma's stuff in the basement. Maybe we'll find something there." Her excitement was contagious. It gave me hope.

As I headed to the basement, I heard Mamie behind me talking on her phone. "Iris, I wanted to call and let you know that your mother is doing just fine ... Yes, Allison left a bit ago, so you're welcome to check with her. But I just wanted to let you know that we're good. So, feel free to take as much of the day as you want. I'll have some kind of dinner waiting for you when you get back, so no need to worry about that." There was a slight pause, and then, "Well, don't thank me yet, you must remember my cooking skills." The next thing I heard her say was, "Okay. I'll see you later."

When Mamie caught up with me, I said, "You're making us dinner tonight?"

"Oh no, I'm a terrible cook, but I can buy my way out of that failing," she said with a wink. "Now, don't go thinking I've become that nicer person just yet. I am trying, believe me, I'm trying, but old habits die hard." I looked at her, puzzled. "I had to keep your mom away while we rummaged through the basement, didn't I?" And with that, she moved past me and down the basement stairs.

For the next hour or two, Mamie and I opened and closed boxes, occasionally rooting through the contents. She told me it was like a pig looking for truffles, but then she had to explain to me what truffles were and how a pig goes poking around in the forest to find them. She also told me truffles were very valuable, but they didn't sound that good to me.

Every so often, one of us would head upstairs to check on Grandma, but she had fallen back asleep and was quiet, not even snoring. I stopped on one of my trips to make sure she was still breathing, which thankfully she was. The ring was still in her fingers. I was afraid it might get lost so I carefully lifted it out of her grasp, which wasn't too hard, and placed it on the table next to her jewelry box. Then I kissed her forehead and returned to the basement.

When Mamie and I decided to call it quits, we had gone through all the boxes with labels that sounded like they contained, as Mamie put it, "something that might jog her memory." To me, it looked like we were just searching for something old. We gathered our finds in an empty box to bring upstairs including old books, pictures, and baby clothes. I carried up a baby doll that didn't look anything like any of Lily's dolls. It had a hard, painted face and fancy clothes. The arms and legs were stiff, but the body was huggable. I had found it and was hoping it would help.

We were surprised to find Grandma sitting up when we returned. She was looking a bit better than before we went to the basement. I ran to give her a big hug, dropping the doll on the bed to do so.

Softly she said, "I love you."

"I love you, too, Grandma." I pulled back, so I could show her what we'd found. "We've been in the basement looking through some of your boxes. We were trying to find something to help you remember more about Abby."

I held up the doll, hopeful. She shook her head, "Antique shop."

"What's an antique shop?" I said, still hopeful.

"It's a store where you buy old stuff," Mamie replied.

"Oh," was all I could say.

After that, Mamie held up one thing after another. Grandma just shook her head, occasionally adding a word or two of detail about where or how it came into her life. None of the items were from her childhood or even remotely helpful with jogging her memory. Dejected, I helped Mamie put everything back in the box so we could return it to the basement before Mom got home.

Mamie picked up Abby's ring. "I guess you are one of a kind, aren't you," she whispered. "Josie, would you like to keep this out, or shall I return it to the jewelry box?"

"Put it away," she said.

Mamie opened the jewelry box and gently laid the ring on top. "What's this?" she said as she held up the bracelet I had noticed earlier.

"Mom told me that's a charm bracelet," I said, a little surprised Mamie didn't know that. It seemed like she hadn't heard me, though, 'cause she had turned and was looking at Grandma.

"Josephine, was this yours as a child?"

I looked past Mamie at Grandma's face. Silent tears were forming and trickling down her cheeks. It was answer enough. Mamie continued, "Did you live in Seattle, or in Washington state?"

Grandma nodded, ever so slightly.

Excited, Mamie turned to me. "Lucas, we've been looking in the wrong place. We need to look for Abby in Washington." She turned back to Grandma. "Was Abby born in Washington?" a nod, and then, "Were you born in Washington?"

Again, Grandma nodded, and then whispered, "Yes."

I was happy, even if I didn't understand everything that was happening. I watched as both of my grandmas hugged and laughed while tears trailed down their faces.

While they were busy, I decided to take all of Grandma's stuff back to the basement. I didn't want Mom coming home and wondering what was going on. I tried to put her things back in the boxes they came from, but all the boxes looked the same. I didn't have a clue where they belonged, so I put a few things in one box and a few in another. I figured if I spread it around, it would be okay. I was hoping Mom wouldn't notice.

When I got back upstairs, Mamie was still beside Grandma, but Grandma had drifted off to sleep. Mamie motioned for me to follow her into the other room where we sat down on the couch. I was anxious for an explanation, but I had to wait a little longer while Mamie called and ordered pizza and wings for our dinner that night.

Finally, Mamie looked at me. "It's simple, really, Lucas. The charm bracelet has figures that are from Seattle." She had it in her hands and held it up for me to see. "There's a crab, a fish, and this is a ferry."

She was pointing to the big boat I had noticed before. "What's a ferry?"

"It's a boat that carries cars. You drive right onto the ferry and then ride across the water to another piece of land or an island and drive your car off onto dry ground. It's common in Seattle, and so are the crab and the fish, but they could also be from somewhere like San Francisco. So, look at the next charm. It's a pine tree, not that unusual, but it's plentiful in Seattle."

"Oh, I thought that was a Christmas tree."

She laughed. "Well, yes, we use them for Christmas trees, but they grow all around Seattle. Now, Lucas, look at these last two things. This is a totem pole. The Native Americans in Washington built totem poles and they are a common symbol in the area. However, it's this last charm the seals the deal."

I looked at it. It was the tower-like thing I had noticed before. "This is the Space Needle. It was built a long time ago, I think for a world's fair that was held in Seattle. So, I figured your Grandma either lived there or visited sometime. Now, she could have come up from Oregon to visit, but … well, that's why I asked her."

My smile matched hers. "So now I'll bet we'll be able to find Abby!" I said.

"Yes, I think so, Lucas. I think so. At least I'm certain we'll be able to pick up her trail there, and once we find the trail, we'll just see where it leads."

At that very moment, I heard a door open and close. My dad's voice called out, "Hello, I'm home."

Chapter 26

"Pete," Mamie called out.

"Hi, mother," Dad said as he walked into the room. He didn't seem exactly happy to see her, but at least he didn't appear mad either.

"Surprised to see me?"

"No. I got a text from Iris."

"So you'd know what was up, or so you could check up on me?"

He stared at his mother and didn't answer. At least now I knew why he was home so much earlier than usual. It got pretty quiet; not even Mamie seemed to have anything to say.

"Mamie, um, Grandma," I finally said, "ordered pizza and wings for us for dinner."

"She did, did she? Okay. So, how has your day been?" He appeared to be asking me, but he was staring at Mamie.

"It was great!" I said it loudly so he'd look at me, but it seemed like he and Mamie were having a staring contest.

Mamie cleared her throat, turned to look at me for a moment, then her face lit up and she smiled. "Pete, I have a great idea!"

"What?" He seemed wary and I was suddenly nervous.

"I know something you can do to help us out." I was getting more nervous, but Dad looked like he was just getting mad.

"What do you want from me, *Mother?*" He was angry, but I had no idea why.

"Are you still mad at me about the other night?"

"Not really. Iris seems satisfied, so I'm satisfied. It's not that."

"Oh, come on, Pete. Let's let bygones be bygones. I said some things, you said some things, she said some things …"

"The 'she' you're talking about is my wife, and her name is Iris."

"Okay, *Iris* said some things, too. Let's forget about that right now. Lucas needs your help and so does *Iris's* mother. Can you help us?"

"Why the change, *Mother*?"

She stared at him silently for a moment. "I may have been mistaken ... about a great many things."

He relaxed his shoulders and sank into a chair. "Well, it's a start, even if it is too late to make a difference." He seemed to be staring at something on the floor, but finally raised his eyes and said, "What do you need from me?"

She looked at me, and I instantly knew what she was going to say. I guess she was asking me if it was okay with her eyes. Honestly, I was desperate enough to try anything, so I nodded my head.

"Pete. I've been doing some checking on your mother-in-law and her family." I could tell she was trying to keep me out of it, even though Dad already knew I'd been talking to her. It would have been obvious anyway, even if he didn't. "It appears that she has a sister named Abby."

"What?" Dad's face was red and he looked angry on the outside, but for some reason, I thought he was pretending. It's like he knew he should be mad but just didn't have the energy to really care. All along he must have been borrowing Mom's anger about the whole Abby thing. It was his hands that gave him away. With his fingers, he was fiddling with the tips of the armrests like he does when he's thinking and far away. Maybe he really was angry underneath it all – he just wasn't sure who or what he was angry at.

"Dad, are you okay?"

He turned his head in my direction, but I could see no light in his eyes. It scared me. Mamie must have seen me out of the corner of her eye 'cause she reached an arm out and put it on my shoulder. It was warm and comforting, and I moved in closer to her.

Dad's expression turned sad when he saw me move. Without taking his eyes off my face, he said, "So, what's this about an Abby? I thought we were done with that." I think he wanted his words to come out loud and harsh, but instead, they were soft and weak. I don't know if Mamie heard the difference.

"Well, Pete," she waited until he was looking at her, "I hired a private investigator to poke around Oregon to see if we could find Abby from when Josephine was a child. He came up empty-handed."

"Okay. Doesn't that prove something to you? Why are you indulging him?"

I didn't like being talked about as if I wasn't there. I was about to say something about it that would probably get me into trouble when Mamie spoke. "Hear me out; I'm not done yet. It just appeared we were barking up the wrong tree. And don't point your finger at Lucas, either. I've heard it from Josie's own lips, and I believe Abby exists."

I realized Mamie was working hard to protect me, especially seeing that about all she'd ever heard Grandma say, that I could remember, was what she heard today, and that wasn't much. She seemed to have silenced Dad for the moment, so she continued, "We just figured out that Josie *and Abby*," she paused, I think to see if he was listening, "that both of them were born in Washington, not Oregon. So, no wonder we haven't found a record of her yet!" She smiled triumphantly. I noticed she was leaving out a lot of details, but I wasn't going to question her methods.

"Okay," Dad said as he stood up, "so let's go check out Washington's records. I don't think Abby will show up there either. Then maybe we can put this behind us." He raised his eyebrows as if he was asking a question.

Mamie didn't say anything. She just smiled, and said, "I was hoping you would say that. We need to see if we can find a record of any Abby Jones, probably near Seattle, but she could be anywhere in Washington."

Dad looked a little surprised – like he'd been tricked – and maybe he had. But I wanted to believe Mamie was just doing what needed to be done, hoping that Dad would finally be convinced that Abby existed.

Dad's mouth was still hanging open, but before he could decide what to say, the doorbell rang. Our dinner had arrived.

As Mamie paid for the food, Dad went upstairs, calling behind him as he went, "I'm not hungry. While you eat, I'll see what I can find on the internet."

It was a lot of food for just two of us. Grandma wasn't awake, and I didn't think pizza would appeal to her anyway. Mom and Lily hadn't come home yet, and I was beginning to suspect they wouldn't until Dad had given them the "all clear" signal.

We ate in silence for a little while, but then Mamie looked at me and crossed her eyes. I started laughing, and she did too. After that, we just talked and laughed like we normally did.

When Grandma woke up, Mamie found a can of soup in the cupboard and fixed it for her. I watched as Mamie gently helped Grandma. She could feed herself, but she was getting weaker and weaker. Even eating seemed to wear her out, so Mamie took care of it, carefully feeding her one spoonful at a time.

Just as we finished clearing away Grandma's dinner, Dad came down the stairs. He pounded down them like I sometimes do when I'm mad and want everyone to know it. So I was surprised to see he was smiling when he entered the kitchen. I should have been worried.

He threw a pile of papers down on the kitchen table. "There. Check it out for yourself. I just paid money and signed up for more people finding websites than I care to recall. A lot of them had duplicate information, but the bottom line is I found 16 Abby Jones with various spellings that had any connection to the state of Washington. I eliminated one right off the bat. It was an A-b-b-i-e spelling and it turned out to be a man. Of the remaining 15, only two were the right age and another seven didn't list an age.

"So, now that I had it down to nine, I paid for reports for them. Only two of them were in Washington as children. The others only moved there as adults. The two I mentioned have families that don't match my mother-in-law in the least." He finished with a smug grin on his face.

Mamie didn't say a thing and neither did I. "Now, can we drop this nonsense once and for all? You're relying on a woman who is delusional." He said it softly, but I could tell underneath he wasn't happy about any of it.

That was the same word Mr. Argent had used. I wasn't sure what "delusional" meant, but I could guess.

Mamie stood up straight. "One day I'll be that delusional woman, but today I'm not. I don't care what you think. I believe that Abby is out there. No, I *know* she is," and with that, she scooped up her purse, gave me a quick kiss on the cheek, and walked past my dad. "I'll get out of your hair now. I am trying to be nicer to you and your family, but I'm not budging on this one."

I thought she might slam the front door, but I was wrong. She closed it gently but firmly, more like a queen would do.

I was a little afraid to look at my dad after that. Quite honestly, when he came back with nothing about Abby, I started to worry that everything I believed about her was wrong. It just seemed like one too many dead ends.

But Mamie wasn't worried. She seemed to believe in Abby even more every time we hit one of those dead ends. If she could trust Grandma, and me for that matter, how could I doubt it? There was no other way about it – Abby *had* to be real.

I was so lost in thought that I was surprised to hear the front door open. Dad looked up, startled as well. I didn't think Mom and Lily would be back so soon after Mamie left. It turns out it wasn't them – it was Mamie.

She walked right into the kitchen where Dad and I were sitting, then focused her eyes on him. "Pete, before I leave I need to talk to you about something else. I realize that this isn't an ideal time, but I fear there never will be, and I'm afraid to wait any longer." Mamie took a deep breath. "Pete, your wife deserves better treatment from you. I know what's going on – about the addition."

Dad looked genuinely surprised. "Really? That seems pretty ironic coming from you."

"Yes, I imagine so. I'm an unlikely source to defend your wife, but as your mother, I felt you needed a kick in the seat of your pants."

Dad let out a scoff. "Did Iris put you up to this?"

"What do you think?"

"Yeah, that wouldn't be likely." He was grinning, but it wasn't a happy grin.

"So, drop it. She needs your support right now. Not only is she dealing with her mother dying, she's got hormones all over the place.

Just love her."

Dad's smile turned to a sneer. "So, you're so smart, huh? It just so happens I had a vasectomy a little while ago. It's not mine. That changes things, doesn't it?" He spit it out at her as a challenge.

I didn't know what they were talking about; I just knew how it made me feel – dark inside. I was scared and snuck into the dining room to be by Grandma's side. She looked at me and grabbed my hand, squeezing it in her grasp. She must have heard everything that had been going on between Dad and Mamie before Mamie walked out and now that she was back 'cause I could see tears sliding down Grandma's face.

It seemed we couldn't escape the voices. They carried clear as could be from the kitchen to us. "I already know about that, Pete. But tell me, how long ago was that?"

"A couple of months before she broke the news to me, which she did shortly after her mother moved in. Convenient, huh? I can't exactly move out in the midst of this, can I? I'd look like a real heel. But down the road ..." He didn't finish his sentence, but his voice sounded sharp, not like my dad's, more like a stranger's. It made me shiver.

"What does Iris say?"

"She swears it's mine, but who's she kidding?"

"Other than this, has she ever given you a reason to distrust her?"

"Well, no, but –"

"Are you that dense?" Mamie sounded angry. "Mr. Smarty Pants, did you take the time to research the failure rate of vasectomies? I think you'll find that in the first few months it's pretty high. Didn't the doctor tell you to use other methods for a little while? Did you do that? Did you go back to the doctor to make sure it's effective yet?"

Dad mumbled something that I couldn't understand.

"Yeah. That's really smart. Your pride just got the best of you."

"But I don't want another one."

"So, that justifies you jumping to the wrong conclusion? You're a bigger idiot than I took you for." She paused. "This is hard for me to say, but Iris is the best thing that ever happened to you. I'm sorry I didn't see that sooner. But don't let this ... this nonsense ruin it all. You owe her an apology and a lot more than that." There was a pause

147

then, "I know you have no reason to trust me, but that doesn't make what I'm saying less important or less true. If nothing else, trust your wife."

I let go of Grandma's hand and peeked into the kitchen. Dad was still sitting, but he was bent over with his head in his hands. Mamie was standing above him. Ever so slowly she reached over and patted him on the shoulder. I barely heard her as she said, "I'm sorry I wasn't a better example to you of how to forgive and let go of things. Your son, your sweet son, is teaching me that life is too short to hold onto grudges. I hope I'm not learning that too late. But he's also taught me to never give up. Please, don't give up on Iris." She bent over and softly kissed the crown of his head then without another word slipped out the front door.

Chapter 27

The rest of that night happened in a blur. Mom and Lily came home and pulled out leftover pizza and wings to eat. I guess Dad was finally hungry 'cause he joined them.

I avoided the kitchen and just sat at Grandma's side, holding her hand. She didn't cry any new tears, but the wet traces on her cheeks remained. I didn't wipe them off. Somehow, I think they were telling me she knew, like Mamie did, that she wasn't as delusional as Dad thought she was and that she was hoping people wouldn't give up - on looking for Abby and with each other.

I put my head down on the bed next to Grandma and laid my arm across her. I'd never known I could love someone as much as I loved her right at that moment. She was the best grandma a kid like me could ever have. But then I had Mamie, too. The corners of my mouth came up in a grin as I realized I was beginning to feel the same way about her.

I must've fallen asleep like that 'cause I woke up several hours later still next to Grandma, still wearing my daytime clothes. I sat up and stretched. That's when I realized it must have been Grandma that woke me up. She was mumbling lightly.

"What's wrong, Grandma?" I whispered. Moonlight was dimly lighting her, and I could see confusion on her face. When she said nothing, I said, "Is it about Mom and Dad?"

She shook her head.

"Is it Abby?"

"Yes, but I can't … I can't …" Her forehead was wrinkled and I could tell she was trying hard to think. "The words, I don't have the right word." She let out a big sigh.

"Can I help you figure it out?" She looked at me, and I could tell she was wondering if I could. After a minute, her forehead relaxed and she nodded.

"Okay, then maybe we can make it a guessing game. Did you hear what Dad and Mamie said last night about Abby?" Another nod. "Was Mamie right that she's still out there?" I hated to ask that, but I knew I had to.

She nodded and picked up my hand to squeeze it. I squeezed back.

"Okay, then. I don't know how we're going to find her. I don't know where she is."

Grandma squeezed my hand. "There's more." Her eyes were reaching out to me, trying to tell me what her mouth couldn't.

"More? More what?"

"More," she repeated.

"More ... Are there more sisters?"

She shook her head "no."

I couldn't figure out what she meant, but she was very determined about whatever it was. I sat and thought for a moment before exclaiming, "Oh, did you remember more?" I immediately covered my mouth, worried that I'd been too loud and that I might wake someone.

Grandma squeezed my hand and nodded her head. "Yes, but the word ... the word is missing," she said and shook her head.

"What word? What kind of word? Is it something about Abby?"

She nodded and her eyes echoed the yes. I didn't know how to help someone come up with a word when they couldn't remember what the word was. It's not like I could play hangman with her and guess the letters.

We both sat puzzling over what to do. Suddenly, Grandma's eyes grew bright and she pointed at a small piece of paper on her nightstand. "I'll show you." I understood immediately. I ran into the kitchen, slowing to a fast tiptoe when I remembered I needed to be quiet. One of the bottom drawers in the kitchen always held scrap paper and crayons. That way, whenever Lily or I wanted to draw, we could.

Grandma snatched the paper and crayons out of my hands when I returned. She drew three stick figures on the paper, two small and one big. Then she crossed out one of the small ones. I didn't quite understand. I only had one guess. "Is that one Abby, the one you crossed out?" I said. She nodded her head. "You already told me she left. Is that it?"

She shook her head, "No ... yes, it's not ... not ..." She made a noise of frustration and grabbed another sheet of paper. Again, she drew three stick figures, but this time, she drew two arms with big hands reaching in from the side of the paper. She crossed out the third stick figure, the Abby, again, but then redrew it in the outstretched arms. I still didn't know what it meant until I saw her draw an unhappy face on Abby.

"Grandma, did someone take Abby?" She nodded vigorously while her eyes burned. "Was Abby kidnapped?" She nodded and collapsed in tears.

"Did it happen in Washington?"

"Yes!"

"When?"

She whispered, "When I was seven."

When I Was Seven

The tide pools always fascinated me, and today is no different. It is low tide and the small amount of water left behind is alive with creatures. I crouch down at a small distance watching, then turn to see if I'm being watched as well, but I am not.

Smells, unique to ocean shores, fill my senses. The salty aroma entices me, reminding me of other beaches, but the underlying scent of decay and death threatens to turn me away.

Curiosity, winning out, leads me to creep just a little closer. As I make my way to the water's edge for a better look, I'm careful, not wanting to step on any spikes or sharp rocks along the way. A boy, older than me, rushes past almost knocking me down. He's laughing and I hear his friends following close behind.

I move out of the way, afraid of them. But I soon realize the boys have no intention of harming me; they don't even notice I am there.

Timidly, I move forward to see what they are doing. I watch as they search for sea anemones in the shallow water, looking for the waving tentacles. As soon as one is spotted, the boys poke it with their fingers. I can't see what happens as they gather round to watch - I only hear their laughter. They do it several times and then, after a call from an adult, race to leave. The last boy stops to pick up a starfish to take with him.

After they are gone, I look for an anemone of my own, then slowly reach out a tentative finger to poke it. I giggle as the tentacles draw in and the anemone closes up on itself. Then I spot a starfish close by. Picking it up like a treasure, I return to the adults.

Later that night I hear the harsh tone. "What was she thinking? It's dead and it reeks." And I hear my starfish being thrown in the trash out back.

Chapter 28

I couldn't sleep after talking to Grandma. All I could think about was telling Mamie in the morning about Abby being kidnapped. I knew Grandma was upset and I figured she wouldn't be able to sleep either, but I was wrong. When she was done telling me what she remembered, she drew in a big breath and almost smiled. Then she closed her eyes and drifted off to sleep.

I wished I could do the same. I heard noises upstairs and realized Mom and Dad hadn't gone to bed yet. Without thinking, I started up the stairs, eager to tell someone what I had just learned. I had only taken a few steps when I remembered why I couldn't tell them anything yet. Dejected, I retreated down the stairs, until I heard their voices. They were talking about Mamie and they didn't sound happy.

"Why did she come?" Mom was saying. "What's she up to?"

"She had a new theory that your mother was born in Washington and that we'd find Abby there."

"You're kidding."

"No, I know the whole thing is ridiculous. I tried to prove it to her by searching for an Abby in Washington, and of course, no evidence of her existed."

"Did that silence her?"

"No. You'd think it would, but it didn't. If anything it made her more determined."

"So, do you think that's why she came? To indulge Lucas and this whole Abby thing?"

"Well, I don't know … she also …"

"She also what?"

"Oh, nothing. She's just hard to understand, that's all."

"Well, I don't like it, but I'm not sure what to do about it." Mom said.

"I'll … I'll do whatever you want me to, but what can we do? I just can't believe she'd –"

"Can't believe what? It feels like she's poisoning our own son against us. But after what she did before our wedding, I wouldn't put anything past her."

"I guess you're right. It's just that she's basically left us alone since then, and quite honestly I was happy about that. But this … I agree with you, it doesn't sit right."

"You know, I wouldn't mind her spoiling him. Let her be a real grandma and feed him too much candy or buy him little trinkets. But she's not doing that; she never has. Instead, she's egging him on with this wild goose chase, and in the process, she gets to be the good guy, and we're the mean, nasty ogres. Why? What does she hope to gain?"

"Well, it's not Lucas, for sure. She never seemed to care about anyone but herself. But …"

"But what, Pete? Why are you looking like that?"

"Maybe she's changing."

"Really? What evidence do we have of that?"

I moved up a step closer, hoping beyond hope that Dad might defend Mamie, tell Mom that she really was nice and that they could trust her, but I was disappointed. Dad didn't respond at first, and then finally said, "I guess there's not much."

"The only thing that makes sense is that she's just trying to get to us, to irritate us just because she can."

"Maybe that's it, I don't know."

"I'll bet Lucas told her right from the start how we didn't believe him. What an invitation for her. She's just using him to get to us. But, Pete, why now? I can't deal with this. My mother is dying, downstairs right now she is dying! I don't know how to cope with that … and everything else. I certainly don't need anything on top of it, especially not your mother worming her way into our lives, working her way into Lucas' heart only to rip it out later on. It's bad enough that she's never been nice to me, but I think seeing her be nice to Lucas is even worse. She's going to hurt him, and he has no idea."

"I'll do whatever you want me to do. Just tell me what it is."

"I don't know! Saying that doesn't help."

I heard my Dad make a noise like my school teacher did when I came up with the wrong answer on my fourth try. "What do you want me to say, Iris?"

"I'm sorry. I don't know. It's just that the real question is what to do. If we cut her off from Lucas, he'll be devastated. He'll hate us. But if we let this continue, where does it end?"

"I have no idea."

They had gone quiet, so I started to tiptoe back down the stairs when I heard Mom again. "Pete, thanks for talking to me. I've missed you. Would you like an extra pillow to take with you into Lucas' bed?"

"Umm, sure, thanks. Well, actually, if it's okay with you, I think I'll stay here."

Mom was slow to respond, but then I clearly heard her say, "I'd like that."

When I didn't hear anything else, I moved quietly down the stairs and into the kitchen to look at the clock. It was almost midnight. I didn't think about what Mamie might be doing right then. I just grabbed the phone and called her cell number. While it was ringing, I crept down the stairs to the basement. I didn't want my parents to hear me.

She sounded tired when she answered. "Hi, Lucas. What's wrong?"

"How did you know something was wrong?"

"Well, the only other time you called me in the middle of the night was when you wanted to run away. I'm guessing you're not going to try that again, but there still must be a pretty good reason for the phone call. Am I right?"

"Well, yeah, I guess so. I'm sorry. Should I call you back in the morning?"

"No, not at all." I was glad she said that 'cause I didn't think I could wait 'til morning. "So, Lucas, what's wrong?"

I was afraid to tell her, but I wanted to know what was going on. "Well, Mom and Dad were kind of mad tonight."

"Mad at you?"

"No, more like they were mad at you."

"Oh. Well, I guess that doesn't surprise me. What did they say?"

"They think that you're just being nice to me to be mean to them, but I don't think that's true." She didn't say anything right away, and I started to wonder if I was all wrong about her. "Mamie, that's not true is it?"

She let out a big sigh. "No, Lucas it's not true, but I guess I can't blame them for thinking that."

"Why? Why would they think that? They said something about what you did before they were married. What happened?"

I heard a small chuckle on the other end. "You remember how I already warned you that I'm not a very nice person, right?"

"Yes, I remember."

"And you remember that I didn't actually like your mother to start with?"

"Yeah," I was beginning to worry about where this was going.

"Well, 'didn't like' is probably too nice of a way to put it. I detested the woman. I thought for sure she was just after your father's money."

"My father has money?"

"Not anymore. He had a fairly large trust fund waiting for him upon his marriage, but I had stipulated that it would only be released if I approved of the marriage."

"So he didn't get his money when he married my mom?"

"You're a very smart little boy. But I'm afraid it was worse than that."

"Really? How could it be worse?"

She chuckled again, "Well, I, uh, I ... I offered Pete a large amount of money, on top of the trust fund, if he wouldn't marry your mom."

"You did? You were going to pay my dad to not marry my mom?" My voice was rising, and I was glad I had slipped into the basement.

"I told you, Lucas, I wasn't a very nice person."

I sat down on the basement steps to think. "I don't understand, Mamie. My mom's a really good person. I mean she yells at me sometimes, but not very often. She takes good care of me and Lily. She used to read me stories before Grandma got sick, and now she's busy taking care of Grandma and all of us. Why didn't you like her? I

156

don't think she'd marry my dad just for his money."

She paused and then said, "You know how I told you she was uncultured and had poor manners? Well, that may not be important to some people, but it was very important to me. And I guess her poor manners made me believe the worst about her, like she was only marrying Pete for his money."

"Well, yeah, but I have bad manners sometimes, and you still like me." Then something dawned on me, "Or *do* you like me?" I knew it sounded like an accusation, and I was afraid of what the answer might be.

"I guess I deserved that. You may not believe me right now, but I do like you, Lucas. I love you. I'm even beginning to believe that I was wrong about your mother. After all, how could someone that terrible raise someone as wonderful as you? I just can't see that being the case."

I thought about it for a moment. I knew I wanted to believe her, I just didn't know if I could. But in the end, I knew I loved her. Maybe that was enough for now. For the time being, I was still going to trust her, and that meant telling her the rest, hoping she was still willing to help me. "Mamie, there's something else."

"What is it?" She sounded curious but worried.

"Grandma remembered something. She said that Abby was kidnapped. Well, she didn't say it exactly, but she drew me a picture so I could figure it out. And she let me know I got it right. She said it happened when she was seven."

"Wow. That changes things, doesn't it? I wonder if they keep records back that far of kidnappings?" All memory of the beginning of our conversation seemed to have vanished. "I wonder if ..."

When she didn't continue, I said, "What, Mamie?"

"Oh, nothing much. I'm just trying to think of a few ideas, that's all. Why don't I call you in the morning."

I wasn't sure how my parents would react to the phone call, but I still had a promise to Grandma to keep. "Okay. I'll talk to you in the morning."

After hanging up, I made my way up the stairs, climbed onto the couch, and promptly fell asleep, still without changing into pajamas.

Chapter 29

It turns out that Mamie didn't call in the morning – she came over instead. There was a small knock on the front door, and I ran to open it. If I'd been worried about how Mom and Dad would react when she called, I was petrified to see Mamie on the doorstep. I let her in and then hustled her into where Grandma was. It felt like I was hiding a candy bar from Mom that I'd been eating right before dinner. I just hoped they hadn't heard the knock on the door.

Then it occurred to me, "Why didn't you use the doorbell?"

Mamie winked at me. "What do you think?"

I nodded my head and smiled. She was smarter than I gave her credit for. At the same time, though, I wondered why there was a problem in the first place. Sometimes adults acted so stupid. It all seemed simple to me – you just say, "Sorry," and go on playing. That's what Justin and I do. I shook my head. Mamie's smile had faded, and she was looking at me funny. I guess she was wondering why I had shaken my head. "Never mind. You wouldn't understand," I said, although I wished for just a moment that she would.

Grandma had already eaten her breakfast and was sitting up in bed. "Hi, Grandma. Was your breakfast good?"

She nodded her head and said, "Yes, Lucas."

"Grandma, do you remember what you told me or I guess showed me last night?"

She nodded.

Mamie had moved in behind me and reached for Grandma's hand. "Josie, was Abby kidnapped? Is that what you remembered last night."

158

"Yes!" Her answer was clear and strong.

"Do you remember anything else?" When Grandma didn't answer right away, Mamie added, "Do you have the words today?"

She nodded, but took a moment before saying, "I think so, but they're slow in coming."

"Is there anything else you remembered?" she said again.

"No, but I get pieces ... I don't know, like pieces of a puzzle. I keep picturing something, something about the ring."

"What do you mean, Grandma?" I picked up the jewelry box, opened it to find the ring, and held it out to her. Her gaze, however, was fixed on the jewelry box. Mamie noticed it too.

"Josie, what is it?"

"I don't know. The jewelry box ..." After a minute, she shook her head. "I can't ... I don't remember."

"What about the ring then? Why did you want the ring?" I said.

She reached up and took the ring in her hands like she had done so often lately. She held it tightly in her fingers, twirling it from side to side. Suddenly her face lit up. "It was Abby's ring, but I loved it. She would let me wear it every so often, but she told me to be very careful and not lose it. I was wearing it when she was ... when she left ... when they took her from me."

"Do you remember anything about that? Do you know who took her or how it happened?" Mamie said.

A cloud crossed over Grandma's eyes. I was afraid she was disappearing again and was relieved when she spoke. "I don't know. It's fuzzy in my mind, like a pain you try hard to forget. I'm sorry."

"It's okay, Grandma." I gave her a gentle hug while Mamie patted her hand.

"Should we let you rest?"

She let out a deep sigh. "Yes, that would be good."

We walked back to the couch to allow Grandma some peace and quiet, but I had forgotten about Mom and Dad. Dad discovered us sitting on the couch playing a game of chess about a half hour later. He was heading off to work, but when he saw us, he stopped suddenly, looking at Mamie and then at me. This time around I knew what I'd done wrong – I'd let Mamie back into our house.

He stood there staring at the two of us like we were an enemy army. Justin had once told me a story about a lady with crazy eyes and snakes for hair who could turn people into stone. I didn't think the story was true, but I almost believed my dad could do it the way he was staring at us.

Right when I decided there was nothing to do except become stone gargoyles, Grandma called out from the other room. I quickly escaped to her side, followed by Mamie. Dad must have seen it as an excuse to get away too 'cause he disappeared as fast as he could.

Grandma was all excited about something. Her eyes were open wide and her hands were shaking. "The jewelry box. I know where it came from."

"Where?"

"They gave it to me to comfort me, right after Abby disappeared."

"Really?" I said.

"Yes! They let me pick it out and I picked one with a picture of a little girl on it." Her eyes glistened, so happy to have captured the memory. "The first thing I did was put the ring inside. I kept asking about Abby. I missed her so much." Then her eyes grew sad.

"What's wrong, Grandma?"

"Something else - they told me something else that made me sad." She paused, thinking, while we quietly wondered what could possibly be next.

Chapter 30

Later, I wondered if Grandma might have been able to remember if we had just given her a little more time, but that didn't happen 'cause Mom and Dad showed up. They weren't happy either.

Mom looked at Mamie with a question on her face. It was the same look I got when I was in trouble and Mom wanted an explanation. I looked up at Mamie, and I could tell she knew what that look meant too.

"Hello, Iris," Mamie attempted. Mom didn't even respond. I thought that was kind of rude, but I wasn't going to say so. "I've just been visiting with Lucas … and your mother. I hope that was okay."

No one said anything for a moment, then Dad finally said, "What are you playing at, Mother?"

"Nothing. I'm not playing you and Iris or her mom, and I'm certainly not playing Lucas." Dad's eyebrows went up in surprise. I wondered if Mamie had just given away that I had overheard them and tattled. But I guess it was too late to worry about that.

"I have a hard time believing that, especially about Lucas. You've never shown interest in him before." Then Dad's eyes narrowed. "As I recall, you told us we were making a big mistake having children. Some reception that was. We call you with the good news that Iris is expecting, and you lecture us on what a mistake we're making." He paused and I saw Mom's eyes confirming that what Dad had said was true. I couldn't believe my ears. What did Mamie think of me? I wanted her to stand up and give my parents what's what like she did to Mr. Argent, but she was silent. "You know, *Mother*," the word didn't sound very nice the way he said it, "I've had a question for you since that day. Was *I* a mistake?"

Mamie raised her eyebrows and said, "Don't you think that's a bit of an ironic question to be asking?" Mom shot a questioning glance at Dad, but he just turned away. I looked in each of their faces hoping someone would tell me what was going on, but nobody did.

Finally, Mamie heaved a big sigh. "No, you were not a mistake, but I certainly made other mistakes along the way." She didn't say anything else. I wanted her to explain what she was talking about, but they all seemed to have forgotten I was even there.

"Really? And what mistakes would those be? The crack about the pregnancy, all the other times you acted like we didn't exist, or back to the original crime - trying to buy me off so I wouldn't marry Iris?" Mamie didn't immediately answer, so he continued. "I think you were just mad that money didn't mean as much to me as it did to you."

Mamie's eyes flew open; she looked like she'd been slapped. "Did nothing I say to you yesterday sink in?" She shook her head looking like she'd just lost the war. "No, I wasn't mad about the money. Although I will admit, I didn't understand your disregard for it."

Dad smiled like he'd won. "And now, suddenly you're here – come to save the day for little Lucas. You're going to be the hero. But why, Mother? What do you want? Are you trying to punish us yet again for not kowtowing to you? Is that it?"

"Oh, and you've welcomed me?! Yes, I admit I made mistakes, but it's not as if you made any of this easy. You could have tried a little harder on your end."

Mom's voice broke through. "What? I did try, but you never once noticed."

"When was that, dear?" Mamie responded in a fake, sweet voice. "Was it the time you told your mother that maybe I'd die young so as not to be a problem?"

Mom just sputtered, "I … I … I didn't mean it that way. How… how did you know I said that?"

"I heard it at your wedding reception."

Mom looked back in control with a smug smile on her face. "Oh, right. You seemed to have forgotten that you didn't have the decency to even show up at our reception. Your only child gets married, and you can't even be bothered to attend the wedding reception. I've never experienced such rude behavior."

Mamie smiled back, but it was a sad smile. "I came early, to see if you needed any help. As I approached you and your mother, I overheard your comment. I know when I'm not wanted, so I spent the evening alone. Your meaning was quite clear."

The room became deathly quiet.

"I'm sorry," Mom whispered. She paused before continuing. "But that still doesn't explain … I mean, it doesn't make up for everything else." She then turned her back and said something to Dad.

He hesitated but then put his arm around her. "Mother, you are not welcome in this home. Iris and I are a package deal, always have been." Mom looked up at him in surprise, but she was smiling. He smiled back at her and continued with a sigh, "I admit you were not a terrible mother, so maybe you didn't really think I was a mistake, but I can never be sure." He shook his head. "I know you tried … well, tried to be different yesterday, but I just don't trust you. There's too much damage that's been done over time for me to think you've really changed. You bring misery with you, and I wish you would please go."

I looked at Dad and then at Mamie. He wasn't looking at her anymore, but she was looking at him. Her mouth was hanging open, but she hadn't moved an inch closer to the door. I wondered what she was going to do next. Finally, she spoke and it was barely above a whisper. "I wish you wouldn't ask that of me."

Dad hesitated and I hoped for an instant that he would change his mind, but before he gathered the courage to speak, Mom stepped in. "I tried to love you, I really did. After all this time, it seems like the best I could come up with was to feel nothing about you – not love, but not anger or hurt either. I could live with that. I could go on and raise my children in peace. But this … I don't know what this is. And you … I don't know who you think you are. What gives you the right to enter our lives, especially now?"

"I don't want your money, Mother," Dad said. It seems Mom's words had helped him decide which side he was on. "I never did, and Iris certainly never did. The only thing we ever wanted from you was your love, and if that was asking too much, we would have settled for your acceptance. Was that so wrong to want?"

"No, of course not!" she was angry now. "How was I to know that? You never said that to me before. I've had people my whole life trying to get my money. How do you think it sounded to me when you announced the pregnancy? You hadn't spoken to me since the wedding, and suddenly you're telling me there's a baby on the way even though you're still in school. You even said to me that you didn't know how you were going to pay for it, but somehow it would work out. Well, I didn't want to be some*how*, I wanted to be some*one*. Was that so much to ask of you?"

Mom and Dad both responded at the same time and I couldn't sort out who was saying what, especially when Mamie joined them. I looked behind into the dining room where Grandma was to see what she thought of everything. She looked like a small frightened child, one who can't save herself even though she's in danger. I looked back at the other grown-ups and wondered who would protect Grandma. For that matter, who would protect me and Lily? I didn't know where Lily was, and I was suddenly afraid for her, worried she was listening from upstairs, all alone and scared.

"STOP IT!" I yelled, startling myself with the sound. I didn't know I could yell that loudly, but everyone looked at me and stopped. "Don't make me pick between you. Please, please, don't make me pick!" Tears started to run down my face, fast and hard. "I love all of you. I love Grandma, and you're scaring her. She's dying in the next room, and you're going to be all I have left." I took a breath, but I wasn't done yet. "I love you, Mom and Dad. I love you, Mamie. Why do I have to pick?" I was bawling by now. They stared at me with their mouths hanging open. I was mad now, and I thought I had a right to be. "And what about Lily? Where is she? Don't you think you've scared her too!"

I guess she was listening 'cause at the mention of her name she came running down the stairs, still in her pajamas. I thought she would run to Mom or Dad for comfort, but instead, she ran to me. She was crying too, and I gave her a hug. Wiping my tears, I nodded my head at the adults as an exclamation point. Lily nodded her head firmly too and added her own, "Uh huh!"

It got really quiet after that. Mamie was the first to speak. "I'm sorry for my part in this outburst. I said I've made mistakes, and I suppose it's time I owned up to a few of them." She took a breath and continued, "I haven't really given you a fair shake, Iris. I would like to try again. Lucas has come to mean the world to me. I love him far too much to lose him now. If that means I have to play nice, I'll try." She looked at me and smiled, but quickly added, "It may take some getting used to, but I'd also like to get to know Miss Lily. Lucas is right. It's time to be done making people pick one side or the other."

I smiled at Mamie, and she moved to my side to give me a hug. With Lily on one side of me and Mamie on the other, things seemed to be getting better. I figured Mom and Dad would join us for a group hug any minute. I was wrong.

Mom and Dad were silent, even though we were all looking at them by now, waiting for them to say something. Mom finally said, "I'm sorry about what I said at the reception. I hope all this," she motioned to me and Lily, "is true, that what you said is true ... but I doubt it." Then she turned and disappeared up the stairs.

Dad stared at Mamie for a long time with a look of confusion on his face. "There's so much hurt and anger inside. I suppose what you said yesterday about me and Iris ... well, I don't like admitting it, but you were right. But if I'm going to pick her, I think that means I don't pick you right now, even if ... even if you're the one we have to thank for saving this, if that's what I'm managing to do." He was looking down at his feet, not willing to look his mother in the eye. "I'm sorry, but I have to stand with her, or at least that's what I'm trying to do at the moment." Then he quickly left, following after Mom.

Mamie looked at me sadly and shook her head. "They say no good deed goes unpunished." When I gave her a funny look, she said, "Never mind, I think I better leave now, Lucas, but I promise you I'll be back." She then reached in her pocket and pulled out a cell phone. "This is probably terrible timing, but I want to be able to call you without going through your parents and upsetting them."

I couldn't believe it when she handed me the phone. "Now, don't go getting all excited. This phone doesn't do a whole lot, and I'd like you to leave it that way. However, I know the number, and I'll call you. I have some things to take care of, so I won't see you for a few days, but I will call you soon."

I nodded my head, but she wasn't done. "Lucas, you don't need to keep this a secret from your parents. I was planning on telling them myself, but I don't think now is the time."

Again I nodded, but then I burst out with, "Are you really going to try to be nice?"

"Yes, but I admit you may need to remind me from time to time. I'm afraid I have some bad habits and changing them won't happen overnight. I told you you were teaching this old dog some new tricks." She winked at me.

"Wheresa dog?" Lily said. She hadn't let go of me yet, but I'd kind of forgotten she was there all the same.

Mamie laughed. "Lily, do you like dogs?"

She nodded but swung around to hide behind me.

"Well, what I said might not make sense, but if you like, I'll take you to play with some dogs sometime. I have a neighbor who has two very soft, very quiet dogs who I'm sure would love to meet you."

"Oooooh," she said while slipping back in front of me.

"But I'm thinking we're going to have to wait just a little for that. At least until your Mom and Dad think it's okay. All right, cutie?"

"Uh huh!"

I sure hoped things would settle down 'cause it looked like if she was given the chance, Lily would fall in love with Mamie just like I had. "Goodbye, you two," Mamie said, and then just like that, with a smile and a hug, she walked out our front door.

Chapter 31

Mom and Dad didn't come back downstairs for a while. When they did, their faces weren't happy or sad, more like they were blank. I had been playing with Lily ever since Mamie left. I wanted to make sure she was happy. Mom smiled slightly when she saw me with Lily. I wanted to help everyone be happy, but I had no idea how to do that. It felt uncomfortable to be in my own house. Dad reached out and gave Mom a small little kiss on the cheek. It seemed awkward and strange, like he was kissing Grandma, not Mom, but I hadn't seen him kiss her at all for a while, so I guess it was good. "I'm going to be really late for work, so I'll probably be getting home late tonight."

Mom nodded. "I understand."

He paused when he saw me and Lily, reaching over to give us each a hug before walking out the door. Mom stared after him with an expression I couldn't understand.

I really wanted to help, but I think I wanted to get away even more, so I said, "Can I go play with Justin?" Mom simply nodded, and I took off out the door.

When I knocked at Justin's house, his mom answered the door. "Hi, Lucas. How are you doing?"

I wasn't sure what to say, so I just shrugged my shoulders. She bent over and gave me a hug. "Justin's out back if you want to play."

I nodded and went to find him. It was nice when grown-ups talked to you and asked you questions, but I was learning that sometimes it was even better when they didn't.

When I found Justin, he was digging a hole. "What's it for?" I said.

He shrugged his shoulders. "Don't know yet. Just felt like digging a hole. Buster's sleeping, and I'm just waiting for him to wake up."

"Okay. Can I help?"

"Maybe you can watch for now. I've only got one shovel, and I want to know how much one person can dig in a day."

"Sure." I sat down at the edge of the hole and watched without saying anything. I pulled out the phone Mamie gave me and looked at it.

The next time Justin lifted his head, heaving out another shovelful of dirt, he spotted it. "What's that?"

I handed it to him. "My Grandma Mamie gave it to me. That way she can call me anytime. Cool, huh?"

"Yeah. I asked my parents for a phone. They said I could have one when I actually need one. Only I don't know when that is because I already need one."

I nodded in sympathy. "My parents don't know I have it yet. I'm supposed to tell them, but I'm kind of afraid to."

"Oh," he said as he handed it back to me.

"Justin, do your parents fight?"

"Sometimes. Do yours?"

"Yeah, they've kind of been fighting, but not out loud, I guess. It's like they're mad at each other, but when Mamie shows up they're just mad at her instead. It's pretty bad." I wanted to explain what had happened at my house, but I wasn't sure how to describe it. "Justin, do you remember that night I stayed over at your house and we heard some cats fighting outside?"

"Yeah, that was crazy."

"I know. That's what happened at my house this morning, only it was the people in my house acting like that."

"Here, I'll let you take a turn digging," he said as he handed me his shovel. I knew he understood after that, even the part about me being afraid to tell my parents about the cell phone.

After we dug a big hole and then filled it back in, because we didn't know what else to do with it, I decided to go back home. I wanted to check on Grandma and I felt a little guilty for leaving Lily.

I found Lily in her room. She was playing with a doll and didn't even notice me. I figured that must mean she was okay, so I went off to find Grandma.

She was just waking up from a nap. I wrapped my arms around her and said, "Grandma, I love you."

Her voice was familiar but weak. "I know, Lucas. I love you, too." She patted my cheek. "Lucas, do you think you might be able to help me go sit outside? I'd like to feel the warmth of the sun on my face. It's been a while since I have."

"Sure!" I hurried to find Mom to see if she could help.

"I'm not sure that's the best idea," she said when I told her the plan. Then she paused, seeing my face. "You know, I guess it doesn't really matter. What would it hurt? Let's do it."

It took a bit of work to help Grandma. She didn't get out of bed much these days, except maybe to go to the bathroom, but she was even doing less of that. I don't think I was much help, but I did move a lawn chair closer to the back door so she wouldn't have to walk as far. When she settled down into it, her whole face seemed to brighten up.

"I think I'd like to stay here until dinner, if that's okay with you, Iris," she said. I thought she was asking Mom's permission, but when I looked at Grandma's face, she closed her eyes and smiled. Then I knew she was just being polite. She was staying there until dinner.

"It's okay, Mom. I'll stay with her and come get you if anything goes wrong."

She simply nodded her head in response, but I noticed she was smiling too, even if it did look like a tired smile. I figured, though, that any smile was good after what had happened earlier.

For the longest time, I thought Grandma was sleeping 'cause she didn't say anything and her eyes were closed, but then she said, "Thank you, Lucas."

"You're welcome. Do you want to talk, Grandma, or are you too tired?"

"I am tired, sweetie, but I can listen."

"Okay." That sounded like a good plan, only I wasn't sure what to talk about. I looked around the backyard and said the first thing that came to mind. "You know, Grandma, I like my backyard."

"Why do you like it?"

"Well, I guess partly 'cause it's ours. It's not like the park where you have to share it." I realized what I'd said, so I quickly added, "I know sharing's not bad, and it's okay if my friends come over to play here, it's just that, well, we get to decide what happens here."

"Do you mean you decide what you play here?"

"No. I'm not sure how to describe it. When Justin comes over, I usually let him pick what to play, but if he's having a bad day and uses bad words, I can say things like my mom doesn't let us talk that way. He knows that it's our yard, so we have to follow our rules. He doesn't get upset about it either, he just says something like, 'You win some, you lose some,' and I know we're okay. I don't talk to him the same way when it's his yard." I shrugged my shoulders. "It doesn't exactly make sense when I say it."

"I understand, Lucas."

"You do?"

"Yes, it's a safe place. Other people can come here, but the choice is yours whether to let them in or not. And if you do, you still have some control over the situation. This is your safe place."

I nodded my head, even though she wasn't looking at me. "I never thought of it that way before, but I guess you're right. I do feel safe here. When you were little did you have a safe place, Grandma, like a backyard?"

She was quiet, but her eyes were wide open now and I saw a tear start to roll down her face. "Grandma, what's wrong?"

She reached up to wipe it away. "Lucas, this is my safe place, right here, right now. It's the best safe place I've ever had." She added, "Tell me what else you like about your backyard," before I had a chance to wonder what she meant.

I looked around and pointed to a back corner of the fence. "Well, right there is where pirate ships often sneak up on me, but I can climb the fence in the corner so they can't reach me or pull me into the water. And over there," I said, pointing to the swing set, "is where I fly to the moon and sometimes Mars." I was going to tell her about the trolls who lived under the house and the buried treasure and the treasure map, but I stopped to look at her. Her face seemed far away but happy, like she was in the middle of her own fairy tales, not mine. "Why do you like this backyard, Grandma?"

She looked around before answering. "Well, I like the flowers." I remembered Dad planting them around the house and wondering if they were for Grandma. I guess I was right. "Sweetheart, I think most of all I like this backyard because it belongs to your family, my family. If I close my eyes, I see you running and laughing all around this yard."

"How do you see that? I'm not running around, I'm just sitting here next to you."

"Lucas, I'm using my imagination. You may be seven right now, but in my mind I see you playing football with your friends when you're twelve, and I watch Lily having a tea party when she's five. I see birthday parties and tents set up for summertime campouts. I see all of those things in my head right now. I'm watching you grow up in this very backyard right now as we sit here."

I didn't know what to say, and my silence drew Grandma's attention. She reached out a hand to touch my cheek. "I hope I'm not making you sad. It's not a sad thought on my part. All those things I imagine make me happy, because in them I see you and Lily being happy. You're going to be fine, even after I'm gone."

I wasn't so sure. If she was trying to cheer me up, it wasn't working. She must have noticed 'cause she stopped trying and just reached out to hold my hand. We sat that way for a long time.

As we did, I noticed how the sun felt on my skin, like a warm towel fresh out of the dryer. I could almost smell how good the sunshine felt. Once, a cloud covered the sun, and the sudden shadow made me shiver. I was glad when it moved and the light returned.

Grandma almost scared me when she started to speak again. "When I die, it will seem to you like that cloud that just passed in front of the sun. But the sun didn't go anywhere, you just couldn't see it for a minute. And just when you think you won't get over being sad, the sun will shine through again. You'll be able to feel it, I promise."

I didn't know if Grandma could handle it or not, but I climbed right up onto her lap, wrapped my arms around her neck and settled my head against her warm body. She tilted her head so that it was resting on top of mine and put her arms around me and held me close.

We didn't talk after that. As I sat there quietly, I tried to take in the world around me, noticing the flowers that Grandma liked. Bees were buzzing nearby, and it sounded kind of like they were singing while they worked. Mom used to sing when she worked around the house, especially when she made dinner. I think Grandma having cancer was like a cloud for her already, even though Grandma wasn't dead yet. I really hoped she would feel the sun again, like Grandma promised.

Looking at Grandma, I saw her eyes were closed again, and her mouth was hanging slightly open, so I figured she was sleeping. I carefully climbed down from her lap so I wouldn't wake her. The backyard seemed different to me now. I was picturing all the things Grandma imagined, but they made me sad. Grandma wouldn't be there when they happened.

I laid down in the grass, making a summer snow angel with my arms. Grass always reminded me I was still a kid. I guess you had to be big to be a grown-up, so you could carry all the worries and problems that you had. I wasn't strong enough for that yet. Being an adult didn't sound like something I was going to like. Justin told me you were supposed to look before you leap. Maybe this was what he was talking about. I was getting a glimpse into being an adult, but I didn't know how to avoid leaping. It seemed like it just happened – you grow old and then it's all over.

Somehow, though, I don't think Grandma thought about it that way. She seemed happy being an adult, even though her eyes were sometimes sad. I rolled over on my side to look at her. Her lips were moving just a little as she slept. I wondered if she was dreaming about Abby.

A squeak caught my attention. One of our swings at the back was wrapped around the side bar of the swing set, but the other swung freely on the ghost-like breeze, creaking ever so slightly as it moved. Grandma, when she'd been stronger, used to push me on that swing, long after I actually needed a push. I could pump my legs on my own, working myself up to a height where I could almost see over the house, but I loved it when Grandma helped me. I didn't have to work so hard, and I could feel the rush of air on my face from the very first push.

We used to have a small sandbox in the back too, but I didn't usually play there when Grandma was around. She said she didn't like the feel of sand on her skin, and whenever I did play in it, she would brush every last grain of sand off my skin and clothes, even rubbing my hair thoroughly before allowing me back in the house. I didn't like it then, but now I was missing it.

I would miss those little things about Grandma. I had been so busy lately worrying about finding Abby and about Mamie and my parents fighting, that I had forgotten about being sad that Grandma was dying, that she wouldn't be here very much longer.

I guess my only choice now was to try extra hard to store up pictures and memories that no one could take away, that would not die with her. A little piece of Grandma would always stay in my mind and wedge itself into my heart. I lay back and fell asleep right there on the grass, thinking about Grandma and feeling the warmth of the sun on my face.

The sound of voices woke me. I sat up, confused, until I remember why I was in the back yard. Looking at Grandma I could see she was still sleeping. Her head was bent down on her chest, and she moved slightly up and down every time she took a breath. Looking past her, I found what woke me.

I could see through our sliding glass door into the kitchen. It must have been getting close to dinnertime because I could smell something good. But what surprised me was Dad. He was standing there talking to Mom. He had come home early after all.

"... I might have to go in early for a few days is all."

Mom looked at him but didn't say anything. She had her hands on her hips, but I don't think she was angry. It's more like what she did when she wanted me to explain why I had left a mud trail through the living room. She might get mad later, but she usually waited for the explanation first.

"You were right, Iris. I've been staying late on purpose, and I wasn't listening to you. I'm sorry."

"Really?" She sounded just like when I told her the mud trail just happened, but I had no idea how.

"Yes. I'm sorry. When you told me, it just really caught me off guard. I never wanted one more, and since I thought we'd taken care of that ... Bottom line is I jumped to the wrong conclusion. I'm sorry. I know I should have trusted you all along."

She was nodding her head, but she was smiling. "Yeah. You've kind of been a jerk about the whole thing."

He smiled back and then reached out to take her hands. "I know. I have been."

"Pete, I didn't know what to think at first either. It's not what I was planning on, but now that it's real, I think I might be happy about it."

"Well, I'm not there yet, but I'm working on it. It just might take a while, okay?" Mom fell into his arms, and he held her tight.

I let out a big breath that I didn't even know I'd been holding.

I generally avoid the beach, and it's been years since I was last here. Being here now makes me cringe, although I can't explain why.

My friends have built a large bonfire to celebrate the start of our last year of high school. No one sees that I am shivering beside the flames.

I leave the group to wander alone. The water beckons me, and as I draw near, I let it tickle my toes. It is so cold. Yet I don't move out of its grasp, and I wonder why. What am I doing here? What am I looking for? Why do I have a sense of loss?

Wading further in, I feel the gentle yet insistent flow of the water. The waves push me back toward shore while the tide pulls me deeper still, both together threatening to wash me off my feet. The uncertainty leaves me unbalanced and confused. Which way should I go?

My days are like this, each one much like the last. I cannot tell if they are bad or good, as I seem to have lost my compass. It is like a pulsing wave moving back and forth, yet never really going anywhere. I am in constant motion, yet always staying put. Will I ever move forward, or even backward? I don't know the answer, and not knowing makes me even more unsure of my footing.

I spot a distant ship on the horizon. I can see it, but I imagine that it can't see me. I chuckle to realize from where I face, I can't see my friends behind me. Certainly they are close enough to be within view, but they are invisible to me unless I turn and look.

Which way should I turn – to an unknown ship or to my friends? Or elsewhere?

While I have been standing, sinking into the sand, the tide has moved in and the water is licking my waist. Is it time to move, to pull my feet up and find my own path?

Chapter 32

I figured Mamie was right, that I wouldn't see her soon. So, I kept the cell phone she gave me close all the time in case she called. Only it hadn't rung yet. I knew I should tell Mom and Dad about the phone, but I was afraid of what they would say. I kept telling myself that I'd tell them tomorrow.

The next afternoon when Justin and I were playing with Buster, I pulled out the phone to look at it. Justin stopped what he was doing to come sit beside me. "Have you heard anything yet?"

"No, but I hope I do soon." I shrugged my shoulders and put the phone back in my pocket. "I never knew that I'd need one grandma to help the other one."

"You like Mamie, don't you?"

"Yeah. When we're not so busy with Grandma dying, you'll get a chance to go to her house with me. I bet you'll like her too." I smiled at Justin, but he must have noticed how my smile went away.

"It sucks that she's dying."

I knew we weren't talking about Mamie anymore, and he was right. I just nodded my head. Usually Justin knew just what to say, but this time, he didn't say anything. He just sat beside me, watching Buster run around the back yard.

―――――――――

For the next few days, when I wasn't with Justin or playing with Lily, I liked sitting beside Grandma and reading a book. She still had good days, but they didn't happen very often. Mostly she just slept when there weren't any nurses or doctors around. Being close by made me feel like I was keeping her company, even if she was sleeping and didn't know I was there.

In between pages of my book, I would look up and watch the rise and fall of the comforter on Grandma's bed. It's the way I knew it was okay to look away and keep reading. The one constant in my life was that Grandma was dying. I didn't like it, but I could count on it. Nothing else and no one else was certain.

Once she woke up with a start, saying, "John?"

I hurried to her side. "Grandma, it's me, Lucas."

"Oh," she breathed deeply, "I see," she said while she patted my arm. Instinctively, she reached out for Abby's ring. She liked to hold it when she was awake.

"I'll get it, Grandma," I said, picking up the jewelry box. I quickly pulled the ring out and handed it to her. I noticed she was staring at the jewelry box, but not saying anything.

"Do you like your jewelry box?"

She nodded. "You said it was supposed to help you feel better after Abby got kidnapped. Did it help?"

Her eyes had clouded over, and I was surprised to see she looked angry. "No!"

"It didn't help?"

She was shaking her head. "No, it wasn't supposed to help. It was supposed to make me forget."

I wasn't sure what to say. I didn't know if she was remembering things right or not. "Really?" I finally said. "You told me you put Abby's ring in there to help you remember."

"Yes, I did, but I had to hide it. They wanted me to forget."

"Why?"

She was quiet, and when she finally spoke her voice was cold, but her eyes were clear. "Because they told me she was dead."

I couldn't believe it, and I collapsed into the nearest chair. Abby couldn't be found after all - she was already dead! I felt so sad that I wanted to cry. I hadn't known Abby, never seen her even, but I didn't expect to hear that she was dead.

Then Grandma's words broke through to me, "But I knew it wasn't true. They just told me the lie so I would forget."

"How did you know it was a lie?"

"I'm not sure; I just didn't believe it. Then one night I overheard them talking. Dad said something about Abby, something about her that told me she was still alive."

"What did he say?"

"I ... I don't remember."

Just then my phone rang.

I didn't know where Mom was, but I didn't want her to catch me with the phone Mamie had given me. So I quickly ran outside before answering it, each ring threatening to give me away.

Even out in the backyard, I hunched over the phone and whispered, "Hello."

"Lucas, are you okay? You sound funny."

I didn't want her to know I hadn't told Mom and Dad about the phone yet, so I straightened up and said in as normal a voice as possible, "I'm just fine."

"Good. I miss seeing you."

"Me too."

"Well, Lucas, I'm calling you from Washington. I decided that this time around I needed to be closer to the problem. I've hired a local private investigator, and I've been checking with him every day on his progress."

"Wow. Did you find anything?"

"Not yet."

"Oh," I couldn't hide my disappointment.

"But we're not done yet, Lucas. Records back that far are pretty sketchy, but we're piecing together what we can. I didn't know this, but the investigator told me that most kidnapping victims are eventually found, so his best guess is that there would have been only two or three that were not recovered from the year when your Grandmother was seven. We just haven't been able to locate the records to find out for sure. So, Mr. Knowles, he's the P.I., has found some old detectives who worked around that time. He's going to talk with them tomorrow to see what else he can learn."

I wasn't sure what to say. I knew she was trying hard, but it all sounded pretty hopeless to me. "Okay, Mamie," I finally said, with as strong a voice as I could find.

"Lucas, if she's to be found, I'll find her. I promise."

I thought that she hadn't heard the worry in my voice, but maybe she actually had. A spark of hope lit in my heart. "Thank you, Mamie. I love you."

"I love you too, Lucas."

"Mamie?"

"Yes, Lucas?"

"Grandma's remembering more, only it doesn't make sense yet. She said she was supposed to forget about Abby because they told her she died." I head Mamie gasp, so I hurried to tell her the rest. "But Grandma says she knows Abby didn't die, only she can't remember why." I took a breath. "Do you think we'll really be able to figure it all out?"

She didn't even hesitate. "Don't you worry. We will indeed."

Chapter 33

The rest of that day and the next I couldn't stop thinking about Mamie being in Washington. Maybe at that very moment she was finding out about Abby. Just when I was staring at the phone in my pocket hoping it would ring, the doorbell rang instead.

When Mom opened the door, we discovered Justin and his mom on our doorstep with Buster right between them. I expected one of them to ask if I could play, but Justin just looked at me with a serious expression on his face. I looked up at his mom and she gave me a small smile, but mostly she was watching Justin with a look in her eye that I couldn't quite figure out.

Finally, Justin thrust his hand at me, giving me the leash he had been holding. "Here. Buster's yours."

I couldn't believe my ears. "What?" I was excited, but also a bit confused.

"I want you to have him. Your Grandma's dying, and I know you're sad, so I thought you could use a pal."

I looked up at my mom to see what she thought about the whole thing. She had the same look as Justin's mom. I looked back and forth between them until I figured out they were proud of Justin and what he was doing. That's when I knew what to do. "Thanks, Justin!" Kneeling down, I hugged Buster. "I think he's awesome." Then I stood back up and added, "But you keep him."

He cocked his head at me, not knowing what to say. Then I saw a smile creep across his face. "I know," he said, "we'll share him. I mean, your dad helped build the doghouse and all."

"Okay, but he'll sleep at your house, you know, at his dog house."

"All right," Justin said, and then we took off to go play with our dog. Our moms didn't say a thing, just stood there on the doorstep watching us go.

When I came back later, I checked on Grandma, wanting to tell her about Buster and Mamie in Washington, and everything, but she was sleeping.

I finally decided to play in the back yard, but only ended up sitting in a chair on the patio, waiting for Grandma to wake up or Mamie to call. Mom came out, only I didn't hear her come. So, when she called my name, I jumped a foot.

"Lucas, are you all right?"

"Sure, Mom. You just surprised me. I didn't know you were there."

"Okay. What are you doing out here? Would you like a book or something?"

I shrugged my shoulders. "I don't know. I was just waiting ..." I almost said I was waiting for a phone call, but caught myself just in time. "I mean I was just waiting for Grandma to wake up. She's sure been sleeping a lot."

With that, Mom pulled up a lawn chair and sat down beside me. She reached up to brush hair off my forehead. After a moment of silence, she whispered, "You're going to miss her, aren't you?"

I just nodded my head, fighting off the tears that had unexpectedly pooled in the corners of my eyes. I got up and climbed into Mom's lap just like I had Grandma's. Maybe other people would think I was too old for that, but it somehow felt right. I wrapped my arms around her neck and rested my head on her chest. She put one arm around me, but with her other hand she continued to brush back my hair. I liked the way it felt.

Just when I thought this must be the most peaceful moment in my life, the phone in my pocket rang. It startled both of us.

I jumped off her lap and fumbled in my pocket for the phone as it continued to condemn me with its ringing. Mom was still sitting, so our eyes met straight across. Before answering the phone, I said, "Mamie didn't want to bother you anymore, so she gave me a phone to call me on. She was going to tell you about it, but then there was that big fight, and I think she was a little scared of you. I was supposed to tell you, but I guess I was a little scared of you too."

Before Mom could respond, I answered the phone and said, "Hello."

"Hi, Lucas. You're sounding better than before."

I guess I was. I really had been afraid to tell Mom about the phone, but sometimes things happen to help give us a little push. It was scary, but it felt good at the same time. "Yeah. I'm okay. What did you find out?"

"The detectives didn't have any specific information for us, but one of them is willing to help us go through the old records. Nothing from that far back is on the computer, so we're going to have to sort through a lot of paperwork. But I got the P.I. and the detective to both agree to let me help. I figure another set of eyes won't hurt."

"Awesome." Despite my worries, I felt like hope was finding a way to creep back in.

We said goodbye to each other, and I turned to walk inside. Mom was still sitting there looking at me. She wasn't smiling and she wasn't frowning. She did seem to be waiting, though.

"Don't be mad at Mamie. I know you don't believe what Grandma's been saying, but Mamie's checking it out. That way we'll know if it's true or not. If there is a sister to be found, then she's trying to help find her. She and a detective and a private investigator are all looking through old records to see what they can find out. Don't be mad at her for that. She's trying to be nice."

Mom didn't say anything, so I quickly escaped inside. I realized I hadn't told Mom all the details about the kidnapping and Mamie being in Washington. I'm not sure why. I guess I thought it would just make it too complicated or confusing. It was a pretty crazy story when you actually thought about it, and that made me laugh.

I was still laughing when I entered Grandma's room. I quieted my laugh, but then realized I didn't need to when I saw her eyes open. I threw my arm around her. "Grandma!"

"Love you."

When I finally let her go, I sat down on the bed beside her. Her eyes were bright and clear. "Mamie's gone to Washington to find out more about Abby. We'll find her, okay?"

She nodded and said, "Yes," but her eyes clouded over.

"What's wrong, Grandma?"

She turned her head towards mine, but her eyes were seeing something else. She reached for my hand and said, "I don't know, Lucas. I don't know."

Grandma was awake for a while after that, but we didn't talk about Abby. I decided to read her a story and she smiled when I started. Soon Lily joined us on Grandma's bed, and all worries were forgotten. It felt like we were having a big sleepover, even though it was the middle of the day.

Dad made it home in time for dinner again that night, which made both me and Mom smile. Mom didn't even seem mad at anyone, so I kept crossing my fingers and saying a little prayer that it would stay that way. When we were clearing the dishes, she said, "Lucas."

I wasn't sure what was coming, but I looked up at her. "Yes?"

"You're going to want to make sure to keep that phone charged. Do you have a charger for it?"

I was so surprised, I almost forgot to answer. "Yeah, I guess so. I just put it in a drawer."

"Well, you'll need to charge it sometime. I'll help you when you're ready."

I stood there, waiting for the rest to come, for the lecture, but it didn't come. I guess she was done. Afraid of my own voice, I said, "Thanks, Mom. I love you."

"I love you, too."

Dad had started washing dishes, but he looked up and smiled his agreement to what Mom had said.

"I can help Lily get ready for bed, if you want," I said.

Mom turned from the food she was putting away to look at me. "That would be nice. Thank you."

I found Lily and hurried her up to her room. She got ready for bed quickly and then we settled on her bed to read stories for the second time that day. Neither of us minded, especially when Mom and Dad both came and joined us, silently sitting on the floor, listening to me read.

I noticed Dad reach over to touch Mom's hair, gently brushing it out of her face and then softly down her back. A memory came to mind, but it was old and faded. When I was little, he used to do that all the time, but I guess he'd forgotten how. He kept watching her while he played with her hair. She was looking at me, but a smile was dancing on her lips.

Chapter 34

I like thunderstorms. I know Justin doesn't. I tried to explain them to him, but he didn't care. He still doesn't like them. I guess I do 'cause of my mom, 'cause of a memory.

What I remember is a really loud thunderstorm. Sudden flashes of light startled me, and before I could get over being scared by the light, loud thunder echoed, sounding like an extra loud drum and cymbal in a parade right behind me. It seems Mom picked me up and held me close. Then she took me over to the kitchen sink. She picked up two blue sponges. Banging the two sponges together, she made a loud noise, telling me that's what the clouds were doing. Then she squeezed the sponges and water, like rain, came spilling out. I laughed.

She let me try the sponges myself and told me I could make as loud of a sound as I wanted when I crashed them together. I played and played with them. I'm pretty sure I was all wet by the time I was done, but by then the storm was done too. I've never been afraid of thunder and lightning since.

Sometimes the noise of a storm wakes me at night, and I lie in bed waiting for my ceiling to light up, then stay still, listening for the thunder to follow. I have a hard time falling back to sleep when the storm stops, waiting and listening to see if it will return.

So, I wasn't surprised to wake to the sound of the summer thunderstorm that night while sleeping on the couch. But as I stretched out my ear to catch every last drop of the storm's sound, something seemed different. I couldn't tell what it was at first, but then I recognized the sound of crying.

Figuring it must be Lily, I jumped up and ran upstairs to her room. I was surprised to see she was still asleep, but then I noticed I couldn't hear the sound of crying anymore. It was pretty dark, except for the broken flashes of the lightning, so I held onto the stair rail as I carefully made my way back downstairs.

As I did so, a loud crash of thunder made me jump. When the sound faded and the shock wore off, I heard the faint sound of crying again. But this time, I could tell it was coming from Grandma's room.

Making my way to Grandma's side, I reached out my hand to touch hers. She jumped when I touched her. "Abby?"

"No, Grandma. It's just me, Lucas."

Just then lightning lit up the room, and for a second, I could see the tears on Grandma's cheeks and the fear in her eyes. She grabbed hold of my hand, pulling me close.

"What's wrong?"

"The thunder and lightning."

"Did it scare you?"

She shook her head roughly, "No! The thunder and lighting. It brought it back. Lucas, I remember! I remember what happened and what they said. I remember how I knew she was alive."

"Really? What was it?"

"I remember what he said, actually what she said."

"Who? Your mom?"

She ignored my question, but continued, "They didn't know I was awake, but I could hear them talking in the next room. He said, 'I like Josie, but I wish her sister were here too.'"

"So, they missed Abby, too?" She didn't respond to me, so I decided to stop talking and just listen.

Grandma's head was up and facing straight out. She must have been looking right past me, even though I couldn't see her eyes. Her voice was clear when she continued. "Then she said, 'No, you don't! Don't even think it! This is enough of a mess as it is. I'm glad you didn't grab them both. Getting one brat was enough. Be happy you have the one.'"

She was suddenly silent, only the sound of the storm continued to scream around us. I finally said, "Grandma, what does that mean? Grandma! Were you the one who was kidnapped?"

Lightning made the room suddenly bright, but her voice, strong and powerful, drowned out the thunder. "Yes, Lucas, I was! It was me! It was me!" Then she fell silent and so did the storm.

Chapter 35

I didn't understand what was so special about nighttime or thunder and lightning with Grandma, but I guess when it gets dark and stormy her mind seems a little brighter by comparison. Maybe it's like how your eyes get used to the dark and you can walk to the bathroom in the middle of the night without bumping into walls even if you don't turn the lights on. It doesn't make sense since it's pitch black, but somehow it works anyway.

Or maybe it's just that Grandma knew I was the only one who would hear her in the dark and the storm, the only one who would come when she cried or called out. And she knew I believed her. Maybe that was enough.

I didn't feel much like sleeping after that, so I climbed up on Grandma's bed. I don't remember reaching out for her hand, but I found myself holding it anyway. For a long time she was quiet except for her heavy breathing. It sounded like Dad after he's gone running. In a strange way, I suppose she had just finished a long run or a long journey. I guess anything that's hard like that can make you breathe just as hard.

I knew she was crying again when her breathing changed to a soft choking sound, and I reached up with my free hand to touch her check and found it wet with tears. "Grandma, I'm sorry," was all I could think to say. I snuggled up next to her and laid my arm across her in a hug. The sounds she was making slowed, softened, and then turned into gentle snores.

I was tempted to fall asleep right beside her, but I knew I had an important clue for Mamie to help us find Abby. I climbed down and started to walk back and forth between the couch and Grandma or into the kitchen and then back. When the sky started to wake up and I could see the outline of the mailbox out front, I figured it was time to call Mamie. It seemed like a good idea to call her before Mom or Dad came down the stairs. Even if Mom was being nice about the whole Mamie thing, I didn't want to take any chances.

It took several rings before Mamie picked up her phone. "Hello, Lucas."

"Hi, Mamie. Are you okay? You sound different."

She cleared her throat. "Yes, I'm fine. I just haven't gotten around to talking yet today, so it will take a few minutes for my voice to get used to the idea."

I wasn't sure what she meant, but then it hit me. "Did I wake you up?"

"Well, yes, but that's okay. What time is it there, Lucas?"

"I don't know. I just saw the sun coming up and figured it was morning."

She laughed. "That's what I thought. Yes, it is morning. It's about 6:00 a.m. where you are, which makes it 3:00 a.m. here."

I could only gasp at my mistake, and Mamie laughed again.

"It really is fine, Lucas. I never explained to you the time difference, so you had no way of knowing. So, what is it you were so anxious to share with me?"

"How did you know that's why I called you?"

"Because you sound like you didn't just wake up, and for that matter, you don't usually wake up at the crack of dawn anyway."

"Yeah, I guess you're right. Well, I was awake 'cause there was a thunderstorm in the middle of the night, but I figured out that wasn't what woke me after all. It was Grandma. She was crying."

"I'm sorry, Lucas. Why was she crying?"

"She remembered something else, something about Abby, or actually something about herself."

"What was it?" I could hear her voice getting stronger and even a little curious.

"She was the one who was kidnapped! It wasn't Abby. It was her!"

It was her turn to be surprised. "Really, Lucas? That's incredible. I guess that changes what we're looking for, doesn't it?"

"Yes, I guess so." Before hanging up, I told her exactly what Grandma had said, and Mamie told me she would start working on finding out what she could first thing in the morning.

Satisfied, I hung up, laid down on the couch, and promptly fell asleep.

The room was fully light when I woke up. I noticed Grandma's doctors and nurses were gathered around her for a regular check-up, and they were whispering. I guess they were being quiet so I could sleep. Since I was in my pj's, I ran upstairs to get dressed. By the time I came downstairs again, the last of Grandma's nurses was going out the front door. I was hungry but first made my way to Grandma's side.

"Are you okay?" I whispered.

She was sitting up straight, not slumped over against her bed like usual, and her eyes were dark and clear. At the sound of my voice, she turned to stare at me with an intensity I hadn't seen since before she'd gotten sick. "Everything is clear for the first time in a long time, Lucas, but I don't think I'm ready to talk about it yet. Is that okay?"

"Yeah, I guess so." With that, Grandma's face relaxed and she leaned back in her bed, looking like a peaceful angel.

When Mom came in, she looked at Grandma and then at me. "What's happened?"

"What do you mean?"

"Something's different with Mom. She looks so calm." Her eyes flew open in alarm. "She's not – "

"No, Mom." I grabbed her arm to hold her steady. "She's not dying yet. She's just happy because her brain is making sense to her again."

Mom looked at me, puzzled, but at least she didn't seem scared anymore. She shook her head like she wasn't sure what to think. "I actually came in to see if either of you was hungry."

"Yes, Mom," I said, but Grandma was still silent. "Grandma, do you want to eat something?" She looked at me and just nodded.

"If she's so clear, why isn't she talking?" Mom said.

"It's hard to explain." I looked at Grandma for help, but she just smiled, encouraging me to continue. "I think she just has so much going on in her head right now, she's trying to figure out what to do with it all."

It was clear Mom wasn't any closer to understanding from the expression on her face. "And exactly how do you know that? Have you become a mind-reader overnight?"

I knew she was just teasing, but it hit me that I was probably the first person Grandma had ever told about being kidnapped. That had to count for something. "I just know, Mom."

Grandma and Mom looked at each other. Grandma simply smiled slightly and then noticeably blinked her eyes. Mom wasn't sure what to think. She looked at me and then back at her mother, finally shaking her head as she left for the kitchen.

The rest of the day was more of the same. It was like Grandma had just woken up from hibernation. I knew bears hibernated, and even though I'd never seen what it was like when they woke up, it had to be something like this. I just imagined they looked around and thought, "Oh, yeah, so this is what the world looks like. I'd almost forgotten."

Grandma was sitting straight up in bed, eyes wide open all day. I almost felt I could see through her eyes into her brain, only it was too dark in there to be sure. The only strange thing was that even though I could tell she was with us, she said nothing, not even nodding or shaking her head anymore. It's not what I expected, but I was happy 'cause she looked so strong.

"Grandma, are you getting better? Like you're not really going to die?" I dared to ask her that afternoon. One look from her serious eyes and I knew the answer. It was too much for a seven-year-old to handle. I started to sob and threw my arms around her. Still silent, she returned the hug, patiently holding me until I had cried my tears dry.

I didn't know if I'd have any tears for later, but I didn't care. Sometimes a boy just needs his grandma.

When I Was Seven

I am standing at the beach, but it's not any of the beaches I grew up near. It's on a different coast altogether, and I'm not sure what led me here – to the strange coast, to a different ocean, to a beach.

I squeeze my husband's hand until he touches me gently on the shoulder, wondering why I'm holding on so tightly. I have no explanation.

I find myself unconsciously looking around to see if anyone is flying a kite, although I don't understand why I care. I don't like kites; I don't ever remember flying one, owning one, or even wanting to. Yet, for some reason, I search the sky above the sand, hoping to spot a kite dancing on the currents. There are none, and I drop my head in unexplained despair.

With my eyes closed, the sounds of the ocean reach me, the flood of water moving toward me, then shushing a retreat. The water beckons, then calls me by name, but I don't answer, afraid of what it will tell me.

Chapter 36

The next morning when I woke up, the first thing I did was check on Grandma. She was awake. Just like the day before, she was completely aware of everything, but silent. I climbed up on the end of her bed and sat down cross-legged, watching her. "You understand everything, don't you?" I said. She didn't nod or shake her head, but just like yesterday, by a single look, I knew. "Okay, then. You're just still not ready to talk yet?" Again the look. She wasn't silent from a fuzzy mind like she'd had recently; it was simply a choice she was making.

I made up my mind, or maybe I was just reading Grandma's mind, but I needed to talk to Mom and Dad. It was still early and Dad hadn't left for work yet. I found both my parents in the kitchen eating breakfast. Their heads were close together, and they were talking softly to each other.

"Good morning," I said to get their attention.

"Good morning. You're up early," said Mom.

Pulling up a chair, I tried to sit taller, gaining courage. They both looked at me as I did so. "What's up, sport?" said Dad.

I didn't mean to say it so bluntly. I was going to lead up to it and prepare them for it, but I opened my mouth and out came the words, "Grandma was kidnapped when she was a little girl."

They just stared at me – no open mouths, no denials, nothing! I didn't know what that meant.

"Did you already know or something? 'Cause I sure thought you would have something to say when I told you."

Dad, at least, raised his eyebrows this time then finally said, "What in the world are you talking about? Was this a dream you had?"

"No." I was puzzled. Weren't they listening to me? I didn't know how to say it any clearer. "Grandma was kidnapped when she was a little girl!" I knew I was repeating myself, but they must not have been listening the first time. I was beginning to understand why Mom got upset at me when she thought I wasn't listening.

"Would you care to explain?" Mom said.

"Well, I don't know a whole lot about it yet. You see, the reason Grandma never told you about Abby, even though Abby was her sister, was because Abby didn't get kidnapped with Grandma. He later wished he'd kidnapped her too, but he didn't. So, you see, she didn't have Abby for a sister when she was growing up 'cause Grandma was kidnapped and living with somebody else." I thought it would be perfectly clear now, but Mom and Dad looked puzzled. At least they didn't look mad.

"Slow down, and start from the beginning. How did you come up with this?"

"Grandma told me."

"When?"

"Well, it's been coming out just a bit at a time, but she told me about being kidnapped the night of the thunderstorm."

"When? We haven't had a thunderstorm for quite some time."

It was my turn to look puzzled. "Night before last. There was a big thunderstorm in the middle of the night. You were sleeping and Grandma was crying. She'd already told me that Abby was kidnapped, but she'd gotten it mixed up. That night she remembered what he said, that he wished he'd grabbed Abby too, and when she remembered that, she remembered that she was the one who got kidnapped, not the other way around."

"First off, Lucas, Grandma isn't really talking much lately, and secondly, being kidnapped isn't exactly something you forget to tell people your whole life."

Dad was making a good argument, but I knew Grandma wouldn't want me to quit trying. "I know, Dad. She hasn't talked a lot, but she talks when it's important. She told me what she needed to tell me, and then she's barely talked or even nodded since. That's why I'm telling you this. I think she wants me to."

I decided to go on before they could say anything else. "She said things like she was raised as an only child 'cause she was. She didn't have Abby in her life. They tried to make her forget her. Grandma thought it was 'cause Abby was taken away from her, but she was the one taken away from Abby. It got mixed up in her brain 'cause she just wanted to see Abby again. So, it didn't really matter who was taken, it only mattered that she and Abby weren't together. She's been so sad 'cause she's been remembering. Only it's been coming in pieces, a little at a time."

Mom had moved beside me while I talked. She bent over and started to play with my hair. "Lucas, you don't just forget something like that. I know you believe this, but it just doesn't make any sense."

"Did you ever meet Grandma's mom?"

Mom stopped playing with my hair and stood straight up. It was a minute before she responded. "Well, no, but she lived on the other side of the country. It was difficult ..."

"Did you ever talk to her on the phone? Did you ever send her presents? Did she send you presents? Have you ever even seen her picture?"

"No."

"You see? It does make sense. Did Grandma tell you stories about being a little girl?"

"A few, I suppose."

"Yeah. I know, right? You didn't even know where she was born. We figured out she was born in Washington state."

"Dad mentioned that. How did you come up with Washington?"

"Her charm bracelet. It had some Washington stuff on it. I didn't know what it was, but Mamie did. So, she asked Grandma about it, and she remembered she used to live there, that she was born there. She said Abby was born there too." I smiled. I thought I was making a good case, like the lawyers I saw on TV.

Only I noticed Mom wasn't smiling. "Of course it was Mamie," she said.

"Mamie just helped. Grandma's the one who told us all this stuff. Mamie believes her, just like I do. That's why she's in Washington right now to see what she can find."

Mom's eyes opened wide. "She's in Washington? Washington

195

state? How did she get there?"

Mom seemed to be asking silly questions, but they weren't too hard to answer, so I did. "Yes, she is. She flew there on a plane a few days ago."

"Really? She spent her own money on something other than herself?" This time, I don't think she was expecting me to answer the question. She seemed to be talking to Dad or maybe just the air, I wasn't sure. She added, more to herself than anyone, "I don't think she's ever done that before."

I wanted to tell Mom about the money Grandma had spent on me for lunch and ice cream and the investigators she'd hired already, but I figured now was the time to keep my mouth shut. She looked puzzled, but then clearly got an idea. "Are you sure she's in Washington?"

"She called me from there. Do you want to see my phone?"

That wasn't the best thing to say 'cause it reminded Mom about the phone Mamie had given me. She may have been okay with it before, but I wasn't so sure she was anymore. "That won't help, Lucas. She would have called you from her cell phone."

"Oh. Well, I called her yesterday morning when the sun came up to tell her about the kidnapping part, and I woke her up. She said it was three in the morning where she was. She sounded pretty sleepy on the phone."

Mom seemed to think about that, but it was Dad who spoke. "She wouldn't have any reason to fake that. Lucas wouldn't have known about the time difference. Maybe she's telling the truth. Maybe they all are." He looked at Mom and shrugged his shoulders.

"I just can't get over the fact that she's spending her own money to help someone else. Do you think she's changed? I have a hard time believing that."

"I don't think you were wrong about her before, but maybe now … I don't know," Dad said. Then he got a funny look on his face, like he was in pain or something. "Iris, I need to tell you something."

"What?" Mom sounded worried. "What is it, Pete?"

Dad was looking at his feet. He let out a big sigh and lifted his head. "Iris, it was my mother that called me out. She's the one who told me in no uncertain terms that I was wrong about you."

"Of course she told you you were wrong about me."

"No, Iris, I mean about the baby. She told me I was making a big mistake, that you were the best thing that ever happened to me, and I shouldn't give up on you."

For once Mom didn't have anything to say. She just stared at Dad with a blank expression on her face.

"What baby?" I said. The sound of my voice made Mom jump as if she'd forgotten I was there.

Mom didn't answer, she just left the room, going in to stand beside Grandma.

Dad watched her leave and then chuckled. "You're going to have a little brother or little sister. Is that okay?"

"You bet it is!" I couldn't believe what I'd heard. I was so happy, grinning from ear to ear. But then I noticed Dad wasn't.

"I'm sorry, sport. There's just a whole lot going on right now, isn't there?"

"Yeah, I guess so," I said, glancing in at Mom and Grandma. Mom was sitting down at Grandma's side, stroking her hand softly. Neither one of them was speaking.

When I felt Dad's hand on my shoulder, I knew he was watching too. He gently turned me around so he could speak to me. "Lucas," he whispered, "I'm not really sure what's true and what's not about your grandmother, and I can guarantee you your mom is even more confused than I am. You have to understand it would be hard for her to accept that her mother had all these crazy things happen to her and kept it a secret for years, and from her only child."

I nodded. "I guess so, but Grandma really did forget, and now that she's remembering, she doesn't have a lot of time to wait for us."

He nodded in return.

Chapter 37

It seemed like for the rest of that day no one was talking. Whenever I saw Mom, she looked confused or hurt or scared or surprised. I was never sure what it was. I'm not sure she did either. But whatever thoughts she was having, she wasn't sharing any of them with me. Dad came home from work right before dinnertime. When he saw me, he just ruffled my hair and gave me a small smile, but he didn't say anything either.

I decided to eat dinner with Grandma 'cause at least I understood why she wasn't talking. Once I left the kitchen, they started talking again, at least a little bit. I could hear Lily's voice mostly, but Mom and Dad said something every once in a while.

Grandma ate all her dinner. It was just frozen chicken patties Mom had warmed up in the oven, with some peas and applesauce. I liked all of it except the peas. Grandma hadn't been eating much lately, so I was surprised when she almost beat me done. I asked if she wanted any more peas, and then I gave her all mine without looking to see if she really wanted them or not. She must have, though, 'cause she ate every last one.

That night before bed, I read a story to Lily on Grandma's bed so Grandma could hear it too. When I climbed into my bed on the couch, I fell asleep before I could even try to go to sleep. I must have been pretty tired.

The voices woke me. It wasn't super dark outside, so it was either early in the nighttime or early in the morning, but I didn't know which. I sat up so my ear wouldn't be buried in my pillow and I could hear better.

"I hope you sleep well, mother," I heard my mom say. So, it still must have been nighttime; I'd just fallen asleep early.

"Thank you, Iris," Grandma said. It took me a minute to realize she'd spoken 'cause she hadn't been talking at all the last couple of days.

I guess Mom was surprised too 'cause she said, "Mom?"

"Yes, Iris?"

"You're back! Where have you been?"

"I've had a lot to think about. I've spent my whole life pretending something that just wasn't true. I'm more awake now than I've been since I was seven."

"What are you talking about? What do you mean since you were seven?"

It was quiet for a few minutes, but then Grandma said, "When I was seven, my life changed, but I don't think you want to hear it."

"Why do you say that?"

"Because you haven't believed Lucas, and he's been telling you all about it."

"You've heard all that?"

"Of course I have. I'm not deaf."

"Well, really, Mom. It's a bit hard to believe. I mean it's not like you've been yourself lately."

"Yes, I suppose that's one way of looking at it."

I heard Mom suck her breath in. She does that when she's frustrated with me. "I'm at a loss. How can I respond to that?" Grandma didn't answer, so Mom went on. "Tell me something. What was the name of the baby you lost, before I was born?"

"Her name was Abby."

I could almost hear my mom smiling. "That's what I guessed. I understand you miss Abby, but making her into your sister has gotten Lucas confused. He's even got Mamie off on a wild goose chase looking for a sister that doesn't exist. I don't even begin to understand where a kidnapping fits into this. If you're thinking so clearly now, why don't you try to sort through how that story came to be? We can talk about it in the morning."

I heard the rustle of the bed, like Mom had stood up to leave. It surprised me to realize that Mom and Grandma had almost switched places. Mom seemed to be the real mom, not just mine but Grandma's too. I wondered when and just how something like that happens. I knew how Grandma felt, though. It's sometimes hard to be the kid.

Just then Grandma spoke. I guess when you're an adult kid, it's okay to have the last word. She didn't sound mad; in fact, her voice came out kind of soft. "Why do you think I named her Abby? No matter how hard I tried to bury Abby in my mind, my heart would not allow it. I couldn't contain that name within my head. Even though I wouldn't let myself fully acknowledge the past, I needed to name my first baby Abby. I needed to bring a part of her back, even if it was only her name. I did it to honor my sister." She paused and then added, "Why don't you spend some time thinking about that?"

I had to smile. It turns out Grandma really was the mom still. Even better, she was my Grandma once again, not just the old lady who was dying in the next room. I don't know if anything happened after that 'cause I laid back down with that smile all over my face. The next thing I knew, it was morning.

Chapter 38

"Lucas, Lucas?" It was Grandma calling me awake. I looked up in time to see Mom clearing Grandma's breakfast dishes. She patted Grandma's hand and smiled as she walked out. I hoped that meant something good.

When I reached Grandma's side, I was reminded how sick she was. Her face looked all worn out and her hands shook as she reached out to me. But for now her voice was strong, and I would hang on to that.

"What, Grandma?"

"I want to thank you for believing me and standing up for me. You're a strong person."

"So are you, Grandma."

"I thought I was." It seemed like she was going to say something else, but then her face changed and a smile replaced the far-away look. "Lucas, I'd like to tell you a story, a story about when I was little."

"Oh, good," I replied and snuggled down next to her, in the bend of her arm to get comfortable.

"When I was about five, my mother bought me a bicycle. My dad had left us sometime before that, and I know she didn't have a lot of money, but somehow she had managed to buy me that bike. You see, my mother taught school, and every day after kindergarten, I would go to her classroom and look at books until she was done grading papers or preparing her lessons. Abby would join us too, only she was reading bigger books than I was. Afterward, we would all walk home together. Except one day Abby wasn't there at first and I was worried, but Mom kept smiling and telling me everything was just fine, not to worry. Just as Mom finished up, in walked Abby with my brand-new bike! It was pink and purple and had training wheels on it.

I rode my bike home that night and every night after that, even if it was raining. It wasn't until summertime when we were all home that Mom took the training wheels off. Most of my friends had been riding without training wheels for quite a while by then, and I thought it would be easy, but it wasn't."

I nodded my head, remembering when I learned to ride my bike. "I know. I fell down a lot when I was learning."

"So did I, Lucas. So did I. My knees were one constant scab or bruise it seemed. I wanted to quit trying, but my mother took me on her lap. She said, 'Josie, life is sometimes hard just like learning to ride a bike, but it's worth it. You just have to decide who's going to win – you or the bike.' I decided I wanted to win, and so I kept on trying until I had it figured out.

"From then on, whenever anything was hard – homework, friends, anything – she would say to me, 'Who's going to win – you or the bike?'"

"But you already won over the bike."

She laughed and it felt good to hear it again, "Yes, Lucas, but she meant – was I going to let hard things get me down, or was I going to keep on trying, just like getting back on my bike. She was teaching me to never give up."

"Oh, I get it now."

"Lucas, I never forgot to get back on my bike. Even when I wasn't with her anymore, I did it, because she taught me to do it. Who she taught me to be was still who I was."

I reached over and hugged her. I could feel how skinny she had become underneath her nightgown, and that made me want to hug her even tighter. I let go only when I heard my phone ring, the one Mamie had given me. I had left it by the couch, so I hurried to find it and answer it.

"Mamie?"

"Yes, Lucas, it's me. How are you doing?"

"Pretty good. I think Mom might be starting to believe us."

"Really? That's great! How did you manage that?"

"I'm not sure, but Grandma's talking more and that's helping a lot."

"I have news, too."

"You do?"

"Lucas, we found the records."

"You did?!" I let out a squeal that probably sounded like a little girl, but I didn't care.

"Your grandmother's mother was named Evelyn, and she reported Josephine missing when she was seven years old. Evelyn also told the police she suspected her ex-husband and his wife, Josie's dad and stepmom, had kidnapped her."

"Wow." I couldn't believe after all this time we'd actually found what we were looking for.

"We had a hard time finding the records, but what we did find indicates Evelyn and her other daughter, Abigail, went to the police station on a regular basis to see if anything new had turned up. But the old detective that was helping us look for the records said it didn't look like the police had done much to find Josie. According to him, the attitude back then was that it was a family matter. Once a child had been taken by the non-custodial parent, that means the parent that she wasn't living with, they thought, 'Well, that's pretty much your problem.'"

"So, no one was really looking for her?"

"No, not except for her mom and sister."

"Boy, I better tell Grandma ... and I guess Mom and Dad, too."

"That would be a good idea. Why don't you do that? You can tell them to call me if they have any questions. Now that we found these records, we'll have a better chance at finding Abby. And Lucas, your grandmother's name was not Josephine Jones, not her real name. Her father and stepmother were named Robert and Patsy, but clearly they changed their last name to keep her hidden. Her real name was Josephine Barrett. We even found her birth certificate, and the birthdates match."

What she was saying made sense, but I hadn't thought about her having a different name. "Wow," I said again.

Mamie chuckled on the line. "It's a lot to take in, isn't it? Her parents were Robert and Evelyn Barrett, so that means her sister was Abigail or Abby Barrett. I'm hoping we'll have better luck finding her now."

"I sure hope so!"

Chapter 39

I could hardly wait to tell everyone what Mamie had found, but I decided to tell everyone together. That meant I needed to wait for Dad to get home. I didn't know if I could keep my mouth shut until then, so I went to find Justin and check on our dog.

He was outside sitting on his front porch eating a snack and petting Buster. When he saw me coming, he said, "So, how's your Grandma? Is she dead yet?"

I sat down next to him and starting petting Buster too. "No. She's hanging in there still, and I think maybe I can find her sister for her before she dies."

"Really? That would be pretty awesome."

"You know what I found out? My grandma was kidnapped when she was a little girl. She never saw her mom or her sister again. The weird thing is she was the same age as we are when it happened."

Justin's eyes got big, and all he could think to say was, "Whoa." I think that about summed it up. There wasn't anything else that needed to be said.

"Would you like to ride bikes?" I said. I didn't tell him the story about Grandma's bike. For a little while at least, I wanted that story to be all mine.

"Sure."

A good bike ride solves all kinds of things, even with a puppy nipping at your wheels. Maybe that's why grown-ups have so many problems, they've forgotten how to ride their bikes.

By the time I went home from Justin's house, it was dinnertime and Dad was already home. I wasn't sure how to get everyone together since Grandma was in her bed and everybody else was in the kitchen, but Grandma ended up doing it for me.

Just as we were clearing dinner dishes, Grandma called us to her bedside. I wasn't sure why until she said, "I think Lucas wants to share something with us."

I dropped my mouth open. "How did you know?"

She looked at me like it was obvious. "Lucas, you were talking to Mamie with a lot of 'Wows.' I've been waiting all day for you to fess up to what's going on. I finally figured out you wanted to tell us all together. Is that right?"

I just nodded my head.

"Well, get on with it then!" I was surprised that it was Mom who spoke. I guess maybe she was starting to believe us.

I took a deep breath. "Okay. Mamie says they found the records about Grandma. Her mom, her real mom, called the police and told them her daughter had been kidnapped, probably by her dad and stepmom, but the police didn't do much to help. They thought it was kind of her own problem to take care of." I looked at Grandma and saw she was crying, so I added, "Mamie says your mom and sister bugged the police a lot."

"Was that right?" Mom said to Grandma. "Was it your dad and stepmother?"

All Grandma could do was nod. Quickly Mom reached over to hug her. "I'm so sorry. I can't begin to imagine what you've dealt with your whole life, the weight you carried alone." They were both crying by now.

"There's one more thing," I said. All eyes turned to me. "Her name was Josephine *Barrett*. They may have changed her name, but we know it's her. She was seven years old, just like me, when it happened."

"That's right! Oh my goodness, that's right!" Grandma said. She was laughing and crying at the same time. "When I was really little, I couldn't get the whole thing out, I would stop at 'Bear.' I thought it was the coolest thing, like being a teddy bear, I was Josie Bear and my sister was Abby Bear."

"That's what you called her in the middle of night. When you woke me up calling for Abby, you called her Abby Bear!"

Grandma nodded, but she was smiling now. "I remember. I remember."

We all gathered around to take turns giving Grandma hugs. When we'd settled down again, Grandma spoke. "They changed my name to Jones."

"That's something very ordinary and nondescript," Dad said. "You would blend in, even disappear."

"Yes. However, I kept calling myself Josie Bear. So, they started saying my new name on a regular basis. 'You are Josephine Jones, now.' They even started calling me JoJo, and it stuck. I didn't mind the nickname, but I abandoned it as soon as I left home. Only I wasn't sure why until this very moment."

She stretched her arms toward me, and I moved into them for a hug. "Lucas, I didn't know until right now that they were looking for me, that they cared that I was gone. I felt abandoned, that they had forgotten all about me, and that made it easier to forget all about them."

I felt her tears drop onto my head, and I looked up into her wet eyes. "Why did you think that?" I said. I couldn't understand what she was saying. My mom, I knew, would never forget about me if I was gone, so why would she think that hers would?

"It's complicated. I didn't think that way at first. Do you remember how I said they told me Abby was dead?"

"Yes."

"Well, I didn't trust my stepmother, but I thought I could trust my dad a little bit. So, one day when I was alone with him, I told him I knew Abby was alive. That was the day hope died. He said, 'We didn't want to tell you, but Abby and your mom didn't want you around anymore. They called and asked us to come get you because you were getting in the way of their lives.'"

No one knew what to say. I had forgotten that Lily was there until she said, "Don't be sad. Me wuv you, Gwamma."

Dad scooped Lily up in his arms and held her close. "You're right, little one. We love Grandma, and we love you, little bug." He looked at me and added, "and Lucas, too." His eyes were shining. I knew all that, but I guess he needed to say it. I got up to give my dad a hug to let him know everything was okay.

"You will never get in the way of our lives!" Dad said firmly. Mom looked at him expectantly, and he nodded to her. I don't know why, but she smiled slightly while rubbing her belly.

We had been so busy hugging each other that we hadn't noticed Grandma reaching for her jewelry box. When we did look at her again, she was holding Abby's ring, the ring that had started all of this. She started talking, and it sounded like she was telling herself the story. "I loved Abby's ring. She let me play with it as long as I promised to take good care of it. I was wearing it that day. I thought for sure she would come looking for me, even if it was just so she could have her ring back. But it didn't seem like she wanted it anymore; she didn't want *me* anymore." Grandma shook her head at the memory. "Deep down, I knew what he'd told me was a lie. That same day he bought me this jewelry box. He said I was starting a new life with new things and he wanted me to forget my old life along with my mom and Abby. It was the last kind thing he did for me, and he didn't even do it out of kindness.

"The first thing I put inside was the charm bracelet I'd been wearing the day he took me. He didn't mind, or more likely, he didn't notice. I'd started to connect several of the items on it with things around Oregon by that time anyway.

"What he didn't know, though, was that the jewelry box had a little trap door at the bottom. As soon as I found it, I hid Abby's ring in it. Somehow, I had a sense I should keep it hidden. Up until then I vaguely remember keeping it in my shoe or tucking it in my sock. I don't know if they would have figured out it belonged to Abby and not me, but I didn't want to risk them taking away the only connection I had to her. I needed to put it in the jewelry box to always remind me what was real and what wasn't … but then I forgot about it."

"But it did remind you, Grandma," I said. "It reminded you *now*."

She smiled at me and nodded her head. Then she pulled the jewelry box to her, hugging it, alternately crying and laughing. Without saying anything, we gradually, one by one, left her alone with her memories.

It wasn't until the next morning that we talked any more with Grandma about what had happened. It felt like we were reading a great chapter book but then had to stop right at the best part when Mom and Dad sent everyone to bed. They said it was just too much at once and we could talk more later. I was disappointed, but I guess they were right.

I woke up eagerly the next morning, hoping Grandma wanted to talk some more. When I went to her bedside, she was already awake and pulled me to her side with a big smile. "It was coming back to me in pieces, but it's finally all there. Thank you, Lucas. Thank you for giving me my life back, my story."

"Even though it's sad?"

"Even though it's sad," she nodded. "It still happened, and whether I remember it or not won't change that. But, Lucas, I've had a hole in my life that I didn't understand. I knew something was missing, but I didn't know what."

"It's the memory of what happened, isn't it?"

"No, it's my family – my mother and my sister. We're not complete without our families." She gave me an extra hug. As she did so, she ran her fingers through my hair, and for some reason, she started laughing.

I pulled back. "What's funny, Grandma?"

"I just realized something. My whole life, I've made sure to keep my hair color exactly the same. Whenever I dyed it, it was just to make it the color I grew up with."

I didn't understand and looked at her funny.

"Oh, Lucas. I wanted them to find me, and I wanted them to recognize me when they did. I guess underneath it all, I somehow knew it was important. Despite everything I thought and everything I tried to forget, I still had hope that they wanted me, that they would find me."

Her gentle laugh rang out again. It must have been like the bell at school saying it was time to start 'cause when I looked up, everyone was there, even a sleepy Lily in Mom's arms, still trying to rub her eyes awake.

Grandma chuckled a little. "Since you're all here, let me tell you my story." And so she began.

When I was seven, my family, that is my mother and my sister Abby, took an afternoon picnic to the beach. It was early spring, and the water was still too cold for wading. Mother was always careful, didn't want us to get chilled, but sand in our clothes she didn't mind. She said it was part of growing up, knowing what it feels like to have sand in your hands and between your toes. My favorite thing to do was to plop down on the beach as soon as we got there.

Abby liked to watch the gulls floating on the wind and brought a kite to fly that day. Mother helped her with the kite, and soon they were chasing it on down the beach. I could still see my mother, and she could see me; I know, because she would turn and wave every few minutes.

Abby had been wearing her favorite birthstone ring that morning but handed it to me just before heading off to fly her kite. She winked and told me to keep it close at all times.

Dad must have been watching me from behind the whole time because when the kite string got tangled and Mother was distracted, I felt his cold hand on my shoulder. He said something about needing me to come to his car to see a surprise he had for Mom. I hadn't been afraid of my father before that moment, but I also rarely saw him.

I didn't want to leave the sand; I didn't want to go with him, but he pulled me up with strong hands and a firm smile and, wrapping his arm around my shoulder, led me to his car. His wife was waiting, but she wasn't smiling.

There was no surprise in the car for Mother, at least not a gift. We started driving and soon we were in the middle of a large thunderstorm. The thunder and lightning seemed to go on forever, and I was cold and scared. I wanted my mom, and I asked Dad about the surprise for her. He told me they had it at the hotel, but the only surprise at the hotel was when Dad told me I was going to live with them now – it had been agreed.

The next day we packed up and moved to Oregon. I was certain that my dad was wrong, that Abby and Mom wanted me, that they missed me. I kept waiting for them to come for me, to find me and take me home, but day after day passed, and it never happened.

I was given a new last name – "Jones," but I was glad they let me keep the Josephine. Father, while he may not have been very loving, at least he was not cruel - unless she was around. I was supposed to call her "Mother," but I called her "Ma" and only when it was absolutely necessary. I suppose I got used to the cold.

As I mentioned, they eventually told me that both my mother and Abby had died, but then Dad admitted they just didn't want me anymore, and I was told I shouldn't think of them ever again. However, they couldn't decide what went on in my mind; they couldn't take that away from me. Or so I thought. The memories faded and became murky, truth mixed with my dreams until I couldn't tell which was which. My past seemed to dissolve before my very eyes.

I began to believe the lies. There was a certain logic to them. Mother and Abby must not have wanted me around, even if they weren't dead, because, as far as I could tell, they never came looking for me. For a time, I wondered if they had forgotten me. But one way or another, either by living their lives without me or by dying, Mother and Abby had abandoned me. That feeling was so strong that an uneasy sense of abandonment chased me the rest of my life, only I didn't understand why.

Growing up, I suppose as a way to cope with what I could not explain, I gave in to what they wanted me to do. I tried to forget everything I had ever known that was true and real. The past was gone, and I would put it behind me. I thought about trying to leave, but where would I go?

They let me out of their stifling embrace to go to college. I think to her it was a good riddance, and he didn't have the courage to fight it anymore. I didn't care how I managed to escape, I was just glad that I had. I picked a college on the other side of the country. I never went back to them, and I never went back to my memories - until I saw the ring.

Chapter 40

We probably would have sat there all day at her side, hardly saying a word, if it weren't for Lily. "Me hungry," she whined. She didn't really understand what Grandma was talking about. I supposed one day when she was older I'd have to explain it to her. But for now, she just wanted some breakfast and didn't want to wait.

Once breakfast got started, the day got started. With school out, I didn't remember it was Saturday, but Mom did. She had a whole bunch of jobs for me to do. I knew she finally believed what Grandma was saying, but that didn't mean she wanted to. Whenever Mom was trying to avoid something, she got busy doing other stuff. I guess accepting what Grandma said was one of those things she had to do, and she knew it, only it wasn't easy.

By the time I was done doing all the things Mom wanted me to do it was afternoon. I'd hardly thought about Grandma all day 'cause I was too busy to think of anything else.

When I went to see her, she was sleeping. I grabbed a book and sat down beside her to wait for her to wake up. I was wondering if she had other stories to tell me, things she might have remembered.

Grandma didn't wake up for a while, and when she did I could tell something was different. She had been so alive lately, that I had forgotten she was dying. I remembered as soon as she opened her eyes. Just since morning, her skin had seemed to change color, or actually lose most of its color. She looked gray and her voice sounded gray and her motions were gray. I didn't like gray.

"Lucas, have you been sitting there watching me?"

"Yes," I said as I hurried to her side, suddenly scared. "Are you all right, Grandma? You don't sound the same as you did this morning."

"I'm not the same. I'm better ... and worse."

"What?" Sometimes adults say strange things, like they don't really know what the words they're using actually mean.

"It's just that I'm at peace, something I haven't been for a long time, but my body just gave me the last bit of energy it had to give. I'm just about done here."

"Oh, but you can't go, Grandma! At least not yet. You haven't seen Abby. We're really close to finding her. You just have to wait, okay?" I pled with her.

"I'll try, sweetheart. I'll try. You've been so good to me. I will try to wait until you finish what you started."

"Will you? Oh, I hope so." I climbed up on her bed, laid down beside her bony body, and started to sob. I didn't know I still had tears, but I had even more than I thought I could.

"Lucas," Grandma said when I started to settle down, "remember what I told you?"

"About what?" I sat up and rubbed my hand across my eyes to clear them.

"About me going to Heaven. It's just like I'm going on vacation, remember, only I don't have to pack any bags."

"Yeah, I remember you told me that, and it seemed to make sense before. But I don't like it anymore 'cause you're not coming back from your vacation. I won't be able to see you again."

"Well, I wouldn't say that. No, I won't be here to read you stories or play games with you, but I haven't been doing much of that lately anyway. However, I will watch over you, and that's something grandmas are supposed to do. I'll be nearer to you than you might think. And, Lucas," she waited until I was looking her in the eye, "I will see you again someday."

I started to cry all over again. I wasn't ready for this. I wasn't ready to be away from her. "But I'm just seven, Grandma. It will be a long time 'til I see you in Heaven."

"I understand, Lucas. I understand," she said while reaching out to hold me.

It was quiet and peaceful in her arms, and when she spoke again, her voice was still gray, but it warmed me like the sun. "Remember, just like my mother taught me, you have to get back on the bike. You can grow and learn and move forward. You can be happy."

"Okay," I said, but I didn't know if I meant it. Then I remembered what else she'd told me. "It's just a cloudy day, right?"

She smiled and nodded. "You remembered. Yes, it may seem as if you can't see the sun when I'm gone, but before long, it will appear again. You'll feel warm and happy." Even though it was kind of a strange way to talk about death, in that moment I completely understood.

I stayed with Grandma until she fell asleep again for another nap. Then I quickly went to find Mom.

"Grandma's not going to make it much longer, Mom. What do we do?"

I didn't say what I was worried about, about not finding Abby in time, but Mom knew. And she knew what to do. "Call Mamie. Tell her how much we need her help and that we need it as fast as possible."

I ran to find the phone and did just what she said. I wanted to explain to Mamie about Mom and how things were better, but I didn't want to waste the time. When she picked up and said, "Hello, Lucas," I blurted out, "We have to find Abby NOW. Grandma's going to die really, really soon."

"Okay. We found them. We found Abby and her family, or at least where they are. She got married, and her married name is Abby Seron. Mr. Knowles, the P.I., and I were going to drive to where they are tomorrow morning, but we'll go tonight. She still lives in Washington state. I suspect Abby thought if she stayed, then Josie could find her."

"Okay. Just hurry, please."

"We will. I'll call Mr. Knowles right now."

When I hung up, I wasn't surprised to see Mom standing right behind me with eyes just as anxious and worried as mine. She wrapped me in her arms. "I'm sorry, Lucas, that I didn't believe you, that I didn't believe my mother. We could have helped you sooner. I hope it's not too late."

"It's okay," I replied, and I meant it. I wasn't mad at her. I was too worried to be mad at anyone.

I didn't like it, but it turns out I was right that she was dying. Her breathing sounded different and she didn't wake up very much. When we tried to wake her for dinner, she just said she wasn't hungry and turned over and went back to sleep.

I wasn't hungry either, but Mom made me eat something. I made it halfway through my peanut butter and jelly sandwich. Dad got some dinner for himself and Lily, but I noticed Mom didn't eat a bite.

Mom and I sat together at Grandma's bedside. Mom pulled a couple of chairs right next to each other and then she got a big blanket, big enough for the two of us. She put it around our shoulders and wrapped her arm around me underneath the blanket. It was warm, which was good 'cause I was starting to shake a little bit. She even whispered a prayer every once in a while.

About one in the morning, I got a text from Mamie. It didn't wake us 'cause we hadn't gone to sleep. It said, "We found the right Abby. Boarding the plane now. See you soon."

Chapter 41

I woke up with my head in Mom's lap, I guess right where I had fallen asleep. When I was little, if I fell asleep in the car or in front of the TV, someone (probably Dad) would move me to my bed. I would wake up in my room in the morning, wondering how I'd gotten there. But I guess now that I was older, they let me stay where I was.

Mom was stroking my head, looking at me when I woke up. I don't think she had gone to sleep at all. "Is she ...?"

She smiled and shook her head. "No, she's still here."

I was really glad. I'd been hoping and praying all night she would hang on until Mamie, and maybe Abby, got here. I was still kind of tired, but I didn't want to fall back to sleep. I got up and started to pace back and forth. Usually, Mom would tell me to go outside and wear a path in the grass instead of the carpet, but she didn't say anything today.

Dad came in a little later and asked what we wanted for breakfast, and he wouldn't accept "Nothing" as our answer. He brought freshly made French toast to us a little later. I hated to admit it, but it tasted good. I was kind of hungry after all. Even Mom ate one or two slices.

I realized it was Sunday so it would be a quiet day – no doctors or nurses. But I guess I was wrong. Mom must have called them, or maybe Dad, 'cause pretty soon they started to show up.

Grandma slept right through all the checking they were doing. When they were done, the doctor turned to Mom. He just shook his head and said, "It will be soon." She nodded in return. "She should pass peacefully."

I knew he was talking about her dying, but I didn't understand why people say that someone "passes" or "passes away." The only kind of pass I could think of is when someone passes a football or you pass your friend in the hallway at school. It didn't make any sense.

The doctor asked Mom, "Would you like a nurse to stay?" She hesitated, but then shook her head. I didn't think she could talk right then if she tried.

The only way I knew that time passed that day was from the sunlight or shadows coming through the windows and Dad bringing us lunch or dinner. Grandma woke up every once in a while, but she just moaned a little in pain, looked at us, sometimes smiled, and then closed her eyes again in sleep.

I'd say she was gray again, but that didn't really describe her. Gray was still a color, and Grandma didn't have any anymore.

She surprised me once, it must have been afternoon 'cause I think we'd eaten lunch, when she spoke my name. I moved to her side and picked up her hand. It was cold. "Lucas," her voice was quiet but clear, "I love you with all my heart. You have helped me so much. Now you need to help your mother."

I turned to look at Mom to see what she'd think of Grandma saying that, but it was clear she hadn't heard it. Turning back to Grandma, I said, "I will."

"Thank you." With great effort, she brought her other hand up to my cheek like she had done so often to gently touch it. If I looked hard, I could still see the light of Grandma in her eyes, but only just barely.

It seemed Grandma was saying her goodbyes 'cause then she called, "Iris."

When Mom came to my side, she whispered, "Go get the others." I knew what that meant, and I hurried to find Dad and Lily.

Grandma took a turn talking to each person, one by one. She spoke so softly that I couldn't hear what she said to anyone else.

She had just finished talking to Lily when we heard a slight knock on the door. Mom hurried to open it and in walked Mamie. They both paused just inside the door. Mom was looking at Mamie and Mamie at Mom, but neither one of them said a word.

Finally, Mom reached out and hugged Mamie. I could tell Mamie was surprised, but then she smiled and returned the hug. When they pulled apart, Mom said, "Thank you for everything you've done, for

Lucas, for my mom . . . and with Pete. Thank you … Mother."

Mamie cocked her head to one side, watching my mom. "Thank you, Iris, but please, call me Mamie." Her face broke into a wide grin and she grabbed Mom in a huge hug again. After a minute, she pulled back and looked down at Mom's belly. Reaching out to pat it, she said, "I'm still not much of a baby person, but Lucas and Lily are a different matter. If you'll let me, I'd love to keep them company while you and Pete take care of this new one. And I'll either get used to the baby or it'll grow up. Either way, I'll try to be a proper grandmother."

Mom tried to say something, but it looked like her tears were getting in the way. Instead, she smiled. Then they both started to laugh, softly as first, then loud and strong.

I can't say I understood why they were laughing, but I knew it meant they were happy. I started to laugh with them, like I couldn't help myself.

At the sound of my laughter, Mamie turned to look at me for the first time. "Lucas, I have much to tell you, and I better tell you quickly." The laughter was gone; it was time for other matters.

Everyone backed away so Mamie and I could talk alone. I guess they figured I had earned the right to hear the story first. We sat down on the couch, and Mamie started to talk immediately. "Lucas, your grandma's sister, Abby, never left Washington. I mean, not ever. She stayed there to go to school at the University of Washington. She met her husband there, and they got married her senior year of college. I met him; he's a very nice man. There were job offers in other parts of the country, but she had made him promise they would never leave Washington. They moved around a bit there, from a small house to a bigger one, but always they stayed somewhere close to Seattle, to the place Josie disappeared.

"I understand when her mother passed away, she made Abby promise to never give up. But a promise wasn't necessary, and they both knew it. Abby had three children. The oldest was a girl she named Myra Josephine."

I laughed. "Grandma had a baby who died, but before she did,

Grandma named her Abby. I guess they were both thinking the same thing." I expected her to laugh with me, but she didn't. Her face had gotten very serious. "Mamie, when can Grandma see her sister? Is she flying out here?"

She looked down, "No, Lucas. Abby died last year, of cancer, just like your Grandma."

Of all the things I could have thought of to happen, I had never thought of that one. We had finally succeeded, and just in time, only to find out we had actually failed. Success had not even been possible. I was too numb to cry, to speak, to move. Abby was dead. Abby wasn't coming. Grandma was going to die without ever seeing her sister again. It was worse than just Grandma dying; she was going to die heartbroken, too.

I looked up, and Mamie met my eyes. She was crying. "Shall I go tell her now?" she said.

Staring into her face, I knew. I knew what I needed to do. "No, I want to tell her myself."

Chapter 42

"Grandma," I whispered, "Grandma." Her head was turned to the side and her eyes were open, but if she heard me I couldn't tell. Her breathing sounded funny, like she was skipping every second or third breath. "Grandma?" She wasn't moving at all, like maybe she couldn't anymore.

I moved to the other side of the bed where she was facing so I could look right at her and maybe she would see me. "Grandma, it's Lucas."

She moved her eyes to look at me without moving her head. "Yes, Lucas, I know."

I was relieved she could hear me, but then my stomach dropped as I remembered what it was I had to say. I looked up at the rest of the family, including Mamie, who were gathered in the room. Mamie and Mom both nodded as if to say it would be okay. Gathering all the courage I could, I said, "Grandma," but then I started to cry before any other words left my lips.

Taking a deep breath, I started again. "Grandma, Mamie went to Washington to find your sister. Abby always loved you, and she never stopped hoping you would come back to her. She and your mom looked, but they just couldn't find you."

Grandma hadn't moved her head, but she was staring at me intently. I knew she understood what I was saying, but I was giving her hope when there was none. "Grandma, Abby's not coming to see you. She can't. She died last year." It was all I could say before sobbing, laying my head down on her frail body, and wetting her blanket with my tears.

I'm not sure what I expected from Grandma, but there was

nothing, no reaction that I could hear. I stopped my crying to look at her face. It was glowing with happiness, and then she spoke, but she wasn't looking at me. She was looking past me. "It's okay, Lucas. I see her. She's come to get me and take me home."

I now know why they say someone passes 'cause that's what she did right then. She left her broken body behind, and Grandma passed right by me. I felt her go, and I knew she was passing me so she could go into her sister's arms.

Epilogue

It was surprising how many people it took to take care of one small, fragile body. It seemed to go in slow motion, feeling like it took forever, but it wasn't even bedtime when they were done.

As the last person left, I watched Mom shut the front door and turn back to where I could see her face. It was marked up with tears and trails of tears. I guess Grandma trusted me with this last mission since I did that first one she asked. I could be her knight one more time now that the dragon had won.

I walked quietly up to Mom and reached out to take her hand that was hanging down. She looked at me, but there was no smile. "Mom," I whispered, "you have to get back on the bike." She looked at me with a confused expression on her face. "You can't let the bike win. You have to get back on."

"What are you talking about?"

"It's something Grandma told me." I wasn't sure how to help her understand - then I had an idea. "I'll tell you the whole story later. Just come here," I said as I dragged her back to the front door and out into the last light of the day. "Put your arm out."

"Lucas, I don't have time for this."

"Trust me. Just put your arm out." This time, she did as she was told. "Can you feel that?" She nodded, and I noticed her eyes were closed, surrendering to the moment. "Mom, I know your insides feel all gray and cloudy and cold, but even when the sun hides behind clouds, it always comes back out." She opened her eyes to look at me. "You'll feel warm again, I promise. The sun is warm and happy, and you will be again too. I promise. Grandma promised."

She threw her arms around me and smiled. "I love you, Lucas!"

"I love you, too, Mom."

I walk along a different kind of shore now, the waters of life ebbing and flowing as I go. It is a peaceful, happy place, and those that walk beside me – John, Abby, Mother, and more – seem always to be encircled in light.

When I look back the way I came, I see them – bumping along with the undulating waves of life's highs and lows. It will be years for them, even Mamie, before they see me, as I am seeing them. But the years will be kind. We keep careful watch, whispering words of guidance, giving protection, being loving and mindful – ever ensuring they will never be abandoned.

View other Black Rose Writing titles at
and use promo code PRINT to receive a 20% discount when purchasing.

BLACK ROSE
writing™